THE RAKISH DUKE AND HIS WALLFLOWER

The Rules of Scandal 1

TESSA BROOKMAN

GROVE
CHRONICLES

Prologue

"Your gentleman caller does not come around anymore, does he?"

Violet's hand that held the pencil froze and hovered over the sketchbook. She had not wanted to listen to the conversation, as frustrated with her cousin's interference as her sister was, but now, she had no choice. Dropping the sketchbook firmly into her lap, she sat straight and pushed the loose curls of blonde hair that had fallen out of her chignon back from her face.

Across the room, she could see who had spoken. Her cousin, Louise, was practically crowing in victory as she walked up and down the room.

"Mama was right. No good comes from encouraging the attentions of a man like Sir Percy Babington, does it?" Louise practically giggled with the words.

"I..." Penelope trailed off.

Violet's eyes shot to her sister to see Penelope was sitting forward in her chair, barely paying attention to the embroidery in her lap.

"No, he does not come around anymore," Penelope said miserably and stabbed the embroidered cloth with the needle another time.

"We knew he was no good. It shows a poor judgment of character, that is what my Mama says," Louise crowed another time as she walked in front of Penelope.

I have had enough of this.

Violet stood to her feet and dropped her notebook so loudly on the table beside her that both Louise and Penelope flinched. Penelope's fair curls turned in Violet's direction and Louise spun around, her red hair whipping with the movement.

"We hear the opinions of your mother from her own lips, Louise. Do you have an opinion of your own to share?" Her tartness earned a warning glare from Penelope behind Louise's back, clearly telling her to be quiet, but Violet did not listen. She strode across the room instead, meeting Louise's gaze.

Violet may have been significantly shorter than Louise, but she would never cower to her cousin's pride.

Louise's lips opened and closed, but no words passed them. Clearly, she had not expected such words to escape Violet.

"No? Well, perhaps we should leave my sister to her embroidery. She is content here in peace, and that peace and quiet is rather being disturbed at present. If you wouldn't mind." Violet spoke with a sweet and kindly tone, even if the words were to the point.

Louise was wrongfooted. She narrowed her brown eyes, clearly wishing to be tart too, but apparently, words failed her. She hurried from the room instead, and Violet followed, being careful to close the door behind her. Once Louise was gone, Violet turned back into the parlor and sighed, leaning on the door.

"Oh, good lord! Save me from our cousin's proud ways," she gushed, rather relieved when she brought a smile to her sister's lips.

"You think we would be used to it by now after how long we have been here," Penelope murmured, looking down at her embroidery once again.

"Used to it? No, indeed. Our cousin is as changeable as the English weather. Sometimes she is kind, other times, like the clouds, she is so ill-tempered that she marches around the house, practically making the floorboards shake beneath her feet."

"Do not let her hear you say that!" Penelope shook her head madly.

"She can hear it. I do not mind." Violet crossed the room and sat down by her sister's side, flopping into the chair. She had hoped her jest would bring another smile to her sister's lips, but it didn't on this occasion. "Penelope, are you well, dearest?"

"Of course," Penelope lied.

"You know I can tell easily by now when you are fibbing to me, do you not?" Violet leaned toward her and whispered conspiratorially, as if it were the greatest secret ever told. "You are my sister, Penelope. I can read you like a book."

"Do not tease me, Violet."

"I am not teasing. I am trying to make you smile, though I admit I am failing in my task at present." Violet sat back again. "You have a habit of flattening your lips together when you lie." Penelope purposefully lifted her head and smiled as if to dispel the illusion of a lie. "It is a good attempt, but you still lied. Would you tell me what is wrong, sister?"

She half-expected Penelope to start speaking at length of Sir Babington, the gentleman caller who had spent months trying to earn Penelope's attention, and when he had it, had frittered off very quickly. Like a bumble bee that persists with one flower, Violet thought Sir Babington just the same. He had waited until Penelope had turned her head toward him, then he had flown away.

"I..." Yet Penelope was not one for indulging in long speeches of what was in her heart. Violet usually had to tease it out of her.

"You can tell me anything. You know that, dearest." Violet reached for her sister and took her hand off the embroidery, clasping her fingers in her own.

"I know." Penelope lifted her head, revealing there were tears in her eyes.

"Oh, what is wrong? Is it Sir –"

"Please, do not say his name. It is something quite different that upsets me."

"Pen, what is it?"

"I feel... Oh, it is all the time at the moment." Penelope flung back her head dramatically. When she accidentally pricked herself with the needle, she cried out and lifted her finger to her lips, sucking on the blood. "Every morning," she murmured once she lowered her hand again, "and this morning, it is far worse."

"What is worse?" Violet leaned forward, feeling her worry begin to burn within her. "Goodness, what is wrong?"

"I feel so sick. All the time." Penelope's words were barely audible, they were so quiet. "Every day, it is like this gnawing sensation in my gut." She gently placed down the embroidery beside her and rested a hand on her stomach. Her other hand was now clutching at Violet's, as if it was the giver of life itself. "Violet... I fear..."

"Fear what?" Violet did not get an answer to her question, for Penelope had lifted both hands to her lips. There was an awful sound within her throat, one that forewarned what was about to happen.

Violet was on her feet within a second. There was no chance they could make it to a privy or a chamber pot in time. Instead, she dragged poor Penelope to the garden door and flung it open.

Beyond the door, late-blooming irises and poppies swayed in the breeze. Penelope pushed them all to the side and bent her head down as she began to retch in the grass.

Violet kicked the door shut behind them, not wanting Louise or anyone else in the house to discover what was happening just yet. Not until she knew the cause of this sickness.

Bending down to her knees, Violet held her sister's hair and rubbed her back whilst she was sick, taking care of her.

"There, there. Let it out, Pen. All will be well again in a minute." Violet made her tone soft. When Penelope finished and sat back, wrinkling her nose when she caught sight of what she had done, she offered a small smile to Violet.

"That is what our mother used to say. 'All will be well again,' she said that so much."

"That she did." Violet wouldn't let herself grow sad at the mention of their mother. At this moment, she had other things to worry about.

Must I call a physician? Is this some passing sickness, or a bad filet of fish that has been ingested, or something else entirely?

"Penelope, we should take you upstairs so you can rest. As mother said, all will be well."

"No, Violet, no, not this time." Penelope's words were rather wild. For one who was usually so quiet and softly spoken, it was starkly against her character. She pulled on Violet's hands, not letting her leave just yet, and tugged her back down to her knees. She entwined their fingers together, latching onto Violet. "I fear I know what the cause of this sickness is, and it will not pass, not before everything becomes apparent."

"Before what becomes apparent?" Violet asked. Penelope didn't answer at first. The tears returned to her eyes, and she began to cry. The tears spilled quickly down her cheeks, running so fast that the drips hung off her chin. "Penelope, you are scaring me. Pray, tell me more before I go mad with worry."

"I know what the sickness is." Penelope spoke so quietly now that Violet had to lean forward to hear her. "It is not food poisoning, nor is it an illness that can be healed. Violet, it is of my own doing. Of mine and Sir Babington's."

Violet felt her body turn cold as she sat back on her knees. She prepared herself to hear the words, even before Penelope could utter them.

"Violet, I am with child."

Chapter One

*B*enedict, when I find you...

Sebastian's thoughts trailed off. As the sun shone down heavily, making his palms clammy around his steed's reins and his back hot beneath his tailcoat, he rode on. He drove the horse forward with a kind of wildness to him, picturing himself as feral as the animal beneath him, with hair loosened by wind and skin buffeted red.

When Sebastian reached Hyde Park, he didn't bother turning the horse in through the open gate. He vaulted the fence instead. The horse managed it easily and passersby squealed, either with delight at how impressive such a feat was, or the shock of the horse traveling so fast.

Sebastian couldn't stop a small smile creeping into his face. He rather liked the idea of ladies giving him a wide berth, and the fans that fluttered across their faces now and the gloved hands that were lifted to lips in shock thrilled him.

Yes, stay away from me! It is for your own good.

When he reached the main path of Hyde Park, Sebastian had to slow down. There were far too many people to ride safely. The steed came to a steady trot, snuffling and snorting in his reins, frustrated at going so slow.

"I know, boy, I know," Sebastian said deeply, comforting the steed as he patted his neck with a strong hand. "I'd rather be somewhere wilder too." The horse had kept him company on his travels abroad to the continent. Like him, the steed seemed to suffer the confinement of London society and the ton too much. "To be back in the wilderness of Spain again, eh?" The horse snorted, as if agreeing with him.

"Your Grace Ashbury! Is that you?" a familiar voice cried.

Sebastian was forced to pull on the reins and put on a polite smile, turning to greet whoever had called to him. A rather rotund fellow with pudgy red cheeks that gleamed in the sunlight. The man was rather a dandy, with so many bows on his shoes that they had to appeal as much to the ladies as they did to him.

"Lord Melbury." Sebastian bowed his head from atop the horse, greeting the man that had once been a close friend to his father.

"Well, well, I did not know we would have the pleasure of your company out here today," Lord Melbury declared and walked toward Sebastian's side, swinging the swagger stick in his hand in emphasis of each word.

"Nor did I," Sebastian muttered before he lifted his voice louder. "I was supposed to be engaged with my brother today. It is the season for the hunt after all."

"Ah, I see by your face that your brother has not turned up. I do believe young Lord Westmond is on a rather different hunt today, and not one that includes searching for foxes." Lord Melbury was clearly thrilled by his own jest, chuckling away and turning his red cheeks a deeper shade of scarlet. He lifted his swagger stick and pointed through Hyde Park.

Sebastian gritted his teeth as he looked forward. Late-blooming flower heads swayed from side to side, dancing in his view, and the early turning autumnal leaves of horse chestnuts got in Sebastian's way. He squinted through the blur where he eventually found his brother.

There you are.

Benedict was standing by the lake in Hyde Park, with no less than two ladies on either side of him, and a cluster of other ladies hovering close by. Each one was fluttering their fan and fussing with the necklines of their gowns.

Sebastian sent a pleading look to the heavens.

Surely, he cannot fall for such tricks.

Yet Benedict was smiling kindly down at the two ladies on either side of him, his eyes rather wide, like a child promised the taste of hot chocolate for the first time.

"He seems rather content, if you ask me," Lord Melbury added with another laugh.

I didn't ask.

"If you would excuse me, Lord Melbury." Sebastian bowed his head another time from atop the horse and moved on quickly, keeping his rather rude thoughts to himself. He crossed the distance to his brother in seconds, pulling the horse to such a halt at the side of the lake that it whinnied loudly into the air and drew the attention of many.

The cluster of ladies nearby all turned their heads toward Sebastian. The fluttering of fans grew faster, and some primped their cheeks and pressed their lips together, bringing more color to them.

Save me from scheming ladies looking for a husband!

"Sebastian! Is that you?" Benedict cried good-naturedly.

"It shouldn't be me. I should be miles away from here on a fox hunt right about now. As should you." Sebastian didn't get down from the horse at first. He fixed a knowing glare on his brother, watching as Benedict offered an apologetic smile.

"I am sorry, brother, I rather got a little... waylaid."

"So I see." Sebastian's eyes flicked to the two ladies beside Benedict. They were both unashamed in their attention to Benedict. One had her arm through his and her gloved fingers were practically clinging to him. The other had adjusted the neckline of her gown so much that Sebastian was forced to lift his eyes elsewhere. "I apologize for interrupting, ladies, but I am in need of the company of my brother."

"Oh! But we were so enjoying Lord Westmond's company," the first lady cried from where she stood on Benedict's arm.

"This is Lady Hayes and Lady Bella, Seb," Benedict said hurriedly.

"A pleasure, your Grace." The young lady, Lady Bella, turned her attention on Sebastian and curtsied so far that she was in danger of tripping over. Sebastian chewed the inside of his mouth to stop himself from laughing.

I must get them away from Benedict! He does not know the danger he is in.

"Careful, Lady Bella. The ground is uneven here and you are likely to trip." He cast a glance down to the earth beneath them. At once, Lady Bella looked down and nearly wrongfooted herself entirely as she stood straight.

Sebastian jumped down off his horse and tied the steed's reins to the nearest branch of a tree before looking back to Benedict. The fool was now offering his other arm to Lady Bella, to stop her from falling over.

"That wasn't supposed to happen," Sebastian muttered to himself, so quietly that the group seemed none the wiser to the fact he had spoken at all.

"The ladies were in need of a drink, Seb," Benedict declared, lifting his gaze from the women at last. His deep brown eyes that were so like Sebastian's own were rather moony as they stared at Lady Bella. "There is a teahouse not far from here."

"Ah, and how do the ladies like their tea?" Sebastian asked as he crossed toward them. If he was going to protect his brother from their advances, then it was high time he was more forthright, even if it became rude.

I do not care what anyone thinks of me, after all.

"Do they take tea only with marquesses and nothing less?" His words clearly hit the mark. As the Marquess of Westmond, his brother was one of the most eligible bachelors of the season.

"I beg your pardon?" Lady Hayes said hurriedly as her sister blushed bright red.

"It is not the tea they want, but the company, Benedict." Sebastian stepped near his brother, practically putting himself between him and Lady Hayes. At once, she was forced to release Benedict and step back.

"Seb, I –" Benedict's tone was pleading, but Sebastian spoke over him.

"I imagine their thirst suddenly came upon them when they saw you. What do you say, Lady Bella? Am I wrong?" His question hit the mark for she stepped back too, also releasing Benedict.

"Come, Bella," Lady Hayes said, striding forward and reaching for her sister's arm. "It seems the Duke of Ashbury does not want our company today." Lady Hayes towed Lady Bella away, though the latter kept looking back to Benedict as she went, offering a sweet smile and a wave that seemed to linger.

Once they were gone, wandering around the lake with other ladies, Sebastian heard his brother sigh beside him.

"Seb, I swear, I do not understand you."

Sebastian smiled a little at these words and turned back to face his brother. Benedict's fair hair was a contrast to his own, not just in color, but in style. Unlike Sebastian's that was wild from the ride, Benedict's was well-coiffed. It went with the pristine nature of his tailcoat and waistcoat. He was even well shaven, and he scratched at his chin now, shaking his head.

"Am I an enigma? Ha! If only, what a man would give to be anything half so interesting as a mystery." Sebastian laughed and walked around his brother before taking hold of Benedict's shoulder and steering him to look at the ladies that had just left. "Those ladies are not for you, Benedict."

"You are becoming worse than a belligerent mother of a young lady of the ton," Benedict said wryly, earning a deep chuckle from Sebastian.

"I suppose I am, but with good cause."

"What good cause is that?" Benedict asked, laughing. Despite his laughter, he still waved after the ladies, and his eyes seemed rather dazed as he watched them. "They were perfectly pleasant, they had charm, and were very handsome. Pray tell me why I could not enjoy their company?"

"Do you want the detail or the quick version?"

"The quick version, please, or we'll be here all day and your horse will be most upset at the wait." They both shot a glance toward the steed that was already pawing at the ground with his hooves, unhappy to be still so long.

"Come. If he sees us walking away, he will calm down. As we walk, I will give you the quick version of this lecture that you wanted," Sebastian said and steered his brother away, aware that Benedict drove the fine heels of his hessian boots into the ground, trying to stall their progress.

"I don't remember asking for a lecture, as such..."

"Then indulge me, for I am your brother." Sebastian encouraged Benedict to walk the other way around the lake. With late summer turning to autumn, more and more trees above them were turning brown and orange, but their leaves hadn't fallen just yet. Sebastian ran a hand through these leaves, snapping off a few of them before offering them to his brother.

"This is an odd gift," Benedict murmured.

"*This* is how the ladies of the ton see you, brother. They see you as something that is easy to pluck."

"Oi!"

"Hear me out," Sebastian pleaded. "You are young, a marquess, wealthy, with your own estate –"

"As much as I enjoy your compliments, is there a point to this?" Benedict asked with one raised eyebrow.

"There is." Sebastian paused in their walk and held his brother's gaze. "Many ladies seek your company for one reason only. They see you as a viable husband."

"What a shame!" Benedict said with thick sarcasm. "Was it not you who encouraged me to marry? I know I am the one who wants to marry, but you seem to have alighted on the idea with keenness. Why should the lady I wish to spend my life with, bother you so?"

"Yes, I am very eager for you to be wed and to see you happy."

"And you? Will you wed?"

"We have been over this before." Sebastian turned his back and continued his walk. He was not in the mood to have that particular conversation today, so he had to bring it to an end quickly. "I have no cause to marry. You should though. I think it will add to your happiness greatly."

"If that is the way you feel, then why do you scare away every young lady that comes near me? Good lord, Sebastian, you're better than a bulldog for a guard."

"Am I?" Sebastian stood taller and adjusted the tailcoat on his shoulders.

"That was not a compliment!"

"I choose to take it as such," Sebastian said with a smile, prompting his brother to shake his head again. "Now, listen, you know I want what is best for you."

"You've said it a thousand times, though I do not always understand your ways."

"Then hear me out a little more." Sebastian took his brother's shoulder once again and urged him to stop. The two came to a halt in the long reeds that surrounded the lake. As they swayed in the breeze, their leaves practically hissing beside them, Sebastian pointed through the reeds and across the lake, toward where the ladies were walking. "You are young, and not yet experienced with ladies."

"How can I be if you frighten them all away?"

"By learning from my knowledge." Sebastian gestured to the ladies another time. "Lady Bella was so keen to get your attention that the neckline of her gown was never fixed, and Lady Hayes was most reluctant to release your arm at all, was she not?"

"And?"

"And? You do not see a problem with these things? Ha! Benedict, you are naïve. Any lady who is truly interested in you will not resort to tricks." Sebastian held his brother's gaze as his voice became solemn. "They will get to know *you* first, not your title, before they decide they like you. As much as I want you to marry, I want it to be the right woman. Marry the wrong one and it could be a life of misery. What kind of brother would I be if I allowed you to do that?"

Sebastian urged his brother on again. They walked around the lake, coming dangerously close to Lady Hayes and her sister.

"I suppose you are right." Benedict sighed with the words. "Though I still do not know how you can judge a lady as being artful and cunning with just one glance."

"One glance is sometimes all that is needed –" Before Sebastian could say anymore, a cry went up from the lake's riverside.

"What was that?" Benedict was already hurrying forward, before Sebastian could stop him.

Sebastian followed behind, though at a much slower pace. He could see Lady Hayes up ahead had tripped on the reeds and was now prostrate on the ground, but at a rather unnatural angle. Her gown seemed to be adjusted just so to flatter her, and the hem of her skirt was lifted a little.

"Subtle, indeed," Sebastian murmured wryly, watching as Benedict caught up with the lady.

"Lady Hayes, goodness, are you injured?" Forever the gentlemen, Benedict took off his top hat and bent down to his knees, offering his hand to Lady Hayes. Beside them, Lady Bella stood, waving a hand in front of her face as if she might swoon from the shock of it all.

This is as good as being at the theater!

Sebastian worked hard to hide his smile as he reached their side.

"I fear my sister is greatly injured, Lord Westmond," Lady Bella said with drama in her tone.

"As do I," Lady Hayes spoke quickly. "It is my ankle, my lord. It is in need of attention." When she lifted her leg a little too easily, urging Benedict to check for an injury, Sebastian hid his laugh behind a cough. He earned merely a glare from Benedict, who knew that it really was a laugh, though the ladies didn't seem to notice.

"Then we must get you to a physician, my lady."

What!?

Benedict's declaration left Sebastian shaking his head, fearing that his brother's rather young and naïve ways would always make him a target of a pretty lady. One smile and he was enamored. Sometimes, Sebastian had to save his brother from himself.

"Good lord, what is that?" Sebastian said and stepped forward, pointing down at Lady Hayes.

"What?" she asked.

"Ah, I see what it is. A spider. It has just crawled under the hem of your dress, my lady."

"Ahh!" She jumped to her feet, so remarkably quickly that Sebastian had to turn away to hide his laughter. Benedict caught up with him and pulled on his tailcoat.

"Seb! That was not funny."

"I think it was remarkably amusing. Look at poor Lady Hayes now, her ankle seems to have miraculously recovered, does it not?" Sebastian gestured back to the lady who was hopping up and down on both feet, terrified that a spider might be under her gown. "See?"

"Ah..." Benedict acknowledged it all with a nod. "I trust you are recovered, my lady?" His words made Lady Hayes freeze with her sister at her side, both attempting innocent looks that no longer worked.

"I am pleased to see your recovery was so fast. If you would excuse us." Sebastian bowed his head and took his brother's shoulder, steering him away once again. "How I wish you had come fox hunting, Benedict. As amusing as this all is, I could have done without it."

"You are better than any chaperone, I'll give you that, Seb. In fact, I hope you will continue with your duties tomorrow evening."

"Tomorrow evening? What is happening then?"

"A ball, at Lord Melbury's house."

"A ball!?" Sebastian scoffed. "You know I am not a fan of them –"

"Yes, I know. Who would go to a ball when the enjoyment of riding their horse wildly is to be had? Did you knock people over on your way here like skittles? The way you ride, I would not be surprised," Benedict added wryly.

"They jumped out of the way, for the most part," Sebastian continued the jest, much to his brother's delight.

"Say you will come tomorrow night, please."

"To a ball?"

"Please. Besides, without you to watch over me, I might just fall for the charms of a pretty woman who is out to marry my title." Benedict's astute words had Sebastian falling still and offering a glare.

"You have played me."

"It has worked though, has it not? Say you will come, brother?"

Do I have a choice?

Chapter Two

"Can Mary spare the time?"

"I am afraid not," Violet said as she stood behind Penelope and gathered her hair together. "It seems the one maid we have has been forced to join the many others that are already attending to our cousin." Violet turned her gaze on Penelope in the vanity mirror above the table where she sat, seeing the nervous way that Penelope chewed her lip. "Have no fear, I'll do a good job."

"I do not doubt it," Penelope said, though her voice lacked enthusiasm. Violet knew how much her sister longed for the assistance of the one maid they had at times.

In the quiet room, Violet began to pin Penelope's hair, preparing her for the ball. She took extra care tonight, placing pearls attached to pins into the curls at the rear of her sister's head, to ensure attention would be drawn to the fairness of Penelope's hair.

"Quite beautiful," Violet said after she stood back and surveyed her work.

"Thank you, but I fear I –" Penelope broke off as she held a hand to her mouth, making that sound that was now so familiar to Violet.

Casting a worried glance toward the door, Violet reached beneath her bed and fetched an empty copper chamber pot, before bringing it to Penelope and placing it on her lap.

"Th-thank you." Penelope stammered, clearly trying to hold in her sickness as she bent over the chamber pot.

"Well, if I have to grab your curls and hold your hair back again, I'll ruin all my good work," Violet said softly as she dropped down to her knees in front of her sister. To her delight, she saw her jest pleased her sister, and a small smile appeared, even if it only lasted for a few seconds. "There, how are you feeling now?"

"A little better." Penelope still stayed bent over the bowl though, clearly reluctant to leave it just yet. "It's not getting any better, is it?"

Violet held her sister's gaze, wishing with everything she had that she could say it was.

Yet it is not.

It had been a challenge indeed these last couple of weeks to hide Penelope's state. The sickness had at first been played off as a passing illness, but now they were forced to hide it, out of fear that if her uncle or aunt, or Louise, saw Penelope was sick so much, they might call a physician.

He could know exactly what causes Pen's sickness. What then if he were to tell our uncle and aunt?

Violet slowly stood to her feet and walked around Penelope as she placed down the chamber pot, apparently done for the moment with her sickness.

"What am I going to do, Violet?" Penelope broke the silence in the room.

They looked at one another in the vanity mirror. Penelope sat down on the stool and Violet stood behind her, with her hands gently resting on her sister's shoulders.

"What will happen to me?" Penelope whispered.

"Have no fear." Violet forced a smile into her cheeks. "I promised I would think of something, did I not?"

"Are you able to think of miracles?" Penelope asked with a laugh, though there was no real humor in it.

"Perhaps I am," Violet said with false pride, then laughed at herself. "Trust me, Pen, that is all I ask, all is not lost yet. Have we not hidden your secret well so far?"

"By the grace of God, luck, and our maid." Penelope gestured to the door, beyond which in another part of the house, Mary was now helping to care for Louise. Violet nodded, knowing how fortunate they were to have Mary's help. She had hidden Penelope's sheets on more than one occasion and washed them herself, to stop anyone from discovering that Penelope no longer bled.

"Well, in these situations, most women marry," Violet uttered the words she had been afraid of saying.

"Marry? Me!?" Penelope spluttered. She stood to her feet and turned to face Violet. "I cannot marry."

"All I am saying is that it would be a way to hide the pregnancy."

"Yes, so it would. Yet I cannot marry. Not now. After I was so fooled by one man, I thought he genuinely..." She broke off, as tears appeared in her eyes.

"I know, I know," Violet cooed softly and stepped forward, taking her sister in her arms and embracing her tightly. "I know what he made you think. We were all mistaken about him. We all thought he cared for you."

Deep down, Violet seethed with anger, though she hid it for her sister's sake. Sir Babington had a lot to answer for. He persuaded Penelope to believe she was in love, and that he loved her too, all so he could have one night with her, then he left, without another word.

He has done this to her.

"The mere thought of marrying frightens me, Violet, I cannot do it," Penelope said miserably as she stepped back again, her eyes red with the effort of trying to quell those tears. "I cannot stand up in a church and vow to love another man forever. How could I?" She laid her hands on her stomach.

There was no swell there yet, but there was a child growing inside her. The thought of what that child was going to be born into made Violet's heart thud harder and that anger swell again.

For Penelope, and for that child... I must do something!

Penelope lifted a hand to her lips. Clearly, in danger of being sick, Violet reached for the chamber pot, the copper cold to the touch, and thrust it into her sister's hands. Penelope took hold of it and bent forward, but nothing came.

"Oh, Pen, perhaps you shouldn't come to the ball."

"I must! Or our aunt will know something is amiss, will she not? I have already missed three events these last two weeks."

"I know, I know." Violet sighed and turned away, her mind thinking quickly.

Penelope is right. She cannot miss any more events.

Yet it was only a matter of time before Penelope's pregnancy started to show. At first, they could play it off as weight gain, but no one would be fooled for very long.

Think of something, you fool! Have you not promised to protect Penelope from all evils of this world? I failed to protect her from Sir Babington. I will not fail again!

"I'll need a new gown, Violet." Penelope's words made Violet look up to see her sister had at last been sick, but some of it had caught on the gown.

"Oh, sister, do not worry. I'll call for Mary and she'll help us to get you changed speedily. Here, sit down, rest." Violet took her sister's arms and steered her to the nearest chair. "I'll be back in two minutes." She bent down and kissed her sister's forehead before she parted. She heard Penelope whimper at that touch, as if she wanted Violet there longer, before she left.

Closing the door softly behind her, Violet wandered into the corridor, wringing her hands together. It was an old nervous action of hers, clenching and releasing her hands, rather like a cat with long claws.

She was on her way to Louise's room to ask for Mary's assistance when she caught sight of another chamber door that was open. It was to her aunt's chamber, beyond which her aunt was striding back and forth, ready for the ball.

"Oh, oh, listen to this, Mavis," she cried to the lady's maid that hurried on behind her.

Well, at least a maid can be spared for someone else other than Louise. Rather a surprise.

Violet kept her thoughts to herself. Louise was the cherished daughter of Mr. and Mrs. Notley, and all their attention and money usually went to her.

Violet stepped back into the shadows of the corridor and peered around the edge of the doorframe, watching as her Aunt Deborah fluttered around the room with a scandal sheet in her hands. The lady's maid hurried behind her, trying to proffer forward a necklace.

"It talks of the Marquess of Westmond," Deborah said with a manic wave of her hand. She waved the scandal sheet so hard in the air, it was almost like a lady's fan, fluttering at her cheeks. "The Marquess, though the younger brother of the Duke of Ashbury, is certainly the much talked of gentlemen of the season. With enough money to his own name and a vast country estate, he has caught more than one lady's eye.'"

"Mrs. Notley, your necklace." Mavis tried to offer the necklace another time, but Deborah was so caught up in her own words, she didn't even seem to notice. Her pudgy hand lifted the scandal sheet another time as she continued to read.

"Whereas the Duke has earned a reputation for travel and can be seen in the corners of balls and assemblies, plainly eager to not be present, his brother is another man entirely. So many dances he has shared with young ladies this season that it is plain to observe his eye could be won by any lady discerning enough to have him. Will the Marquess of Westmond find a bride this season? This writer is sure to write of the gossip when she hears more.'"

Deborah ended her speech by closing up the scandal sheet. "Oh, Mavis, what a thing that could be for the girls."

"The girls?" Mavis said in surprise, lowering the necklace on her palm.

"Oh, think faster, Mavis. You must realize I am thinking of one of the girls catching his eye. There are three young ladies under this roof that we must see wed." Deborah crossed the room and threw the scandal sheet down on her dressing table before turning back to take the necklace from her maid.

Violet slowly crept closer to the door, to better listen to her aunt.

"Lord knows it will not be an easy task," Deborah declared with a grimace. "My Louise is a beauty and has already charmed many a gentleman. Penelope may be a little plainer, but she has demureness I suppose. That will work in her favor. As for Violet, oh! My sister left me with a challenge when she bestowed Violet into my care."

The words made Violet flinch and reach for the wall beside her. She planted a palm to the plaster, hating the way Deborah spoke.

It was hardly my mother's choice to pass away, was it?

"That girl can speak without thinking. Heaven knows what some gentlemen think of her."

"Yet she is a beauty, is she not, Mrs. Notley?" Mavis' words were clearly unwelcome, for Deborah snatched a ring out of her maid's hand and made her scurry back.

"I suppose she has a certain charm," Deborah added reluctantly. "Yet the girls must marry. How can I not think of this Marquess of Westmond? So wealthy, so desired, and respected. Oh, imagine if he caught the eye of young Louise? What a happy thing that would be!" Deborah clapped her hands together in delight, making the extra fat on her arms jiggle.

Violet stepped back away from the door, creeping away on her tiptoes, yet she listened on, reluctant to disappear completely.

"Hear what else it has to say, Mavis."

"What of your bracelet, Mrs –"

"Shh!" Deborah said firmly and returned to her scandal sheet. "Whichever lady turns her eye on the Marquess of Westmond might be in for a greater challenge than they thought. Allow me to warn any young lady readers out there, for though the Marquess can clearly be charmed by his smile, the older brother does not look so easy to charm. The Duke of Ashbury may have only recently returned from his travels, but he seems reluctant to let his younger brother dance with every lady at a ball.' How troublesome," Deborah continued on. "Well, with Louise's charms, we must hope she can slip by this Duke."

Violet crept away. Walking on the tiptoes of her shoes, she moved onto Louise's room, though she paused outside of the door, not quite knocking, for she was deep in thought.

The Marquess of Westmond...

Here was an interesting prospect. Here was a man that was wealthy and had a country estate. It could be the perfect way to hide Penelope away from the worrisome gossip of the ton. With money to their names, Penelope would be well taken care of. Who would care then if she had a child? The rumors would struggle to travel far from the country, and they would have the fortune to care for the child.

"They could be happy," Violet murmured to herself under her breath. "Penelope and the child... they could be happy." She lowered her hand from where she had raised it to knock on the door and crossed to the nearest mirror on the landing.

Framed in gold with a beveled edge, the mirror reflected back her image. Violet fussed at her reflection a little. She brushed back the loose golden locks from her updo that framed her face, peering at the green eyes that stared back at her. She had never thought of herself as particularly pretty, rather plain in comparison to her sister, yet Mavis had described her as a beauty.

Violet had always found her green eyes were rather too large on her face, and her lips were far too plump. They were nothing like Penelope's that were slim and had this habit of curling into an elegant smile.

Could it be possible for me to catch a gentleman's eye?

She adjusted her Pomona green gown, so bold in color that it matched her eyes, then she tweaked a few of the golden gems in her hair. Once content with her appearance, she stepped back.

"This could work," Violet muttered to herself. So caught up in her thoughts, she neglected to knock and call for Mary after all. She shot back across the corridor, hastening to her room, and bustled through the door.

She moved so fast that Penelope jumped on the other side, nearly dropping the chamber pot she had balanced in her lap.

"Let me guess, Louise cannot afford to spare Mary?" Penelope asked with a wry smile. "You would think two maids were enough for her without taking the one we shared."

"Pen, Pen!" Violet said enthusiastically, hurrying forward, "I have had an idea."

"You certainly seem excited by it."

"I am. Nervous too, but oh, determined as well." Violet grabbed the nearest chair and pulled it forward, sitting down in front of her sister and taking her hand.

"Do not come too close, Violet, I don't want to ruin your gown too."

"Tush, if it happens again, I will hold back your hair for you. Now, listen to me." Violet leaned forward. "To take care of you, we need money and a house. To get either of those things, we need a husband."

"Violet, I told you. I cannot marry. Besides, how am I supposed to convince a gentleman to marry me in such a short space of time?"

"No, Pen, I do not mean you. I mean that *I* shall marry. If I could catch the eye of a gentleman and persuade him to accept my hand, well, you would be safe. Is it not a wonderful idea?"

"Wonderful? My thought was reaching for impossible!"

"Pen!" Violet sat back, affronted.

"No, I didn't mean why would any man want to marry you. I meant how will you get a man to marry you so fast."

"Well, I suppose I will have to make a plan." Violet moved to her feet and clasped her hands together. "Here is what we shall do."

Chapter Three

"I pray the Lord will save us from the behavior of our aunt and uncle," Violet murmured so that only her sister could hear her as they stepped through the doorway of the grand house, ready for the ball. Penelope hid her giggles behind her gloved hand before quickly lowering her fingers.

"They are not so bad..." she said with a kindly tone.

Violet raised her eyebrows and looked forward. In front of them, Mr. and Mrs. Notley were leading the way, with Louise closely behind them. Despite the fact they had no title between them, and it was certainly a kindness to be invited to an event as grand as this one, in a house so fine, they seemed to act as if they were at home. Deborah tossed her pelisse toward the poor footman beside her, who caught it in a kerfuffle, and Walter waved his hand incessantly at the butler in front of him.

"Hurry up there, we cannot be late, you know."

As if that was the butler's doing and not our own!

"Your goodness does you credit, Pen," Violet whispered to her sister, "but you and I are not blind. Look how the butler and footman exchange glances with one another." She cringed as Penelope did the same. They watched the staff together, seeing how they were silently dismayed by the rude behavior before them.

"Violet? Penelope? Come, we are much later than the rest." Deborah beckoned them forward and wafted a fan in front of her hands. The smile on her face showed that it was all part of her plan.

"Strange... we seemed to leave late from the house," Violet murmured. Her words were noticed by Louise who turned an angry glare in Violet's direction, momentarily flattening her fan and waving it at Violet, as if she were a bee that could be dismissed from her presence.

"Well, one must make an entrance, mustn't one?" Deborah said with a happy smile as she turned to her husband.

"Just so, dear. Just so."

"Oh, good lord," Penelope whispered, clinging to Violet's hand as they hurried forward behind their aunt and uncle. "Just whose house are we at? Who are we intending to make such an impression on?"

"An impression! I think this is more likely to look like the height of rudeness, is it not? To turn up late and command attention by walking through the door when everything is already underway −" Violet was cut off as the door to the ballroom opened.

Inside, heads turned in their direction. Ladies' hair dressed in tall ivory feathers, and men's heads slicked with wax, all angled their way. The butler stood by the door and announced their names, but no one hastened forward to greet them.

"Is it not perfect, my dear?" Walter said to his wife with excitement. "All eyes are on us."

"What a fine thing for Louise," Deborah whispered excitedly. "Think of all the gentlemen now looking at her." On cue, Louise stepped forward and fluttered her fan so much that the loose curls of her hair wafted in the wind she created.

"Ever wish you could disappear into the shadows between the candlelight?" Violet whispered with a mischievous smirk. Beside her, Penelope laughed, though she tried to hide it as a hiccough when Deborah turned a glare on them.

"Come, girls, with me." Deborah beckoned them all forward.

Slowly, the guests went back to their business, turning away from the incomers they had not cared to greet.

"We must find someone to speak to. I wonder why no one comes forward to address us," Deborah said, her wide eyes on her large face showing her surprise.

"I wonder why," Violet murmured.

"Shh," Penelope urged and stood on her toe, pleading with her to be quiet.

"Whose house is this, Mama?" Louise said a little too loudly for comfort as she walked alongside her mother. "What a house it is indeed! These furnishings... those chandeliers... look how much staff he has too."

Violet saw it all too, though she did not see it with the greedy gaze Louise saw. She was busy looking back and forth between the candelabras and myriad of crystal glasses set on tables. She was searching for a man she had only seen once before in passing.

The Marquess of Westmond... I must put this plan into action! As soon as possible.

"Oh, I shall point him out to you when we see him. What a surprise it was to have an invitation from *him* of all people. I can only presume his brother knew of your father and persuaded our host to invite him."

"Who is she speaking of?" Penelope whispered in Violet's ear. Before Violet could answer, Deborah stepped forward and accosted a countess. The movement was so sudden, and the curtsy so deep that Penelope clutched harder at Violet's hand. "Did she just...?"

"Well, nothing can be undone now. Have they even been introduced before?" Violet's question was answered by the countess' agog expression.

As Deborah pulled the countess into conversation, Violet stepped back. She felt a sudden need to extricate herself from this world and the embarrassment of her aunt and uncle.

"Where are you going?" Penelope uttered quietly in her ear. "If you are to go ahead with this plan of yours, then you must find a man to set your sights upon."

Violet offered an apologetic smile. Though she had told Penelope she would marry in order to save her from being destitute with her child, Violet had not yet revealed that she had the Marquess of Westmond in mind for a husband.

"I know, but first, I need a minute to myself. I will be back shortly. I promise." Violet squeezed her sister's hand in comfort, receiving a smile in return, then she hurried off.

Slipping between other guests, she did not lift her chin and neither did she let her gaze search for the Marquess of Westmond in the crowd. Her hunt could wait for a little while yet. She needed a moment to herself first.

Stepping through a door set in the side of the ballroom, she hastened down a corridor, in need of an empty room. When she found one, a smile lit up her features. With so much artwork inside, she could not have picked a better room to escape to.

This is my true home.

Violet sighed as she stepped into the darkened room, lit by just one candle. It was plain to see this was an area that should have been off-limits to guests, yet Violet couldn't help herself. She needed to take a breath, not just away from the behavior of her aunt and uncle that made her cringe every few seconds, but away from the ball entirely.

"Can I really do this?" Violet muttered as she clasped and unclasped her hands together.

It is for Penelope. I must do it!

Yet ensnaring a husband in a trap made her feel a little sick. Determined to think of something else for a while, she wandered the room, realizing what a joyful space she had stepped into.

Every wall was full of paintings. Far from being a sitting room or a parlor, this chamber seemed to be a kind of personal gallery. On one wall Violet found Constable paintings, then Gainsborough's too. She moved from one to the next, so excited by each one that her eyes were restless, darting between them.

When floorboards creaked behind her, she didn't notice at first. She was too caught up in admiring a dramatic painting of a ship caught in a storm by Rembrandt that was resting on an easel, that the growing light in the room went unnoticed.

"Hiding in corners like a mouse, my lady?" The deep voice startled Violet so much that she whipped around and stepped back. Her shoulder collided with the Rembrandt painting on the easel and sent it flying to the floor, the bang so loud that it echoed across the room, making the candle the stranger was carrying flicker. "Not as quiet as a mouse, I see."

"I didn't mean to do it," Violet spoke quickly and reached down to the painting. She was on her knees, lifting the painting up when she grew aware of the figure crossing toward her.

"Here, let me. It's a heavy thing." The gentleman discarded his candle, then bent down too and took the painting, only his hand clasped over Violet's instead of the frame. When he did so, neither of them pulled away, they both just froze, staring at each other.

Violet looked properly at the gentleman for the first time. He was tall, significantly taller than her, and with such dark brown wild hair that it looked as if it had been tousled, as though he had recently left a lover's bed. Brown eyes stared back at her, above a square jaw that was dappled with stubble.

"*That* is my hand. Not the frame," she said coolly, trying to extricate her hand.

"I noticed you did not pull back right away." The gentleman chuckled and moved his hand, shifting it on the frame before lifting the painting and putting it back on the easel.

"You stopped me from doing so," Violet said as she hastened back to her feet.

"Ha! You think so?" The gentleman seemed humored by the idea. "Believe me, my lady, I am not the kind of gentleman that is so artful with a lady."

"You do not need to address me like that," Violet spoke hurriedly.

"Well, I do not know who you are, though you are creeping around the corridors of this house, unescorted, so I presumed you are someone who feels entitled to do so." He turned his back on the painting and gestured to the room.

Violet flinched when his eyes met hers again.

This is inconvenient!

Never had she seen such a handsome face. The way something coiled in her chest made her rigid and fold her arms across her body, wanting to distance herself from him.

"You think me rude?" she said, raising her eyebrows. He mimicked her action, folding his arms and raising his eyebrows too.

"I did not say as much."

"You implied it."

"Astute of you."

Why are we arguing?

Violet let her eyes wander over him quickly, wondering how she had come to arguing with a stranger in the art gallery of this house. All she had wanted was an escape, now she was here alone with a man. If anyone saw, it would certainly be scandalous!

"I could accuse you of being just as rude." Violet's quick words, she could have sworn, brought a smile to the handsome face, though he appeared to try and hide it. "Let us start again then." She curtsied. "I am Miss Violet Hathaway." He bowed to her, but as they both stood straight, he did not utter another syllable. "This is usually where a gentleman would introduce himself." Violet gestured toward him.

"This is usually where a young lady scurries off, frightened to be caught alone with a man." He gestured to the door. "Yet you are not in a hurry to leave, are you?"

"This was my hiding place first." Violet turned her back on him and returned her focus to the paintings.

"I beg your pardon?" he spluttered with laughter and began to follow her around the room. Violet grew aware of the scent he was wearing as he came near, following at her heels like some sort of guard dog. It was earthy and spicy, perhaps it was some foreign scent. Her body yearned to turn back toward him, but her mind overruled her.

What is wrong with me?

"You are hiding from a ball, Miss Hathaway?" the stranger said as he followed her. Violet couldn't help looking his way, even as she tried not to. He was tall with wild hair, and the way he was dressed certainly suggested affluence.

He has to be a man of considerable position, or fortune.

"I am." She came to a stop by a constable painting, admiring it. "If you wish to escape the ball, then it is you who can go elsewhere, sir. After all, I was here first."

"Well, I suppose that is a fair stance to take." He moved his hands to rest on his hips. "Other than the fact this is not your house."

"I am not harming anyone by being here." She gestured to the paintings. "Would you be so cruel, stranger, as to ban me from a few minutes' enjoyments?" Her question seemed to change something between them.

The fast words and quick bickering faded, and he cocked his head to the side, as if he was analyzing her. Under the intense dark gaze, Violet shifted between her feet.

"You are fond of art?" he asked after a few seconds of silence.

"Immensely. I certainly enjoy looking at it more than I do a ball." She shifted her gaze to the painting.

"You would be the first lady I have ever met to declare such a thought. Here, if you want a painting to observe, then let it be this one." He beckoned her to follow him across the room. In the recesses of her mind, Violet knew she shouldn't follow him, yet her body went of its own accord anyway, rather wanting to be near him. "This painting describes ladies of the ton, to my mind."

Violet had to fight the small smile that tempted her lips. She did not recognize the artist, but the painter had created a ball in which all the ladies were reaching toward one fine gentleman. Rather than appearing as fine, elegant women, they looked a lot more like vultures, with fingers outstretched as talons.

"What a cynic you are, stranger," Violet murmured, shaking her head and pretending to tut at him. "You think this describes every lady in that ballroom?"

I suppose tonight I will be one of those vultures, will I not? Reaching for a man with nothing else in mind other than the money he calls his own.

"I know it does," the man spoke firmly as he returned his focus to Violet. "So, I ask you again, why are you really out here alone in this room? Perhaps you are waiting to meet a man? To trick him into marriage?"

"Good lord!" She stepped back from him. "I do not think I have ever met a gentleman so outspoken."

"I speak of what is on my mind, that is all." He waved a hand toward his own temple.

"Then allow me to speak mine." Her firm words made him turn back to face her, that intense gaze returning to meet her own. "I came here for peace, privacy, and quiet. *You* are rather spoiling it." He smiled a little at her. "Are you proud of it?"

"No, I am not. I am merely rather impressed by you." He gestured toward her. "Either you mean your words, or you are a fine actress."

"I have never been so insulted." She walked away from him and returned to the Rembrandt painting resting on the easel. To her surprise, he followed her once again and stood by her shoulder, so close that the pleasant scent he was wearing brought goosebumps to her skin. "You do realize our rather unpleasant encounter could be terminated right now if you left the room?"

"Unpleasant? Is that what you call it?"

"It's as stormy as this painting is." She gestured toward it.

"Actually, I am rather intrigued by this meeting." The gentleman's words made Violet slowly turn back toward him. He was staring at her now with such a mischievous smile on his face that she narrowed her gaze at him, wary of him. "I rather think you do not dislike this meeting as much as you pretend to either, or you would have run away by this point," he whispered and gestured to the door. "Is it the bickering that keeps you here? Or something else?"

"What would that something else be?" She couldn't resist teasing him. She had never known this feeling before, nor this kind of conversation. It seemed to be that nothing was off-limits, nothing out of bounds. She didn't dare guess what he would say next, for he was impossible to predict.

"Well, a beautiful woman is keeping me in this room," he said, his voice deep. "Is it so mad for me to hope that you rather like the look of the gentleman before you, and that is why you stay here?"

"Oh, should I call that arrogance?" She laughed and shook her head. "I wonder why you bother trying to charm me at all, sir, when you have just insulted all of my sex with reference to your painting over there." She gestured to the painting of the ladies being like vultures.

"Challenge me then. Prove to me not all ladies are like that." He stepped toward her as he said it, his chin tilting down toward her.

Such tension filled the air that Violet quite forgot herself. She didn't think of the ball, nor what her plan was for that night. She thought only of the little distance that was between her and the mysterious gentleman, and how near his lips were to hers.

"I cannot." Her whispered words made his brows lift further.

I am one of them.

"Why?" he asked, tilting his head to the side.

"I have stayed long enough, sir." She tried to step back, but she bumped the painting on the easel yet again. Her gasp filled the air, as the gentleman reached toward her. His hand went for her waist and jerked her forward, stopping her from toppling the painting any further.

The easel wobbled in its place, but the painting didn't fall.

Violet was breathless, staring up at the gentleman as one of her hands fell to his chest. They were so close now, impossibly so, with his lips near to hers. His eyes flicked downward, finding her lips.

"Stay another minute more, Miss Hathaway." His voice was deep. She found she could not refuse him and stayed there in his hold. When she did not move away, he inched down toward her.

When his lips met hers, Violet heard her heart thud in her ears and felt her hand curl around the lapel of his jacket.

Oh, so this is the thrill of a kiss...

Chapter Four

Sebastian couldn't resist Miss Hathaway. His lips moved against hers with a kind of urgency, a need that had overtaken him. It was a desire most passionate. How he could feel such a thing for a stranger was unknown, but all he knew was that he could not end this kiss yet.

Kisses should not feel like this... should they?

His mind was wandering to places he knew it should not, but he couldn't help himself. As Miss Hathaway placed her hands on him, he was imagining how those hands would feel if they touched his bare chest, not his clothes.

He had kissed ladies before on the continent, but not a single one had felt like this. Miss Hathaway's hand clutched to his lapel as one of his palms slid across her back, holding her to him. When he angled the kiss, deepening it further, he felt her whimper in a sort of pleasure, her lips soft against his own. When her tongue came out to meet his, participating with vigor, he felt breathless, not wanting this heat to end. He could have sighed with the desire that stirred in him, then the kiss changed. She bit him on his lip.

Sebastian jerked back, both humored and shocked. His hands were still on her and there was fire in that touch. Her hands on his chest were still playing on his mind, making him want to feel that touch against his skin. She seemed equally affected by it, glancing down at her hands against him.

"What the —"

"You should not have done that." There was fire in those bold green eyes as she stumbled away from him.

"The painting!"

She knocked into it for a third time as she hastened out of his hold. She didn't reach to catch it, leaving Sebastian to jump forward and grasp it before it could topple over. Yet Miss Hathaway tripped on the edge of the easel and nearly fell over. The way she twisted her ankle made it plain it was injured.

"Miss Hathaway?" he called to her, but she was already hastening out of the room, practically limping with the effort. "Miss Hathaway?" he called again. This time, she froze in the doorway and looked back at him. Her gold hair appeared almost orange in the two candles that kept them company in that room.

"Not another word, sir, I beg of you," she said in a harried whisper. "That should not have happened."

"Because of propriety or because you did not enjoy it?" He couldn't resist asking the question, just as she shot him a glare and ran off. The moment she was gone with the door closing behind her, Sebastian felt his good sense return. "What did I just do?"

He thrust his hands into his hair and pulled on the ends as he looked around the room. When he had first seen someone was in this chamber, he had merely wanted to encourage them back to the ball. He didn't want guests wandering around his house, uninvited. Yet there had been something about Miss Hathaway that had been quite intoxicating to him.

Sebastian hadn't yet had a claret or a brandy that evening, but he felt as if he'd had two or three. It had been all too easy to bicker with her, feeling mischievous and playful at the way those large green eyes kept shooting back to him.

Oh, she liked the kiss though, did she not?

He rubbed a thumb across his bottom lip as he lowered his hand and thought of that kiss. She had returned it, with passion, and when he had asked her to stay, she had done that too.

"Whatever this feeling is," he muttered to himself, "I am not the only one to feel it."

He was quite certain of that. Turning his eyes on the painting she had admired so much, he cast a gaze over the ship caught in a storm. He rather imagined a storm had just taken place in that very room. There was the crack of thunder in their argument and then the flash of lightning in that kiss.

Sebastian found his feet controlled him. He blew out one of the candles and took the other, carrying it out of the room and into the corridor. When he reached the ballroom and stepped inside, placing the candle with the others, he looked over his guests.

There were so many people here tonight, he wondered if anyone had even noticed his absence for a few short minutes. He looked between ladies' headdresses that were trussed up with feathers, and between fluttered fans, looking for one pair of deep green eyes.

Where are you?

Sebastian didn't think about why he was searching for Miss Hathaway. He only thought of the thrill of the argument, and that kiss.

Traipsing through the guests, people tried to stop him more than once, encouraging him to be introduced to their daughters and nieces. He smiled and politely greeted them, but he would not be ensnared so he moved on. At last, he saw Miss Hathaway. He stumbled to a stop by the violins as she stepped into the ballroom, limping, with her arm resting through another gentleman's.

"I do not believe it," Sebastian muttered in a little anger. The excitement Miss Hathaway caused had suddenly deadened and numbed within him, for she was on the arm of Benedict. Not only that, but she was clutching to him, looking up at him with such a false smile that Sebastian didn't want to believe the proof of his own eyes.

I knew it! All women, they are just the same.

He crossed quickly toward the two of them, so determined to intercept Miss Hathaway before she could lay a trap for his brother, that he nearly slipped up at one point on the floorboards. The sounds of his near trip caught her attention then. She looked away from Benedict and those dark green eyes found Sebastian's across the room.

Do not let that thrill begin again now, you fool. You can see what sort of a lady she is now.

"Well, well, what is happening here?" Sebastian said and stopped at their side, with his eyes only on Miss Hathaway, though he spoke directly to his brother. "Benedict, it seems every time I look for you these days, I find you with a lady clinging to your arm."

"Do not cause trouble now, Seb," Benedict said tiredly, then turned a big smile on Miss Hathaway at his side. "The lady is injured. She has hurt her ankle and I was offering to help her to a chair."

"How thoughtful of you." Sebastian kept his eyes on Miss Hathaway. She returned that stare, momentarily, before she shifted her gaze to Benedict where her expression softened. It was such a happy smile, so easy in appearance that Sebastian found something jolted in his chest.

She didn't look at me like that, even when we shared that kiss.

"You are most kind, my lord, I must thank you for your help." Her hand seemed to curl more around Benedict's arm, clinging onto him. When Benedict's hand came up to tap her fingers in comfort, something in Sebastian raged.

Do not fall for her charms, Benedict!

"What a to-do this is. How did you find the injured lady, Benedict?" Sebastian asked, crossing his arms over his chest as he waited restlessly for the answer.

"Quite by accident just now in the corridor. She was returning to the ball, and tripped, causing her ankle to twist. Fortunately, I was there to catch her before she could fall further."

Wait, I thought she tripped over the easel?

Sebastian returned his glare to Miss Hathaway another time. It seemed like any other lady he had met, she was cunning and artful after all. She must have tripped on purpose when she saw his brother, in the attempt to make him catch her and establish some sort of touch between them. From the way Benedict's eyes drifted over her, her plan was working.

Save us all from artful women!

"Ah, my lord," Miss Hathaway said with a smile and gestured to a young lady who had approached them. "May I introduce my sister to you? This is Miss Penelope Hathaway." Benedict turned his focus on the younger sister.

Rather like her sister, Miss Penelope had fair hair, but her features were more petite. She was also rather demure in nature as she curtsied, almost afraid to lift her eyes to meet either Benedict's gaze or Sebastian's own. She was unlike Miss Hathaway, who continued to boldly look straight at Sebastian.

When he caught her staring, he smiled at her, mischievously, showing he had seen her looking.

"How do you do, Miss Penelope." Benedict bowed politely with his words. "I am afraid your sister has gained an injury. We must get her somewhere to rest."

"That is most kind, my lord. Here, I shall help her from here." Miss Penelope stepped forward to take her sister's hand, but

Miss Hathaway was clearly not in a hurry to release Benedict just yet.

I must get them apart from each other!

"No, no need for that." Sebastian stepped forward before any more damage could be done. "I have heard the best thing for an injury is sometimes to exercise."

"Oh, have you?" Miss Hathaway asked, her tone challenging as she lifted her chin in his direction. "Where did you train to be a physician, sir?"

"Well, one picks up a few scraps of information on their travels. All you need is a little exercise to loosen the ankle, Miss Hathaway." Sebastian could see he had angered her. Her cheeks had blushed pink, and her brows furrowed together.

"I suppose I –" Before Benedict could make the offer, Sebastian cut him off.

"Share a dance with me, Miss Hathaway? Something tells me in one dance I could make sure your ankle is miraculously healed."

Now we shall see how you have faked the injury.

"I do not think that a wise idea, sir." She was shaking her head, animatedly, urging her golden curls to whip back and forth around her face.

"Oh, Violet, one cannot refuse a gentleman's offer," Miss Penelope said hurriedly, with a look of horror on her face at the thought of such a thing.

"Ah, am I in company that worries so about propriety?" Sebastian was humored by the idea. "Then I will work the situation to my advantage." He spoke with further mischief as he offered his hand to Miss Hathaway. "You would not turn down a gentleman's offer, would you, Miss Hathaway?"

She frowned at him further, those green eyes full of fire once again. Sebastian could see there was danger in those eyes. It could be easy for a man to become entranced when staring at such enchanting fire. He had to get her far away from Benedict before he could fall under such a spell.

"Very well." She huffed as she placed her hand in his. Stepping back from Benedict, her expression changed, and she offered him a rather sweet smile. Sebastian sighed loudly as he led her away, pointedly groaning at her action, but she was clearly the only one who had noticed it, for Benedict had already turned his attention on the younger and far quieter Miss Hathaway.

"You are a persistent sort of gentleman," Miss Hathaway murmured as Sebastian led her toward the dancefloor. Through her gloved hand, he could feel the warmth of her palm, and he suddenly had no wish to let her hand go, even as they took to the floor and had to bow and curtsy to one another.

"Why do you think that? Just because I would not let you trick Benedict into giving his attentions to you? I fell for it, Miss Hathaway, I will not let him fall for it too." He uttered the words quickly before releasing her to bow.

As he did so, he held her gaze, watching as her jaw slackened in shock at his words. As the music struck up, he found it was an upbeat cotillion, fast and rather sharp in tone. It matched his mood perfectly, for when he took Miss Hathaway's hand and walked around her, beginning the rather complicated choreography, their hold was firm upon one another.

"I did not trick you into doing anything, sir," Miss Hathaway declared, her words hurried and quiet as they circled each other. "You were the one who spoke to me, may I remind you of that?"

"Yet you could have left."

"You were also the one who…" She trailed off and looked at the other dancers as they parted from one another. They were forced to circle other couples separately before they came back together. This time, Sebastian took her waist and one of her hands. She gasped at that touch, with her gloved fingers resting on his shoulder.

"I what, Miss Hathaway?"

She didn't say the words, but flicked her eyes down to his lips, reminding him exactly of what he had done.

"Well, you did not pull away."

"Neither was it my doing. I will not be accused of enticing the attention of a gentleman, not when you were so forward."

"Then tell me this, why did you fall into poor Benedict and force him to practically carry you back to the ballroom, hmm? You seemed capable of walking away from my company just now."

"Did you not notice my limp?" she asked, her eyes wide. He led her back and forth, completing the galloping steps.

"I did, but you seem to be dancing on it remarkably fine now, do you not?"

"Then you do not know what an expression of pain looks like, sir." She released him as they walked around one another. There was not a touch between them, though he was tempted to reach out toward her. He yearned for it.

"I thought that was a look of dislike."

"Perhaps an easy mistake to make." Her words tempted him to smile as they turned away from each other. Once again, they circled other dancers before they came back together.

As Sebastian found it hard to tear his eyes away from her, that realization made his heart thud harder. She had power over him. If she had such power over Benedict too, then it would not be long before his brother was standing at the end of an aisle in church, about to marry a woman who had ensnared him in a trap.

"Allow me to speak plainly, Miss Hathaway."

"Strange for you to ask permission now after you have already been so bold this evening," she murmured, revealing a smirk of humor that he could not help returning for a moment, before it faded.

"Stay away from Benedict."

"I beg your pardon?" She leaned a little away from him. He was forced to step toward her again and place his hand on her waist, drawing her back for the close section of the dance.

"I have met plenty of ladies like you. They all approach Benedict with the same thing in mind. They want him for his fortune and his title. I will not let any lady trap him so."

"Who are you to him to guard him so?" she asked. He blinked, realizing that in all their hurried conversations tonight, he had not once revealed he was Benedict's brother, nor even his name. Before he could answer her, Miss Hathaway winced and looked down.

Oh... is she actually injured? Or is it an act?

"I should compliment you on your fine acting again, Miss Hathaway."

"It is not an act," she said through gritted teeth. Guilt began to sway within him, realizing she could truly be injured.

"Then lean on me." His words urged her to do just that. He tried not to think of the thrill that coursed through him as one of her hands rested on his upper arm and the other clutched to his hand. Sebastian had her weight entirely, and in that moment, they merely stared at each other, with not a word passing between them.

There was a serenity there, even if it only lasted a few seconds. A moment of peace where he admired the woman's beauty and allure.

Do not fall for the very act you are trying to protect your brother from, you fool!

"I noticed that you have not denied trying to capture the attention of Benedict," he whispered, watching as those green eyes sharpened upon him. "I see. I'm reminded of that painting I was showing you. The one with the ladies all vying for one man's attention."

"Do not pretend to know me, stranger. You do not."

The dance had a sudden shift in music, and he released her to perform the next part. Her words had angered him, and it made Sebastian release her without much care. As she stepped away, her weight shifted backward.

"Miss Hath —" He leaned toward her to catch her, but she fell to the ground so loudly that the violin music paused, and other dances all stepped back.

There was such a commotion in the room that Sebastian felt gazes swing toward them. Without hesitation, Sebastian dropped to his knees and offered to help her up.

"You really are injured," he murmured, proffering his hand. She didn't take it but glared at him still.

"No, I'm not, I just wished to fall to the floor for my own amusement," she whispered with thick sarcasm.

"I am offering to help you up."

"I do not trust you not to drop me again."

Sebastian was hurt by the words. He didn't know why. Had he not been attempting to drive this lady away? Should he not be pleased he had angered her?

"Violet! Violet, are you all right?" Miss Penelope was suddenly at their side, along with Benedict. The two had been dancing together before coming to Miss Hathaway's aid.

"Merely an accident when dancing, Pen." Miss Hathaway moved to her knees and winced. With her face turned down, she seemed to be hiding her blush of embarrassment, but Sebastian saw it all. "Clearly, my lack of dancing skills has caused me to worsen my injury."

"Nothing to do with your dance partner then?" Benedict said knowingly, looking to Sebastian. Once again, Sebastian tried to help Miss Hathaway to her feet, but she took her sister's hand instead and stood, before wincing as she put weight on her ankle.

"Sister, would you help me away, please? I think I have had quite enough of dancing with this gentleman for one night. Perhaps for good."

As she turned away, Sebastian watched her go. He ignored the curious looks of Benedict and the others in the ballroom, for he was too caught up in his own thoughts.

"Seb, what exactly just took place?"

Chapter Five

"I have invited the Miss Hathaways for a promenade in Hyde Park." Benedict's sudden words made Sebastian crumple the newspaper sharply in his lap.

"You did what?" Sebastian sat forward, watching as his brother opposite him at the breakfast table was humored, smiling as he drizzled honey on his bread. "This was not part of the plan."

"You mean your plan? Whatever plan that was." Benedict shrugged, clearly not caring for what Sebastian thought on this matter. "Listen here, brother, I'm more than happy for you to advise me as to what lady is worthy of my time. However, I will not have you embarrass a lady as you did last night." He froze and shook his knife in Sebastian's direction.

Sebastian let the crumpled newspaper fall limp on the table beside him as he lifted a hand and pinched the brow of his nose. Guilt swelled inside him, so much so that he shifted on his chair until it creaked.

"It was never my intention to embarrass Miss Hathaway last night," he murmured.

"Was it not? Pah! You think I believe that?"

"It was an accident, Benedict."

"You knew she was injured, yet you asked her to dance, then promptly let her fall." Benedict was clearly outraged, moving so quickly with his knife now upon his bread that he tore the bread into chunks.

"Careful, you'll have nothing but crumbs soon," Sebastian said as he lowered his hand and gestured at his brother's plate. Benedict dropped the knife and held Sebastian's gaze.

"Are you proud of what happened at your ball?"

"No. Not for a single second." Sebastian shook his head. As he had watched Miss Hathaway walk away from him, the guilt had only become worse. "Benedict, I was trying to protect you. I believe Miss Hathaway turned her attentions on you last night because she is looking for an advantageous match. I wished to be sure."

"So, you threw her on the floor?"

"That is not what happened!" Sebastian sat forward, upset at the mere suggestion. "She was leaning on me because she was injured. I was only just beginning to understand that she was indeed hurt when I released her for another part of the dance. I did not realize quite how much she was leaning on me, but then her ankle gave way, and she..." He gestured to the floor beneath them, imitating her fall.

"Hmm."

"Do you believe me?"

"Yes." Benedict sat back in his chair and sighed. "I have invited Miss Hathaway and her sister to Hyde Park today, because she deserves an apology for the way you behaved last night."

"I know. Believe me, I know she does." Sebastian thrust his hands into his hair, feeling the truth of just how badly he had behaved. Yet Benedict was not the one who should be giving that apology. "I shall come to your promenade too."

"What?" Benedict spluttered in laughter. "You? You always say you'd rather ride your horse through the Thames itself than come to Hyde Park."

"I would." Sebastian nodded. "I am not like you, brother. When I go for a walk, I go to the countryside. I look at the birds, the deer, the wildlife. You, well, you go to look at ladies."

"I am not that bad."

"You are easily enamored." Sebastian shook his head with a sigh. "Yet you are right. Miss Hathaway deserves an apology, and I should be the one to give it to her."

"Then this has nothing to do with you wanting to keep an eye on her, does it?" Benedict asked, his voice knowing.

Sebastian chose not to answer, though he smiled as he picked up his coffee cup.

I'll protect you, brother, even from Miss Hathaway.

"Good lord, Seb, you really are becoming my guard dog." Benedict laughed at his own words and picked up his honeyed bread.

"I just want you to be careful." Sebastian made his voice solemn. It clearly caught his brother's attention, for all humor in the air dissipated between them and they looked at one another across the breakfast table. "You are my brother. I want you to be happy, Benedict. If Miss Hathaway turns out to be the thing that makes you happy, then very well. I will come to the wedding and be deliriously happy for you both."

"Hold on! We are hurrying ahead a bit here."

"That we are, but the point still stands. If she will not make you happy, then I want to be sure we know it fast. Before any attachment can grow." Sebastian's words clearly struck a chord with Benedict, for he nodded and returned to his breakfast.

With Benedict's eyes turned away, Sebastian attempted to return to his newspaper, but he could not. He kept seeing in his mind's eye the way that Miss Hathaway had clung to him in his gallery room the night before as he had kissed her. It didn't make sense to him how a lady could return such a kiss and then move her attentions to another man within the space of minutes.

No. There is no honest intention there, even if I do owe the lady an apology.

Chapter Six

"I beg your pardon?" Louise was on her feet as she stared around the sitting room in wonder. Her head turned back and forth so much that Violet feared she rather looked like a chicken, with her head bobbing back and forth.

"You heard me right, Louise, I am sure of it," Walter said from where he sat by the fireplace in the room, staring down at the note in his hand. "The Marquess of Westmond has invited Violet and Penelope to accompany him in Hyde Park."

Louise clearly did not believe the proof of her ears, even for a second time, for she turned to where Violet and Penelope were sat together on the settee.

"How did you manage to trick him into this?" she asked wildly.

"Louise! Is that any way to talk to your cousins?" Deborah's sudden defense of Violet and Penelope made the two sisters exchange a look. Violet could see the same shock in her sister's face that she was sure was on her own. Their aunt didn't usually stand up for them in such a manner. "We should be thrilled for them. Oh, how exciting this is."

Deborah moved to her feet and clasped her hands together. "You have the attention of a marquess!"

"It says here in the gentleman's note that he wishes to make reparations for the incident that occurred last night at the ball." Walter peered over the spectacles that balanced on the edge of his nose, looking straight at Violet. "It seems he wishes to pay a compliment to you, Violet."

She tried her best to return the smile. After all, was this not good news? Had she not wanted to secure the Marquess' attentions toward her? Penelope seemed to notice her odd behavior, for she subtly elbowed Violet when she sewed another stitch into her embroidery, urging her to speak.

"Yes, it is very kind." Violet found her voice at last, though she was still restless. Attempting to turn her focus down to her sketchpad, she found her pencil began to create a face on the page, one in profile with a strong jaw and stubble upon his chin. When she discovered it was not the Marquess' face she was drawing, but the mysterious gentleman she had danced with instead, she closed the book sharply, making both Deborah and Penelope in the room jump.

Who was that man? He must have been either a good friend or even family to the Marquess of Westmond, for he addressed him with his first name.

Violet had barely slept all night. She kept trying to tell herself it was from the guilt of attempting to catch the Marquess of Westmond's eye, but deep down, she knew the true reason. She kept seeing the mysterious gentleman in her sleep and imagined that kiss once again. Each time she saw it, she stirred from her sleep and passed her fingers over her lips, tempted to relive the moment.

"If this is to go well, then you must appear at your best." Deborah crossed the room toward Violet. When Louise was in the way, she was hastily pushed to the side. This was so unusual that Louise was not the only one whose expression was agog, for Violet's matched it. Deborah took hold of Violet's hands and pulled her to her feet. "The gown will do I suppose, but perhaps you should change into your ivory gown? It certainly flatters you well."

"Aunt, I am sure such a thing is not necessary," Violet pleaded, trying to extricate her hands from her aunt's, suddenly uncomfortable at how close her aunt had come.

"Perhaps I could go too?" Louise declared and walked toward her father, leaning down over his shoulder to read the letter that was clutched in his hand. He proffered it up to her and rested back in his armchair.

"Louise, dearest, it does not mention you, only your cousins." His words made Louise's bottom lip quiver, like a child rather put out and ready to cry.

Violet turned and looked at Penelope, who was trying her best to hide her smile of amusement in her embroidery.

"Oh, aunt, what are you doing?" Violet abruptly cried as Deborah reached her hands toward Violet and started fussing with her gown.

"It must sit right. A gentleman's eyes go to certain places when they look at a lady."

"Good lord, this is not to be born," Violet muttered as Deborah continued to adjust the gown. Next, she pinched Violet's cheeks, trying to bring some color to them. "I am fine, aunt, truly."

"Penelope, you need some color too." Deborah dropped down to her knees in front of Penelope and pinched her cheeks, so harshly that Penelope winced and whimpered. "Hmm. You are rather pale still. I wonder if your sickness is still lingering."

"I am fine, aunt," Penelope lied and turned a pleading look on Violet, clearly wishing for her to change the subject.

If only Deborah knew the true cause of Pen's paleness.

"When is the promenade to be, uncle?" Violet changed the subject, much to Penelope's relief as she sat back again.

"Any minute now, it would seem." Walter checked the pocket watch that rested in his waistcoat and nodded down at the watch face. "He must be eager to see you again to make an appointment to come so early. Not to mention to send this ahead of him." He gestured once more to the letter that was now clutched in Louise's shaking hand.

"Why is this?" Louise asked abruptly. Eyes in the room turned to her.

"What was that, dear?" Deborah asked. She had now returned to Violet and was fussing with her hair so much that Violet feared she looked like a baby bird in a nest, with its mother preening its feathers.

"Why would the Marquess take a liking to Violet so? It is not fair!"

"Louise, that is hardly kind, is it?" Walter asked, his voice deep. Once again, Violet looked to Penelope who appeared equally amazed. The transformation their aunt and uncle had suddenly undergone did not make sense at all.

In a distant part of the hour, the bell for the front door was rung.

"Oh! That will be him." Deborah released Violet and hastened forward, standing in the middle of the room and adjusting her own gown so that there were no creases in it. Walter stood too, straightening his cravat and the pin that held it together.

Violet reached for Penelope's hand and pulled her to her feet, feeling better to whisper to her now that everyone was looking at the door and no longer at them.

"Do you think our aunt and uncle are quite well?" she murmured to her sister.

"It seems the prospect of you gaining a marquess' attention has altered everything." Penelope shuddered at the words. "You know our aunt and uncle. They like advancement in this world."

"You are right." Violet was prevented from saying any more as the door to the sitting room opened. The butler was the first to step in before he bowed and stepped to the side.

"May I introduce the Marquess of Westmond, sir." Behind the butler, the Marquess stepped in.

Violet had to acknowledge the gentleman was handsome and certainly had an affable countenance, for he turned smiles on everyone in the room, including Violet. He parted his lips, apparently eager to speak to her, when Deborah bustled forward, her quick feet limited by the narrowness of her gown so that she seemed to totter.

"You are most welcome, Lord Westmond. Please, please, do come in." Deborah smiled so much that it was gushing and made the atmosphere of the room quite uncomfortable. "You do us a great compliment by coming to see us. Does he not, dears?" She turned to look at Violet and Penelope, but she didn't wait for an answer and shifted back to look at the marquess, still eagerly speaking. "How was your journey? Not long, I hope?"

"Was she really talking to us then?" Violet murmured to her sister.

"She was."

"She never calls us 'dears'."

"She does now," Penelope pointed out. Before any more could be said, Louise moved to their side and stood tall with a large smile on her face. Violet had to hide her laughter, humored by her cousin's attempt to gain notice.

Violet suddenly grew aware of a shadow moving in the doorway.

"We have a second visitor too, sir." The butler continued and gestured a hand to the gentleman that moved forward. "The Duke of Ashbury."

Wait... the Marquess of Westmond's brother?

Violet felt her jaw fall so far that it might as well have hit the floor. In front of her, with his dark eyes shooting straight to meet her own, was the mysterious gentleman she had met the night before. His lips curled into a playful smile, for he was clearly taking pleasure in her shock.

He is the Duke!? I kissed the Duke of Ashbury!

Chapter Seven

Violet was struggling to take her eyes off the Duke. Shortly after the gentlemen's arrival at the house, Deborah had ushered them all outside, eager to see them on their way to the promenade. Louise had hinted lots of times to go but was soon quietened when her father had taken her hand and held her back.

Now, as they walked into Hyde Park, Violet was standing between the two gentlemen. Her eyes kept lifting to look at the Duke, though her arm was looped through the Marquess'. On the Marquess' other side, Penelope stood quietly, barely uttering a sound.

"I see I have shocked you today, Miss Hathaway," the Duke said with clear humor as they all strode into Hyde Park together. The sunny day shone down boldly, making the Duke's dark hair seem brighter. He turned a mischievous smile toward her as they passed through the flower borders.

"It would not be the first shock you have given," Violet murmured, knowing the words had a dual meaning. To her and the Duke, they meant something else entirely. He winked at her, showing he knew exactly what she meant.

How dare he!?

She snatched her gaze away.

"On that subject, my brother and I owe you an apology, Miss Hathaway." The Marquess took up the thread of the conversation. "My brother's manners seemed to abandon him last night at the ball."

"I can make the apology for myself, Benedict," the Duke said good-naturedly, though the Marquess shook his head, apparently in disbelief.

"Then hurry up and say it before I do it for you." The Marquess pulled them all to a stop. Violet turned her eyes back to the Duke, waiting for the apology to pass his lips.

He shifted between his feet for a second, looking a little uncomfortable. Unlike his brother, he did not bother wearing a top hat. With his wild hair rather loose, he ran a hand through it, apparently feeling rather stressed.

"Something tells me you are not used to giving apologies, your Grace," she said with humor. "There is nothing to fear in an apology, I assure you."

"I am sorry." His words came quickly now. "I stepped out of line last night. My attempt to look out for my brother may have come across as ill intentions toward you. That was not my wish, Miss Hathaway. Your fall was my doing and I apologize unreservedly for it. Plus... for any other impropriety that may have been of my own doing last night."

Ah, he is apologizing for more than just the fall. He is apologizing for the kiss too.

She smiled a little, appreciating how he could so easily say the words and yet keep his true meaning hidden from Penelope and the Marquess.

"Thank you," she said with a smile. "I appreciate that, and you are forgiven." Yet she jerked her head away sharply and moved forward, encouraging them all to walk again with her.

Why does the thought of him apologizing for that kiss upset me so?

"Well, now *that* is done, let us talk of something else," the Marquess spoke quickly, his tone buoyant and upbeat.

Violet was distracted. She was too aware of the way the Duke hurried at her side, so close that she felt enveloped by that exotic scent once again. It was as if she was immune to the scents of the jasmine and wisteria from the park, all she could think of, was him.

"What do you say, Miss Hathaway?"

"I'm sorry?" Violet looked up at Lord Westmond and offered a smile, realizing she had managed to ignore him with her focus taken so much by his brother.

"I was saying that a violin quartet are supposed to be playing in the park today. I would be glad to hear them if you two ladies would be interested."

Violet kept her smile in place. In truth, she was not particularly fond of such music. She sometimes found a violin a little whiny for her liking, and would have infinitely preferred looking at a painting, yet her gaze shot to Penelope who looked rather eager at the Marquess' side.

"We would be glad of that, my lord. My sister is a particular fan of such music."

"You are, Miss Penelope?" the Marquess seemed intrigued by the idea, turning his focus on Penelope. Yet she merely blushed and nodded, then looked away. "What are your thoughts on art? I am afraid I have little liking for it."

"That is down to your stubbornness alone, brother," the Duke spoke up.

"It is not stubbornness."

"You merely are not a fan of it because I have amassed a huge collection of it." The Duke shot an apologetic glance Violet's way. "Forgive my brother. He has not been amused by the number of times I have pushed a painting under his nose and wanted an opinion on it."

"It has rather made me tire of the whole art form. Miss Hathaway, what are your thoughts on art?" the Marquess asked, seeming eager to have her answer.

Violet paused nervously, making a quick decision. She loved art, through and through. It was why she spent every day with her sketchpad and was always dragging Penelope to Somerset Gallery, but could she say as much now?

I need the Marquess to like me, do I not?

Violet's gaze shot to Penelope and down to her stomach. She knew it wouldn't be long before Penelope began to show.

"I am not a great fan myself, my lord," Violet said.

"You are not?" The Duke's voice was humored. Violet swallowed past a nervous lump, suddenly realizing what she had done. She lifted her gaze to meet the Duke's to see he had another mischievous smile in place. "A conversation we had last night could have truly persuaded me to believe you had a fondness for it."

Violet cursed inwardly, remembering how she had professed a love for art in front of him the night before.

"It does well for distraction, your Grace. If I praised it, that is merely what I meant." She shrugged, as if it was no great thing to talk of.

"Ah, here we are!" the Marquess declared with vigor. "The violinists are here."

Violet looked away from the Duke to see they had appeared in a square within the center of Hyde Park. A bandstand draped in late-blooming boughs was currently bearing host to four musicians who were stepping forth, carrying their violins with them. Around the bandstand, people gathered, looking for seats and places to stand on a lawn.

"If you would excuse me, momentarily, I wish to greet the violinists."

"You know them, my lord?" Penelope said, speaking up for the first time.

"I do. I am a particular fan of this quartet and often like to hear them. I will be back soon." He bowed to the two of them and hurried off. Violet could see the rather eager look on Penelope's face, as if she too would have liked to have spoken to the violinists, yet Penelope said nothing and moved to Violet's side instead.

Violet offered her arm to her sister and Penelope took it, leaning on her.

"Your ankle seems to be holding up well today, Miss Hathaway." The Duke's words made Violet look sharply at him. Once again, he had a playful look in his expression, as if he was out to cause mischief.

"It is heavily bandaged, your Grace. I would prove the case to you and lift my hem so you could see it, but we both know how improper that would be, do we not?" she said, teasing him. He nodded in approval.

"I admit, you rather reminded me of that painting last night. What's it called? Oh yes, *The Nightmare*. The one with the lady prostrate, flung down in shock. Painted by Boucher. It was quite the fall."

"Fuseli."

"I'm sorry?" The Duke turned his head to her.

"Boucher did not paint that, Henry Fuseli did." Violet realized a second later the error she had made when Penelope squeezed her hand.

"Violet..." she murmured, silencing her. Violet grimaced and looked up at the Duke.

"Not a fan of art, eh?" he said, chuckling away. "Something told me you would not be able to resist correcting me."

Violet seethed as she stared at him. She wasn't sure which part of him angered her more. Was it the fact he had caught her out in her deception? Or was it that infernally handsome smile that she kept gazing at, when she knew she should be looking at the Marquess of Westmond?

"If you would excuse us for a moment, your Grace," Penelope spoke up before Violet could invent a lie to explain herself. "I must speak with my sister."

"Of course." The Duke bowed to them and let them escape.

Violet stumbled behind her sister as Penelope led her to a space on the lawns. To any observer, it would have appeared as if they were taking up a place, ready to listen to the music, whereas Penelope actually had such a tight hold of Violet's hand that it was plain she wished to speak.

"What are you doing?" Penelope cried in a hurried whisper.

"Attempting to bond with Lord Westmond. Yet I am failing miserably, am I not?"

"Lord Westmond?" Penelope blinked a few times. "You mean to say that when you spoke of trying to marry a man... you have set your sights on Lord Westmond?"

Violet looked around the two of them, ensuring no one else was nearby before she continued.

"Yes, I have."

"Oh, Violet!"

"What? What is wrong with that?" Violet glanced down at her sister's stomach, thinking only of the child for a minute. "Pen, you and I know we must do something. Lord Westmond is a good prospect, is he not? He is kind, caring, wealthy, and has a good estate in the country where you could go."

"Y-yes, I suppose, it is just..." she stammered with the words.

"Just what?" Violet murmured, seeing her sister was nervous to say something.

"Well, it is not going very well, is it?" Penelope said, her manner rather strained.

Was that really what she wished to say to me?

"The Duke has noticed you are lying, even if Lord Westmond has not. How long do you think it will take him to tell his brother?"

"I know, I know." Violet sighed and turned her eyes to the blue sky above them, wishing she could plead with the heavens for help. "Forgive me, Pen, I am hardly practiced in the art of seduction, am I? What you see is a fool's attempt to try and capture a man's attention. What else am I supposed to do though?" Her question seemed to silence her sister.

Penelope said nothing for a minute before she shrugged, clearly unable to offer any more thoughts.

"Well, that is settled then." Violet linked their arms once more. "Now, come, you must help me to think of a plan of how else to capture the Marquess' attention."

Chapter Eight

"Benedict?" Sebastian called to his brother as he crossed toward the bandstand. His brother turned away from where he was laughing with the musicians that were preparing themselves and faced Sebastian.

"Where are the ladies?" Benedict said, his smile dropping from his face. "Seb, did you say something?"

"Worry not, brother. I am able to talk to ladies and handle myself with courtesy when you're not around." Sebastian's words earned him a suspicious look from Benedict. "Well, I am able to when I wish to."

"What does that mean?"

"Nothing. May I speak with you a moment?" Sebastian took Benedict's arm and pulled him back a few steps from the bandstand. He glanced across the lawn in the direction of the Miss Hathaways who seemed intent in their conversation with one another. It gave Sebastian the freedom to talk to Benedict without fear of being interrupted. "I fear what I thought of Miss Hathaway last night is true."

"Seb, please." Benedict lifted a hand and pinched the brow of his nose.

Sebastian recognized the action – it was something they both did when suffering frustration.

"I think she just lied about –"

"Seb!" Benedict's tone was unusually sharp, prompting Sebastian to fall quiet with raised eyebrows. "Do you have any categorical proof that Miss Hathaway is anything but a kind lady who has accepted my invitation to promenade today?"

Sebastian stood still, his mind racing. He could tell his brother about the fact he knew she liked art, but that was hardly proof of a grand deception. It was merely a white lie.

"Well?" Benedict urged him on.

"I..." Sebastian trailed off. There was something else he could tell his brother. He could reveal that *he* had been the one to share a kiss with Miss Hathaway last night at the ball. He could point out how odd it was for Miss Hathaway to go from kissing him so passionately to clinging to Benedict's arm and smiling sweetly up at him, but to admit to such a thing would be a scandal.

I cannot tell Benedict of it. To do so would be to ruin Miss Hathaway's name.

He glanced her way across the lawn and felt guilt writhe within him, as if it were an asp, trapped in his gut.

I cannot do that to her, even if she is guilty of trying to catch a husband.

"No, brother. I have no proof."

"Then leave your suspicions to yourself for the time being, please," Benedict begged. "The moment you know without a doubt what she is up to, then fine, tell me of it, but not beforehand. Now, I will return to my conversation with the musicians." As he moved back to the violinists, Sebastian felt a muscle in his jaw tick as he looked back at Miss Hathaway and her sister.

For a minute, he replayed that kiss in his mind. It wasn't just about the heat of that moment, though that had certainly been all-encompassing, it had also been the seconds leading up to it.

She is bold, outspoken, and not afraid... I liked that.

Sebastian was convinced he was a fool. It seemed he was fascinated by one of the very women he had always wanted to protect Benedict from.

Circling the lawn and those that had gathered to hear the music, he hurried across the park, heading in the direction of the ladies. When he approached behind them, it was plain they had not noticed he was there yet, for the two were speaking easily and quickly with one another.

"It is a good plan, Pen, please believe me."

"The nature of a good plan is debatable on this subject."

"I agree with you, but we have no other choice, and you know it. I must set my cap at someone and who else should it be other than Lord Westmond?" Miss Hathaway's words made Sebastian stumble to a halt. Fearful of the sisters turning around to notice his presence, he stepped back and hid behind the nearest tree that was placed at the very edge of the lawn. With his back to the rough bark of the trunk, he strained his ears to better listen to the sisters.

"Why Lord Westmond in particular, may I ask?" Miss Penelope asked, her voice rather taut. "Why must he be ensnared?"

"I am not ensnaring him. Good lord, you make me feel quite horrible about myself."

"That is not my intention. I simply mean that we do not know the man very well and he seems a very good man, a very kind man. Do you not think so?"

"I do." Miss Hathaway's words had vigor in them. "He does seem kind indeed. What more could a lady want in a husband than a man who is kind?"

Sebastian felt his lips flicker into a small smile in spite of himself.

Is it possible she looks for something more than money and a title?

"How about love?" Miss Penelope professed. "How about the ability to laugh and enjoy each other's company. To think alike and enjoy similar things. To want to spend every day in such a man's company and no others. Isn't this what someone should want from a husband?" Her impassioned speech cast a quietness between them.

Sebastian held himself as still as he could, nervous that if he moved, even shifted his weight, he might make a noise with his hessian boots in the grass and alert their attention.

"It is." Miss Hathaway clearly agreed with her sister, but her tone was shaky now. "I wish that for you, sister, but time is not on our side. I do not have the luxury of wanting such things from a husband, and you know it."

"But –"

"What else can I do, Pen?" Miss Hathaway's voice was pleading.

Sebastian was growing restless now. He fidgeted with the cuffs of his tailcoat, understanding that his suspicions had been right about Miss Hathaway all along.

"I must find a husband." Miss Hathaway spoke with conviction. "It must be done, and Lord Westmond seems a good man. He has the wealth we need too."

Sebastian felt sick. He shook his head and gritted his teeth together.

How can a woman who had turned my head so, enough to kiss her after a first meeting of just a few minutes, be so materialistically minded?

He couldn't bear to hear anymore. Sebastian staggered away, making a path through the trees and back round to the bandstand. He practically shook with anger as he waited for Benedict to be done with the musicians.

"Something wrong, brother?" Benedict asked, looking back at him.

Much!

"Come, let us join the ladies again." Benedict drew Sebastian away, though Sebastian went reluctantly, for his mind was a whir.

I must make a plan. From today, Miss Hathaway will not succeed in her plot. I will do whatever it takes to drive her away from Benedict.

Chapter Nine

"What is it you are doing so secretly?" Penelope called across the room. Violet kept her head bent down over the sketchbook. She had no words to offer, but neither was she prepared to let her sister see what she was drawing. Usually, she shared every secret with Penelope.

This one is too big to share.

"Violet?" Penelope called to her.

"It is nothing, sister. Simply some doodles."

"Perhaps you are writing down more of your plot." Penelope sounded saddened at the words. Violet paused with her pencil on the page and looked up, finding her sister's gaze with her own across the room.

Penelope was pale today, reclining on a chaise longue near the window of the garden room. Basked in sunlight, Violet thought how beautiful her sister looked, surrounded by potted palm trees, though the view was somewhat marred by the flattening of her lips together.

"Pen, I am not proud of myself either," Violet muttered, "but I do not know what else to do. Do you?"

"No." Penelope shook her head after a minute and sat back on the chaise longue once again, allowing her eyes to close softly.

Good, she needs some rest after her sickness this morning.

Violet returned her attention to the sketchbook, seeing exactly what she had drawn. It was the Duke, but as he had been in Hyde Park just a few days ago. He was striding across the page, as if the drawing was alive with movement, with autumnal leaves above his head, swaying in the breeze and teasing his wild hair. His tailcoat was flung open with the buttons undone, revealing the waistcoat that was tight across his narrow stomach and broad shoulders.

"Why am I doing this?" Violet muttered to herself as she turned her attention to his face. She took extra care with his expression, drawing in the handsome lines with eagerness.

Because I cannot stop thinking of him. That is why!

"Look, look! Is it not thrilling?" Deborah's voice bustled into the room. Violet hastily closed her sketchbook and Penelope sat forward, her eyes shooting open, clearly disturbed from her nap. "Violet, have you seen this?" Deborah asked and thrust forward a scandal sheet in her hands. Behind her, Louise hastened, like a puppy at her heels.

"Mama, I have not read it yet."

"Dearest, do you not think Violet wants to see her name here first?" Debora giggled and thrust the scandal sheet toward Violet. "How thrilling this will be! Imagine this, a marchioness for a niece." She turned and took her daughter's hand, spinning her around in a circle. "How much we will go up in the world then!"

Violet shot a look at her sister, only to see Penelope was just as uneasy at hearing these words, fidgeting in her seat. Violet took the scandal sheet and laid it down over her sketchbook to better read the article that had delighted her aunt so much.

'Will the Marquess of Westmond soon marry? Those with eagle eyes would have noticed the Marquess of Westmond's attentions to the Miss Hathaways as of late.

Not only did he dance with the younger sister at the ball, but he was most atten-tive to the elder with an injured ankle, and he was seen to escort both sisters through Hyde Park for a promenade this week. If Miss Violet Hathaway has set those large eyes of hers on the marquess though, her goal could be a pointless one.

'She may have shared a dance with the elder brother, the Duke of Ashbury, at his ball, but he is not a man whose head will be turned easily. The Duke has declared never to marry, and his rather watchful eye over his younger brother suggests he intends to stop his brother's intentions too.'

Violet lowered the scandal sheet, feeling her hand tremble around the paper. The snide remark about her appearance was one cause of pain, but there was another cause within the article.

"Is it not wonderful?" Deborah exclaimed again.

"Wonderful, aunt? What is wonderful in it?" Violet asked in surprise. There seemed to be little good in the sheet.

"Oh, Violet. You do not understand how such scandal sheets work." Deborah scoffed at her, waving a belittling hand in Violet's direction. "The mention of you and Lord Westmond together is enough. Ignore their warnings, they mean nothing." She grasped the scandal sheet and fluttered it in the air, where it was swiftly grabbed by Louise, who was most desirous to read it. A few seconds later, Penelope appeared at her shoulder, reading it too.

Violet swallowed nervously, thinking of what she had just read.

The Duke intends to never marry? Whyever not?

She peeled back the cover of her sketchbook, seeking out the image of him she had recreated. To her mind, though the image was just the same, his expression was no longer inviting with that mischievous smile, but turned away, ignoring her.

"Enough drawing, dear." Deborah placed a hand on the book and closed it. "If you are to impress the Marquess, then you must work on your accomplishments that can impress him. Take the pianoforte."

"Mama!" Louise dropped the scandal sheet in outrage, where it was quickly snatched by Penelope so that she could finish reading the article. "I always practice the pianoforte at this time of day. It is what is done."

"You may take the piano, Louise." Violet had no wish to practice. She had no skill for such a thing, and she already felt she was pretending to be someone she was not in her attempt to impress Lord Westmond. She didn't fancy putting on a new identity entirely and suddenly developing an interest in the piano.

"Nonsense." Deborah clasped Violet's hand and pulled her to her feet. The movement was so sudden that Violet stumbled, nearly falling over the chair entirely.

"Careful, aunt. My ankle, it has still not healed."

"Tush. One can go through a little pain to catch a marquess' eyes. Now, sit." Deborah thrust Violet into the piano stool, where they were followed by both Louise and Penelope. Louise snatched up her own music from the piano, clearly not inclined to share, and Penelope watched with an eager gaze.

"Aunt, please, I am awful at this instrument," Violet pleaded. "One would sooner listen to a cat shriek than hear me play."

"Then you must practice."

"Aunt?"

"Practice!" The sudden sharpness of Deborah's words startled them all. Violet froze, as did her sister and cousin. The heavy jowls of her aunt shook as the beady eyes rounded on her, and a hand was waved at the keys. "Now, Violet." Her tone softened.

Breathing deeply, Violet pressed her fingers to the keys. She had to play from memory with no music before her and it soon transpired how awful she was. She played the wrong notes and became certain she played out of key. When Louise sniggered, Violet broke off completely and shot a pleading gesture at Penelope, who shook her head, not knowing what to do.

"On second thoughts..." Deborah paused and took the piano cover, slamming it down rather loudly. "Perhaps he should not hear such an attempt at the piano after all. It might make the gentleman run a mile."

"That's what I feared," Violet murmured, to which Louise laughed all the more.

"God have mercy, that was truly awful," Louise said through her giggles. "One would think you had never played before in your life."

"Louise, it is your talent, not mine."

"What is your talent then?"

Violet shot a glance to the sketchbook on a table nearby, but she said nothing. There was not a chance she was going to show anyone the drawings from within that book.

A bell rang in the distance of the house.

"Are we expecting callers?" Penelope asked, looking quite afeared at the idea.

"Oh, did I not tell you?" Deborah giggled, almost with childish delight. "Your uncle invited the Marquess to come for tea. It seems he has accepted." She clasped her hands and hurried off, rather raucously calling to the maid to bring tea at once.

Violet winced at the awful sound along with Penelope, before Louise ushered Violet out of her place on the piano stool. Louise primped her cheeks, bringing color to them, then lifted the cover, clearly intending to play and try to catch Lord Westmond's eye with her fine playing.

Penelope took Violet's hand and led her across the room.

"Have you noticed how eager our aunt's attentions are to you at the moment?" Penelope whispered.

"One would have to be blind not to see it," Violet murmured in agreement. As they turned to face the door, Violet noticed how eagerly

Penelope stepped forward with a sudden smile on her face, but Violet's attention was quickly pulled away.

It seemed Lord Westmond was not the only one who had accepted the invitation to tea. Behind Lord Westmond and Deborah as they entered the room, the Duke of Ashbury walked in. The sight of him made Violet's palms clammy and she reached for her sketchbook, where she hid it firmly behind her back.

God's wounds, why is he here?

THIS IS INSUFFERABLE.

Sebastian could think of many reasons why he did not wish to be here, sharing tea with the Miss Hathaways, their aunt, and Miss Notley. For one thing, he now knew Miss Hathaway's true character, and it made an anger burn within him, for another, he couldn't stand the way Benedict kept turning his gaze upon her.

Why does it bother me so?

Sebastian sat back in his place around a small circular table, glancing toward Miss Notley who was still at the piano, trying desperately to capture Benedict's attention by playing as charmingly as she could. The way she primped her cheeks when she thought no one was looking made Sebastian hide his laugh behind his teacup, before returning his focus on Miss Hathaway.

She was sitting forward at the table, eager in conversation with Benedict, but at her side, there was a small book that she kept laying a hand over, as if not wanting anyone to see it.

Hmm. What is in that book?

"How fares your ankle today, Miss Hathaway?" Benedict asked, leaning toward Miss Hathaway so much from where he sat on her other side, that Sebastian's hand curled tightly around the handle of the teacup he was holding. It bothered him. Not just to see Benedict giving attention to a woman who was out to ensnare him so, but the fact he looked at Miss Hathaway at all.

That kiss still burned in Sebastian's memory, and every time he looked at Miss Hathaway now, he found his eyes flitting down to those lips, wondering what it could be like to steal another kiss.

"It is improving, my lord. I thank you for your concern." Miss Hathaway smiled sweetly. There was something so false about it that Sebastian tutted under his breath. Miss Hathaway appeared to be the only one to notice, who glanced his way with a narrowed look.

"Lord Westmond, we are so delighted you could come today," Mrs. Notley said, her tone gushing as she leaned toward Benedict across the small table set for tea. "We hope this will be the first of many visits for tea?"

Sebastian lifted his head and tried to communicate silently with his brother across the space between them, hoping his warning look would be enough, but clearly, it was not. Benedict looked purposefully away from Sebastian and smiled at Mrs. Notley.

"I hope for that too, Mrs. Notley."

Sebastian tutted a little louder this time. In answer, Miss Hathaway at his side pushed a plate toward him.

"Cake, your Grace?" she said quietly. "It is a fine honey cake."

"Did I look hungry?" he asked, turning a mischievous gaze on her. "Or are you trying to stop me from speaking my mind?" he whispered the words, so only she could hear him. She glared at him once again, as the conversation was taken over by Benedict and Miss Penelope Hathaway.

"You are fond of concerts, my lord?" Miss Penelope said gently, with reserve, and sat back in her chair as she turned a polite smile on Benedict.

"Oh yes. What joy is there in this world than to hear a good piece of music?" Benedict asked with a smile.

"What of art, brother?" Sebastian's wit earned a stare from his brother.

"You simply praise art above all other cultures of this world." Benedict shook his head and laughed at him. "You must acknowledge there is space for other talents too."

"That I do." Sebastian nodded. "But surely art is like no other form of artistic talent. The creation of the image on a page is quite miraculous. Miss Hathaway, what do you think?" He was trying to get her to speak, desperate to see her reveal the lie she had told to Benedict about being disinterested in art.

"I…" She paused and laid a hand on the book beside her again. Sebastian frowned as he looked down at that book.

What is she hiding?

"I think there are many art forms that deserve praise, your Grace."

"How diplomatic," Sebastian murmured, earning another harsh gaze from Miss Hathaway.

As Benedict turned his attention back to Miss Penelope, and the two began to talk at length of music, Mrs. Notley stood to her feet.

"Let us have a demonstration then, as you are so fond of music, my lord." She smiled gushingly and rushed to her daughter's side. "Louise, play the Vivaldi piece you have been working on."

"But… Mama."

"Vivaldi, Louise."

Miss Notley put a smile on her face and at once played a more dramatic piece at the piano. With the attention of the room shifted, Sebastian took his opportunity, for he couldn't resist. As he reached forward to take the plate Miss Hathaway had pushed toward him, he lifted the cover of her book with one finger.

The sight that greeted him shocked him. What was supposed to be a mere glimpse to discover her secret ended up being a long stare.

It is a sketchbook! Who is that face I see here?

He found himself lifting the cover a little higher. Across the page strode a familiar image, surrounded by autumnal leaves and bristled by wind. Sebastian could see his hair on the page, his cheekbones, his dark eyes, and his mischievous smile.

Miss Hathaway didn't appear to have noticed his transgression. Her focus was on Miss Notley, instead, at the piano. It made Sebastian bolder, lifting the cover of the book a little bit more as he felt his smile growing.

The sketch she had made of him was not only spectacular in its skill, but it had also been done with great care. Had she not drawn each line with devotion? Had she not recreated that smile with particular attention and many pencil lines?

So, she thinks of me more than my brother after all.

Sebastian found his smile grew all the more. Now, he knew another of Miss Hathaway's secrets. She may have set her cap at his brother, but she could not stop thinking of him, no more than he could stop thinking of her.

The book cover was suddenly pressed down, out of Sebastian's grasp. He chuckled under the cover of the music and turned a smile on Miss Hathaway. She was staring straight at him, her cheeks blushing madly red and her chest heaving up and down with breathlessness as she pulled the book out of his reach.

"I do not know what to say first, Miss Hathaway." He leaned toward her and whispered. Both he and Miss Hathaway glanced at Benedict, ensuring he was not paying attention, but he had more interest in talking to Miss Penelope and praising the music.

"Then say nothing, I beg of you," Miss Hathaway pleaded, though she leaned toward Sebastian too. The proximity of her made that familiar sense of heat rise within him again.

It is like she is an addiction...

"You are fond of art, after all, and have great talent."

"Of all things, that is not what I thought you were going to say," Miss Hathaway murmured, biting her lip in the effort to hide a smile, but Sebastian could see it.

"Oh? Shall I talk of your subject matter instead?" he asked, tilting his head to the side. She snapped her gaze away from him and looked down at her sketchbook. "Or perhaps you will tell me why you are sketching me when you are pursuing my brother?"

"Your Grace... I..." Her words were shaky. Had no one else been in the room, Sebastian would have happily snatched that sketchbook from her hand and kissed her again. Not just to feel that thrill another time, but to prove to her that her heart didn't lay with Benedict. As it was, he had to hold himself very still in the seat.

"Sebastian? What do you think?" Benedict's sudden question made Sebastian and Miss Hathaway flinch in their seats, turning their attention on him.

"What was that, brother?" Sebastian said, planting a false smile on his face.

"Miss Penelope and I were just talking of a concert tomorrow night. I am inviting the Miss Hathaways to accompany me to see the violin quartet, *The String Angels*. Say you will come too, brother?"

Sebastian looked at Miss Hathaway, noting the way she subtly shook her head, pleading with him to say no. Sebastian glanced down at that sketchbook again and found his answer tumbling easily from his lips.

"How can I say no?"

Chapter Ten

"It is not fair! Why do they get to go to the concert, and I do not?" Louise's voice shrieked from the corridor.

As Violet and their maid, Mary, helped Penelope into her gown, they all exchanged uncertain looks.

"Louise, dear, you are beginning to sound like a child," Deborah's voice followed, the warning tone plain.

"But... Mama..."

"Enough, Louise!"

When the slam of a door followed, Violet returned her focus to Penelope, seeing she was very quiet this evening.

"Think nothing of it," Violet whispered to her. "Louise simply wants attention herself. And she will soon enough have it."

"Yes, but perhaps not from a marquess." Penelope kept her eyes averted from Violet as she spoke, stepping into her new gown. "You should hear the way our aunt talks of you when you are not in the room, Violet. Nothing could excite her more than the prospect of you and Lord Westmond being married."

"Then we must ignore our aunt's words for now," Violet insisted. She left Mary to fasten the gown as she stepped away to collect Penelope's jewelry.

"How can we?" Penelope called to her. "It is all anyone thinks about in this house at present."

"Not everyone," Violet murmured, so quietly that neither her sister nor the maid could hear her. Violet knew that thoughts of marrying Lord Westmond bothered her a little. How could she think of marrying the Marquess when all her mind wanted to think of was his brother? Was it possible she could consider marrying the brother instead? Or was it a hope too far?

With her face averted away from Penelope, Violet looked in the mirror over the vanity table, seeing the expression that greeted her there. It was uncertain, and nervous.

What does he think of me now?

She thought of the way she had slammed the sketchbook shut after he had seen the drawing that she had made of him. His mischievous smile had announced his thoughts plainly enough. He had been thrilled by that drawing, for it had caught her out in what she was trying to hide.

I think more of the Duke than of the Marquess.

"Miss Penelope, do smile," Mary said sweetly as she finished fastening Penelope's gown for her. "You look quite beautiful this evening for the concert. The gown is very elegant."

Penelope didn't answer but turned to face a floor-length mirror. Sensing something was wrong, Violet fixed a smile in place and hurried back to her sister's side.

"Mary is right. You look quite stunning, sister." Violet straightened out the creases of Penelope's skirt, admiring the shimmer of the cream lace that fell to the floor.

"How long do you think it will be until I..." Penelope trailed off and laid a hand over her stomach.

Violet exchanged a look with Mary, both sensing what Penelope was trying to ask without having to hear the words.

"Until you show?" Violet finished the question for her, prompting Penelope to nod. "A couple of months yet, sister. Please, do not worry about that now. We are off to a concert. You love your music, is this not a quartet you have wanted to see for a long time?"

"Yes, it is. It is just..." Penelope petered off again. Violet came to stand beside her sister and fussed with her hair a little more, as Mary went to fetch shoes.

"It is just, what?" Violet asked, encouraging her sister on. To her surprise, she found Penelope couldn't meet her gaze in the mirror. She seemed to be avoiding looking at Violet at all, lost in her own thoughts. "Pen, is something wrong?" Violet whispered.

"It does not matter." Penelope's words made Violet's stomach knot.

Something is very wrong!

"Sister, please, tell me what it is." Violet walked around Penelope, determined to have her gaze. "Is it the child? Are you feeling well?"

"I am feeling fine." Penelope forced a smile into place. "Shall we go? It will not be long before the Marquess' carriage will arrive for us." With these words, Penelope walked toward the door and stepped out, taking the shoes from Mary as she went.

It left an awkward silence in the room, with Violet and Mary looking at one another.

"Did I do something wrong, Mary?" Violet asked quietly to which Mary shrugged, none the wiser. Violet shifted for a minute, clasping and unclasping her hands nervously before she too looked in the mirror.

It must be the baby. Pen must be worried about her future. I cannot afford to dally with thoughts of the Duke anymore!

Violet felt her determination grow as she stared at her reflection. Tonight, she was wearing a pastel green gown, almost white with the slightest hint of color to it. The neckline was deep and beaded too, accenting the curve of her bosom and the slenderness of her neck. Violet tried to admire the dress, but when she should have been wondering if the Marquess of Westmond would like the gown, she found herself thinking of the Duke instead.

Enough!

She turned away and forced a smile in Mary's direction.

"Thank you for your help once again, Mary. What of the sheets?"

"The bedsheets, Miss?" Mary smiled. "Do not worry. I have hidden them away again."

"Thank you, Mary. I do not know what we would do without you." Violet wished the maid a goodnight and hurried out of the hallway, determined to find Penelope. In the end, she found Penelope standing at the bottom of the staircase, with a hand on her stomach, that she dropped the moment Deborah appeared in the hallway beside them.

"There you two are! Oh, pretty as a picture," Deborah said gushingly. Meanwhile, Louise followed her into the room, a glare set on her face. "Do not forget, Violet." Deborah turned her attention on Violet and pinched her cheeks, trying to bring more color to them. "Smile sweetly at Lord Westmond, agree with his opinions, and flatter him. That is what gentlemen want. Flattery."

"Is it?" Violet was shocked by the idea. She thought back to the night she had kissed the Duke of Ashbury.

There had certainly been no flattery then!

Chapter Eleven

Sebastian stepped into the concert room, trailing behind his brother as Benedict escorted the Miss Hathaways into the space. He had Miss Violet Hathaway on his left arm, and Miss Penelope on his right. Both were smiling up at Benedict, laughing at his jests, a little too eagerly for how funny the jokes really were. Sebastian scoffed under his breath, shaking his head as he followed them.

The concert room was packed tonight, with chairs pressed closely together, and so many people that it was difficult to even see the violinists at the front of the room. As Benedict led the Miss Hathaways to two chairs, Sebastian couldn't resist. He found himself taking one of the chairs beside Miss Hathaway, something that seemed to surprise her, for her eyes widened as she turned her focus on him.

As Benedict and Miss Penelope fell into conversation, Sebastian and Miss Hathaway just kept staring at each other. Sebastian imagined it was rather like a competition to see who would crack first.

"Why did you come?" she asked, whispering so quietly that Sebastian had to lean across the distance between them to better hear her. Around them, people were sitting, with their words quiet as they waited for the concert to begin. "You said you were not fond of concerts."

"I have to protect my brother, do I not?" Sebastian said with raised eyebrows. "There are ladies everywhere tonight, Miss Hathaway. Who knows when one woman will turn her focus on him, intending to capture him in marriage?"

Miss Hathaway spun her attention forward, looking toward the violinists and waiting for them to begin. As they did so, the room fell quiet and was then filled with sweet music. Sebastian could acknowledge it was a beautiful piece, with the quartet playing excellently and with vigor, yet he grew distracted. His eyes were soon on the paintings around the room.

In the dim candlelight, some pictures were harder to see than others, with orange glows reflecting off the oils in the paintings, but it wasn't long before he noticed he was not the only one looking at the paintings. Miss Hathaway beside him had stopped watching the musicians. Her eyes were flitting between the paintings as well. She even sat forward in her seat at one point to better see a certain picture.

Sebastian couldn't help himself. He glanced first at Benedict, but finding his brother was enchanted by the music, Sebastian felt safe enough to speak freely to Miss Hathaway. He leaned toward her, practically whispering in her ear.

"Have you lost interest in the music already?" At his words, she flinched in the chair. Something burned happily in his gut when he noticed she didn't lean away from him, yet merely turned to meet his gaze with her own. "You were staring at the paintings."

"As were you."

"Yes, but I never professed to loving music more than art." He chuckled under his breath, showing he had caught her out. "Which one do you like?"

"The William Hogarth." She nodded her head at a particular painting in the corner of the room. "His paintings have such wit and satire in them, don't you think?"

"That they do." Sebastian turned his focus on the artwork she had pointed out to him. "*Marriage-a-la-Mode, deux.*" Sebastian gave the painting its full name, prompting Miss Hathaway to jerk her head in his direction once again.

"You know it?"

"Of course. One of my favorites of his. It speaks volumes, does it not? Of what can really happen in a marriage."

"Yes, but he comments on marriages of convenience, does he not?" Miss Hathaway asked. She abruptly leaned closer toward Sebastian. He was so entranced by that proximity that he looked away from the painting entirely, thinking only of her. "Marriages of love, now, Hogarth always approved of those."

"And how common do you reckon those are, Miss Hathaway?"

"In truth?" she asked, her large eyes wide. "Not as common as we would all wish them to be." There was something sincere in her words that wrongfooted Sebastian entirely. For a moment, he was not looking at a lady who was scheming, trying to capture Benedict's attention. No, he was staring at the same woman he had met the night of his ball. The one who had wandered around his painting gallery.

"What other paintings do you like?"

"Here?"

"Anywhere." He encouraged her on. Sebastian shifted forward in his seat and whispered so no one else could hear them. "Forget the music for a minute, Miss Hathaway. Tell me what you really love about art." His pleading tone must have connected with her, for those enchanting pink lips curved into a thrilled smile.

"We'll be here for hours if you wish me to talk of such a thing."

"Well, you and I must have some way to pass the time, mustn't we? Go on, Miss Hathaway."

Sebastian didn't know how long he sat there in the end, talking with Miss Hathaway about art, but he learned many things. He learned of her favorite artists; Hogarth was amongst them. He also learned of the styles she loved, and that she preferred portraits to landscapes. When she turned the focus on him with questions, Sebastian was startled to find himself talking willingly. He even spoke of his new acquisitions, and what more he wanted for his collection.

They had to be nearing an interval in the music, for people were shifting in their seats, desiring a break. Sebastian didn't want that break, for he knew the moment they stood again, Benedict would talk to Miss Hathaway, and this moment between them would end.

Strangely, I do not want it to stop.

"Before we must end this discussion, Miss Hathaway, tell me this," he pleaded with her. "You are fond of painting and drawing yourself, are you not?" She winced at his words and looked away, as if in pain.

"I thought for a few minutes there that you were going to do me the courtesy of not bringing up what you saw in my sketchbook."

"How could I not bring it up?" he asked quietly. "First off, I will happily praise your skills."

"You will?" Her voice was full of surprise, and her lips parted. "You thought the drawing was good?"

"I did. You have talent, which is plain to see." His words made her cheeks color. "Yet the subject matter interests me all the more."

"Please, do not say it," she begged, glancing back in Benedict's direction before turning her focus on Sebastian once again.

"Then I will say something else entirely." Sebastian waited until he had her full attention. "Miss Hathaway... leave my brother alone."

She froze. Her eyes had gone wide and the color that had been in those high cheekbones a second ago began to melt away.

"Why?"

"How blind do you think I am?" Sebastian muttered quickly. "You try to charm my brother in public, yet you draw of me in private."

"It means nothing." She closed her eyes and turned her head away from him as if trying to hide in this very public space.

"No? Nothing? I know it means you do not care for him."

"How can you be sure of that?" Miss Hathaway's voice may have been quiet, muffled by the music, but it was full of vigor too. "I could care for your brother very deeply. If I had set my cap at him, what would be so awful in that?"

"He deserves love. *That* is why it would be awful." Sebastian subtly gestured at the Hogarth painting. "Take a leaf out of your favorite painter's book, Miss Hathaway. Like him, do you not think marriages should be for love?"

"What makes you think I could not love your brother?" she asked boldly, lifting up her chin in such a way that her lips were closer toward his. Sebastian found himself glancing side to side, around the chairs, but no one was focused on them. They were all too busy watching the musicians.

"Shall I refer to the sketch you made? It was of me, not my brother." Sebastian's words made her chin lower again. The temptation of those lips was still near enough though. "Or perhaps I shall refer to that kiss instead."

"Shh!" she pleaded, looking around, yet like him, she seemed to notice no one was interested in their discussion. They were at the back of the room and everyone else was much too interested in the music. "Your Grace, that kiss was momentary madness."

"You returned that kiss."

"I did, because my head had been turned by a charming smile and a man with wit." Her words made Sebastian flinch in his seat.

That is how she sees me?

"I was carried away in the excitement of a moment. It was nothing more than that." She shook her head heartily.

"Nothing?" The disappointment grew within Sebastian. He couldn't reason it to himself. After all, he wanted nothing to do with Miss Hathaway, but her words now cut deep and made a numb feeling stretch through his chest. "So, if I kissed you again, would you not return it?"

"Shh!" she pleaded another time, glancing back and forth. "You wish me to speak the truth in this moment?"

"It would be refreshing, compared to the lies and the ruse of trying to charm my brother."

"Fine, then you will have the truth." She leaned toward him, coming so close that he was encapsulated by her scent. The honeysuckle and rose teased his nose. "You may be exciting, your Grace."

"Ah, a great compliment."

"Yet that is all." Her words made that numbing feeling stretch within him. "Your brother is a kind man, and a true gentleman. Is it so awful that when I am in need of a husband, I should turn my attention to a man such as him? Tell me, what is so truly terrible in that?"

He couldn't answer her. All the words had been stolen from him and his jaw hung loose.

"We cannot all marry for love, as Hogarth, or any other good man would wish us to." She spoke with such passion that Sebastian hung on her words, desperate to know more.

Why must Miss Hathaway marry?

"You have not married yourself, have you?" She added, her tone still ardent. "Surely you have seen marrying for love is a difficult thing."

"I have not married because I do not intend to ever marry."

"That is what the rumors say, but why is that?"

"It is because I have made a vow. One I intend to never forget, for Benedict's sake." Sebastian realized the words had escaped him so freely with horror. He froze in the chair, his back going rigid, just as Miss Hathaway stared at him, her hands fidgeting in her lap.

"What did you say?" she asked, her voice soft.

"Nothing. It does not matter."

"You have hinted at a secret here, your Grace."

"And that is what it will remain. A secret." Sebastian couldn't stop cursing himself. In the ease of talking with Miss Hathaway, he had almost revealed something he had vowed to take to the grave with him.

I am a fool! Hoodwinked and charmed by her.

The music ended abruptly, and Benedict got to his feet.

"Wasn't that wonderful? Shall we find some refreshments?"

"Yes, that is a good idea." Sebastian jumped to his feet too and offered to be the one to go and fetch the drinks. He was glad for the escape, but he kept glancing back in Miss Hathaway's direction, aware that she was watching him.

My god... how close I came to telling my secret then.

To his surprise, someone followed him. Sebastian was busy with the drinks when Miss Hathaway appeared beside him, prompting him to chink the glass of a carafe against another.

"Did I make you jump?" she murmured at his side.

"Well, perhaps you have more of an effect on me than I am always willing to acknowledge." His words made her smile.

That smile...

It was intoxicating to him. Sebastian didn't think. He found himself glancing back to the room. Seeing that Benedict and Miss Penelope were distracted in talking with one another, he beckoned Miss Hathaway to follow him.

"Come with me." To his thrill, she didn't object, but followed on behind him. They crossed quickly out of the room and into a corridor. Sebastian looked left and right, with agitation, waiting until a member of staff had left before he found another door, leading to a separate room. Hurrying inside, he took Violet's wrist and pulled her in.

"What are you doing?" she said in surprise. When she didn't pull away though and followed him as he closed the door, Sebastian was reminded of that night in his picture gallery.

"Showing you that you need to stop your attentions to my brother." He moved toward her. Unable to stop himself, he reached for a kiss.

When her lips molded to his without restraint, he felt every fiber of his being come alive. It was as if she had sung a perfect song, to which his body was listening attentively. When her hands curled on the material of his waistcoat, pulling him down toward her, he couldn't resist deepening that kiss. He took her tongue with his own, dominating the kiss, until she panted against his lips, making a breathless sound.

"We shouldn't... be doing this..." she murmured between kisses.

"I know. And yet... we are." He kissed her again. "Tell me why you are trying to charm my brother, when you feel *this*. Please."

"I can't." She parted from the kiss. That need was still there, this yearning to have her kiss him again, yet the moment was slipping away. Already, she was pulling back from him. "I'm sorry." She hurried for the door.

Sebastian let her go, trapped somewhere between the guilt of what he had done and the need to repeat it.

What secret is it she is keeping?

Chapter Twelve

"What did you say?" Sebastian was distracted. It had been two days since the concert and in that time, he had not stopped thinking of Miss Hathaway and the conversations they had shared together, not to mention their illicit kiss. Sitting in his library, he was clutching the sketchbook he had bought the day before in Bond Street, unsure why he had purchased it at all.

Miss Hathaway's was torn and old, she clearly needed a new one.

The thought didn't quite explain why Sebastian felt the need to be the one to give it to her.

"Sebastian, do listen. You seem to be in another world at this moment," Benedict said as he walked around the library, leafing through the sheet music he had in his grasp.

"I am sorry. Go on, you were saying something about inviting some people over for dinner?"

"Not just some people." Benedict laughed, clearly amused by Sebastian's distraction as he turned the sketchbook over in his hands once again.

Would she like it?

"I am intending to ask the Miss Hathaways to come for tea, along with their aunt and uncle, and their cousin, of course."

Sebastian nearly dropped the sketchbook. He had to catch it in the air to stop it from falling before he leaned on the mantelpiece once again beside him, doing his best to look nonchalant, as Benedict watched him.

"Are you well, brother?" Benedict asked.

"Perfect. And why are you inviting them for dinner?" Sebastian's voice was wary. "I thought I had warned you about Miss Hathaway —"

"And I warned you to keep your opinions to yourself, did I not?" Benedict asked, smiling as he shook his head, apparently humored by Sebastian's interference. It merely made Sebastian clench his hands around the sketchbook.

"Why are you inviting them?"

"Because I like the family. What is more, I still wish to make amends for the way you treated Miss Hathaway the night of the ball."

"What do you mean!?" Sebastian spluttered, thinking of that kiss.

"Have you forgotten the way she fell down?" Benedict looked up accusingly from the sheet music he was surveying.

"Oh. Of course not. It's just that Miss Hathaway has already accepted my apology for that. Do they really need to be invited for dinner? For another apology?"

"I wish them to come." Benedict's words put an end to the matter.

Sebastian turned around, trying to find something to do with his hands to look busy as he stepped away from the mantelpiece. He continued to fidget with the sketchbook in his grasp, wondering what to do with it.

I bought it for Miss Hathaway, I should give it to her, but what would she think of such a gift?

Sebastian turned his focus on his brother, watching as Benedict looked at the papers before him. Benedict seemed unaware of Sebastian's keen gaze. It allowed Sebastian to watch his brother, seeing the crease in his forehead as he concentrated and that keen look.

"Brother, could you tell me something..." Sebastian built himself up to ask a question. "Are you inviting the Miss Hathaways here because you are fond of them?"

"Well, yes, they are both charming."

"No, Benedict, you misunderstand." Sebastian fiddled with the sketch-book once again. "I mean to say that despite my warnings, are you charmed by Miss Hathaway?"

A smile appeared on Benedict's face.

"So what if I were? Would it matter if I were charmed by her or any other lady? We talked about this, Sebastian. You are my brother, not my guard dog when it comes to me marrying someday."

"I know. It is just that I want you to be happy in your marriage. I am your brother; can you blame me for being protective of you?" Sebastian's words made Benedict look up from the sheet music with another smile.

"You're a good brother." With these words, Benedict got to his feet. "I will send the invitation then, if you have no objections?"

Sebastian stood still, trying to think of any excuse, but nothing came to fruition. He had no meaningful objection to give to the invitation, and the thought of seeing Miss Hathaway again was making him hold onto that sketchbook much harder than before.

"No. Invite who you will, Benedict. I will ensure the staff prepares the dinner for when your guests arrive."

"Thank you, Seb." As Benedict hurried off, Sebastian sighed and flung himself down into the nearest chair, tapping his forehead with the sketchbook in frustration.

"What am I doing?" he muttered in anger. Deep down, he knew there was another reason why he had not objected. He wanted to see Miss Hathaway again for himself. He wished to know her better, to escort her around the painting gallery properly this time and have her true thoughts, to sit with her and talk to her with freedom as they had done at the concert.

I am a fool.

The mere thought made him drop the sketchbook on the table beside him, for he had made up his mind. He may have been charmed by the beautiful Miss Hathaway, but he was not going to lose his head to her, and certainly nothing so foolish as his heart. Buying the sketchbook was a moment of weakness, yet he wouldn't follow through with it. That sketchbook would stay here, and it would not be gifted to Miss Hathaway, no matter the temptation that Sebastian felt.

Chapter Thirteen

Violet stepped into the house, feeling awkward and walking on her toes so that the soles of her shoes did not tap loudly on the marble floor. The last time she had been in this grand house, she had kissed its owner, and the mere thought of being back here had her heart beating fast in her chest, so quickly she imagined it was rather like a bumble bee's wings.

"Violet? Is all well?" Penelope asked at her side, with their arms looped together.

"Of course." Violet lied and put a false smile in place as she looked around the house. It was truly beautiful, and very grand indeed, with such fine paintings on the walls that Violet could have spent hours at a time admiring them in their gilt frames, yet she could think of none of it now. Her gaze was flitting between the doors, in search of their owner.

"Imagine being the mistress of a house such as this." Deborah's rather loud words made both Violet and Penelope groan before looking in their aunt's direction.

Deborah was on her husband's arm, and the two were admiring the entrance hall with vigor, pointing out ornaments and paintings without demureness or subtlety.

"You would think they were moving in," Violet whispered to her sister, relieved to see when Penelope giggled at the words. Behind them, Louise walked in, flattening the skirt of her gown incessantly.

"How can they not see how embarrassing this is?" Penelope murmured, so only Violet could hear her. "Look at them." On cue, Deborah reached for a fine vase on a hall table and picked it up, admiring it as if it were her own. Violet held her breath, nervous Deborah would drop it, before she placed it down again at her husband's instruction.

"Soon, we could be here a lot. This could be our second home," Deborah giggled, prompting Violet to shudder at the mere thought. "A niece married to a marquess? This would be thrilling indeed!"

"Have they forgotten this is the Duke's house?" Violet whispered to Penelope.

"Lord Westmond stays here, does he not?"

"Yes, but it is the Duke of Ashbury's home."

"Violet, Violet!" Deborah said excitedly, moving to her side. "Could you imagine yourself living here?"

"Shh!" Violet pleaded, urging her aunt to fall silent as a door opened in the distant part of the hallway.

Together, the Marquess of Westmond and the Duke of Ashbury walked in. Violet's eyes shot straight to the Duke. She couldn't help smiling a little when his eyes found hers. He seemed to return that smile, before it faded once again.

Could I imagine living here?

Violet found the question lingered, for she wasn't imagining living in the house or with these things, she was imagining living beside the Duke of Ashbury. Never had a thought given her such a thrill or made her shiver with delight as this one did.

"Welcome!" the Marquess hurried forward to greet them. "We were worried your carriage might have got lost in the storm."

"Oh no, my lord," Deborah spoke up. "Nothing could have stopped us from getting here. One is willing to brace the thunder and rain when such friends are to be met." Her effusive tone made the brothers exchange a look, something that was noticed by Violet.

"We apologize for being late, my lord," Violet said, wishing to stop any possible awkwardness. "The storm made for a treacherous path." She was not going to tell them that Penelope had been a little ill before they had come. Already, Deborah was growing suspicious and had commented on Penelope's lateness to the door.

"Of course. Please, do not concern yourselves with being late. You must be hungry. Come, I will show you to the dining room." As the Marquess stepped forward, he offered his arms to Violet and Penelope. Violet took the proffered arm, though her gaze lingered on the Duke as she walked past him. He stared back at her with just as much intensity.

How can he look at me like that? As if I am the one thing that matters in this room.

She tried to shrug it off as if it was all in her imagination as they walked into the dining room.

The dinner began rather inelegantly at first. The food was delicious, but Deborah's and Walter's lack of manners was very noticeable at times. They constantly drew attention to the grandness of the plates and leaned their elbows on the tables. Violet tried her best to engage the Marquess in conversation to distract him from the display of poor manners, but it was clearly all observed.

In the end, Violet felt Penelope tap her hand under the cover of the table. It was a silent comfort, urging her to give up in her attempt.

You are right, Pen. Nothing will create the illusion of a refined Aunt and Uncle when they are behaving like this!

"Goodness, Walter, look at this," Deborah said, not quite swallowing her mouthful before she spoke. "Are these crystal glasses?"

"Yes, they are." The Duke spoke up for the first time.

Violet turned her attention on him, feeling rather breathless each time she looked his way. Since the concert, she had not stopped thinking of their conversation. For a few minutes, it had been freeing, as if there were no walls, boundaries, or pretenses between them. Now though, as he looked between her and her aunt, with clear wariness, that wall was back up again.

What must he think of me and my family now?

"Miss Penelope," the Marquess said, clearly eager to change the conversation. "What did you think of the concert the other night?" Penelope lit up at the question and sat forward.

"I loved it, my lord. I have longed to see such a concert for some time."

"She is just like her mother was, my lord," Deborah said, speaking up as she lifted the crystal glass once again and took a hefty swig of the claret inside. "She always had her head in the clouds too, listening to music and talking of such things to a great extent."

Violet heard the insult. It made her fingers clench around her cutlery. She judged her aunt to be in her cups, having drunk a little too much, and it was making her tongue loose.

"You remember, Violet, your mother was just like Penelope, wasn't she? They could talk for hours about a violin!"

"Yes, they could," Violet said calmly. "I always enjoyed listening to them talk so." She added the latter sentence with purpose, but it did little good to stop their aunt from speaking.

"Your mother was often like that, talking of odd things."

The words made Violet and Penelope look at each other, both horrified, but dumbstruck, unsure what to say to such things when they were in public.

"I would have liked to have met your mother," Lord Westmond said very kindly. He bestowed a sweet smile on both Violet and Penelope, looking between them. "There is nothing I love more than a conversation about a good violin or a piece of music."

What a kind man he is.

Violet approved of Lord Westmond even more because of these words.

"You would have liked her very much then, my lord," Penelope said conversationally. Violet couldn't help noticing that Penelope was more up for conversation than usual tonight, smiling back at the Marquess.

Perhaps the wine has given her some confidence?

"I'm sure I would have done." Lord Westmond nodded, with his tone soft.

Violet was still uncomfortable. The mere mention of her mother made her itchy and fidget in the chair. She found she missed her mother greatly, and the discussion of her was making Violet miss her all the more.

I must escape this place!

"If you would excuse me." Violet stood to her feet. She wasn't sure what excuse she was going to make. Her hand shook as she placed it on the back of the chair and pushed it back in. All she knew was she had to escape, to get away from the discussion of her mother.

"I think it a good idea we retire to the other room," the Duke declared standing too. "Ladies, perhaps you will go to the withdrawing room where we will have coffee prepared for you. We will join you shortly."

They all moved to stand. In the bustle that followed, Violet looked to the Duke to find he was staring straight at her. He had conveniently given her a reason to escape. She mouthed 'thank you' across the space and he nodded, clearly having read her words.

They retreated to the withdrawing room where coffee was prepared, but still Violet could not stay with the others. Deborah was pulling on her arm, warning that she had not captured the Marquess' attention enough tonight.

"Good lord, Violet, I would say it is as if you are no longer interested in Lord Westmond."

"Enough, Aunt," Violet pleaded as she moved to her feet and walked toward the door. "If you would excuse me, I must visit the privy."

"Then I will accompany you, for there is much that needs to be discussed." Deborah followed her out. Violet shot her sister a pleading look, but Penelope shrugged as she sat down beside Louise, clearly not knowing what to do to help. "Now, listen to me, Violet. Here is what you must do to capture his attention."

Violet listened to her aunt with dismay all the way to the privy.

"You must flatter him, capture his attention, don't let him look any other way."

"I am not a courtesan, Aunt," Violet muttered in anger as she reached for the door.

"Well, at least a courtesan would know how to seduce a man." Deborah's snide comment made Violet close the door angrily on her aunt.

Violet stayed in the privy for longer than she needed to, breathing deeply. In a mirror, she could see the tears threatening as she thought of her mother.

"Mama would not wish me to be like this," she whispered looking at the mirror. "She was always one for finding happiness in the world." Somehow, saying the words aloud helped her. She sniffed and stopped the tears, thinking of the happy times she'd had with her mother, rather than the sadness of her parting.

By the time Violet had found the courage to step outside of the privy once again, she found Deborah excitedly in the corridor.

"I have had a wonderful idea!" Deborah clasped Violet's arm and dragged her down the hallway.

"Ow, aunt!" Violet tried to pull Deborah's pudgy fingers off her, but with little success.

"I have just seen Lord Westmond enter the library. You must take this opportunity to see him. Alone together, you could charm him."

"Aunt! That is scandalous," Violet muttered as they came to a stop near the door, both of them glancing at the closed library door.

"Only if someone were to discover you," Deborah whispered and then giggled, like a child reading a naughty novel. "Have no fear, I will not disturb you. Now go, quickly. I will return to the withdrawing room and invent a reason for your absence to Louise and Penelope. Go, now!"

Deborah pushed Violet toward the door so harshly that Violet had no choice but to place her hand on the handle.

I cannot do this!

The mere thought of going in and finding the Marquess alone was a shock to her. She knew she should have jumped onto this opportunity. After all, Lord Westmond was the man she had set her focus on. Was he not the perfect husband to find when faced with the challenge of Penelope's pregnancy? Yet the thought of seeing him alone made Violet uncomfortable.

I know what I will do. I will go in just long enough for my aunt to walk away again, then, I will leave and make my escape.

With her mind made up, she nodded at her aunt and turned the door handle, stepping inside. She was still in the doorway when Deborah stepped down the corridor, humming to herself happily, though she didn't go away very quickly. It prompted Violet to close the door, to cement the illusion that she intended to stay.

Pressing her ear to the door, Violet waited, trying to hear her aunt's footsteps retreating completely. The humming gradually disappeared, as did the steps.

"What do you think you are doing in here?"

Wait... that is not the Marquess' voice!

Violet turned around, her hand still on the handle, to see that it was the Duke who was alone in the library, not Lord Westmond after all.

Chapter Fourteen

Violet couldn't speak, not for a full minute as the Duke stood from his chair beside the fireplace. Behind him, the fire roared bright orange, revealing the fact that the Duke was not fully dressed. He had come in here clearly to escape them all, for his jacket was gone and his waistcoat was nearly completely undone. Violet's eyes flicked down, seeing the loosened cravat and the glimpse of his bare skin beneath.

Look away!

"Miss Hathaway, I ask you again, what are you doing in here?" the Duke said. There was something in his tone that froze her to the spot.

"I wished to escape." That much was the truth, and she was happy to admit to it.

"From whom, I wonder?" the Duke asked as he tossed the book he had been reading onto the side. "From your aunt and her odd comments about your mother? From my brother who you are supposed to be engaging in conversation? Or from me?" He added the latter one in a whisper and stepped forward a little.

From all of it!

"On second thought, don't answer that." He turned away from her and thrust his hands into his hair. "I do not think I want to know the answer."

"What does that mean?" she whispered. Violet found herself stepping away from the door and crossing toward him. She kept watching the way he was pulling at his hair in frustration, imagining herself pulling at those locks instead.

Stop it!

Yet her thoughts could do nothing to halt her mind's wanderings.

"It doesn't matter." He turned back to face her, lowering his hands from his hair. In the dim light, with the fire beside them, his features were bathed in the golden glow. "Miss Hathaway, return to your family, please."

"Why?"

"I feel as if we are reliving our first meeting," he said suddenly with a sharp laugh. "Do you wish me to repeat how scandalous it would be for the two of us to be found alone together?"

"Perhaps so." She glanced to the door, but she thought it unlikely anyone was to come to find them now. Louise and Penelope thought all the gentlemen were still in the dining room. And Deborah thought Violet was in here seducing Lord Westmond. One brother must have looked much like the other in the darkness of the corridor.

"Then why are you still standing here?" the Duke asked. Violet turned her focus toward him, watching as the Duke gestured to her, urging her on for an explanation.

"Because I do not want to be anywhere else." She shrugged as the words fell from her lips, as if it was an easy thing to say. "Is that so awful?"

"Yes! It is."

"Why?

"Because for starters," he stepped toward her, "you are here under the pretenses of charming my brother, are you not?"

"Your Grace, I –"

"I have had enough of this." The Duke's words were abruptly sharp, yet he did not walk away from her. He stayed very close, prompting Violet to lift her chin toward him, feeling as if there was a tension between them in the air. It was as if the fire didn't crackle in that grate, but in the space that separated them. "Admit it for me, Miss Hathaway."

"Admit what?"

"That you are intending to trap my brother in marriage, and for what? Simply an advantageous match."

"That is not what this is."

"Then what is it, exactly?"

"I cannot tell you." Violet chewed the inside of her mouth, thinking only of Penelope and her predicament. She could not speak of such things to the Duke, not just because he would tell his brother, but also because he would no doubt throw them out of his house. The thought of not seeing the Duke again gutted her.

"Then tell me this. Why have you chosen my brother?"

"I told you at the concert." Violet lifted her chin higher and placed her hands on her hips. The Duke may have been a formidable presence, but she wasn't going to back down, not now. "He is a kind and good man. What more could a woman want in a husband?"

"It has nothing to do with his position then? Nor his money? The estates that are in his name?"

"I am fond of him," Violet spoke through gritted teeth. She was startled to see the words made the Duke laugh softly as he tilted his head to the side, watching her.

"Not that fond. I can prove it."

"How?"

"Like this."

Violet held her breath as the Duke came closer. He stopped a mere hair's breadth in front of her, moving his head nearer to hers. His lips hovered over hers, promising a kiss that didn't quite come. Violet felt a tingle pass over her body, because of the longing of wanting that kiss.

"What does this prove?" she asked after a second, wetting her lips.

"You have not left, Miss Hathaway. You have not walked away, and you have not even moved an inch from me. That tells me everything I need to know." He didn't wait any longer. The Duke moved his lips to Violet's and kissed her.

The moment that kiss happened, Violet felt any resistance to the Duke crumble within her as if it had shattered into pieces. She lifted her hands and clung to his arms, feeling his biceps move beneath the shirt sleeves as he moved his hands to her waist. She was pulled toward him by those hands, with a passionate embrace, as he deepened that kiss.

This time, there was nothing chaste about that kiss. He parted Violet's lips as if they had done this a hundred times before, taking her tongue with his own to tease her, make her feel such pleasure that her toes curled within her shoes.

When his hand slid across her waist, bringing her closer still so that she was nestled against his body, Violet at last found some sense in her head.

What am I doing? Am I about to ruin my reputation with the Duke of Ashbury?

"Hmm!" She moved back from the kiss, jerking her head away, though she didn't step out of his arms. "We shouldn't be doing this."

"Why not? Because you're afraid of being caught, or because you do not want to?" he asked with a sultry smile, clearly knowing it was not the latter. "We won't be caught, Violet."

He used my Christian name!

The mere sound of it on his tongue made another tremble of excitement quiver up her spine.

"How can you be so sure?" Her answer was apparently all he needed. He stepped away from her. At the loss of his touch, she felt cold, wanting him back again. He strode toward the door of the library, where he grabbed a nearby chair and jammed it between the handle and the floor, blocking the door from opening, then he crossed the room back toward her again.

She met him in the middle without restraint. This time, she was the one to initiate the kiss. As he angled her head backward, lifting his fingers to her cheek to brush the loose locks of her hair out of the way, Violet chose not to think.

She didn't think of Penelope's situation, nor of Lord Westmond. She thought only of the Duke of Ashbury and the way he was with her now, kissing her, as if it was the very thing keeping him alive.

Violet was backed up. She went willingly, her hands reaching for the buttons that were already undone on the Duke's waistcoat. All she knew was that she wanted to feel more of him, to experience this excitement at its most. He didn't stop her. On the contrary, he let her pull at his waistcoat as he continued to back her up.

When she collided with the wall, she made a sound of surprise into their kiss. It prompted him to leave her lips and make his way down her neck, kissing her all the more. She was stunned at the feeling. Not just the sensation of pleasure that was ricocheting through her, but the way his lips molded to her skin, creating a sizzling path that ended at the top of her gown.

"After that first kiss, I thought... I thought you didn't like me very much." The words escaped Violet, prompting the Duke to stand straight.

"You were wrong," he murmured. "I liked you the moment I found you in my painting gallery and you refused to leave. You want to know how much?"

Violet nodded, not wanting the feeling to end.

"Then hold onto me," he pleaded, and wrapped an arm around her waist. She did as he asked, clinging to his shoulders. In one easy movement, he lifted her from the floor, pressing their bodies together. Their hips brushed against each other's, and their chests were flattened. The Duke smiled as he carried her across the room, bringing her to a settee. He sat down first, before resting her over him, so that her knees fell on either side of his hips.

Violet's breath hitched at this intimate position. There was something incredibly scandalous about it, yet at the same time, natural. As if there was nothing wrong in the world about being with the Duke in such a way.

"You can tell me to stop at any time," he whispered.

"Stop what?" At her question, he began to lift the skirt of her gown. It was a slow movement, so that the silk teased her legs. The entire time, he held her gaze, clearly waiting to see if she would turn him down. It was the furthest thing from Violet's mind. She wanted to know more of these touches and stolen kisses. They gave her an excitement she had not known was possible, and she didn't want to stop now.

When the skirt reached her hips, revealing her legs, his smile grew wider. He reached up to her then, finding her lips with his own. Violet practically whimpered into that kiss as he rested his hands on her thighs. The touch was intimate, but too gentle, she wanted something more from him, though she didn't know what. All she was aware of was this ache in her very core, one that made her long to be closer to him.

As one of the Duke's hands began to move, teasing her with the softest brush of his fingers to the top of her leg, she moaned into the kiss, pulling on his shoulders in order to deepen that kiss. He must have sensed her urgency, for his fingers slid across her thigh and reached between her legs, to where she was hovering above him.

With the first touch to her center, Violet pulled back from the kiss, feeling a small breathy moan escape her lips. The Duke smiled at her reaction and then slid his free arm around her waist, holding her chest to his. It was such an intimate position that Violet felt herself rock her body toward him, wanting more of that friction.

The Duke was not so gentle this time. When he returned his fingers to her, pleasuring her in the center, Violet lost all sense of time. All she cared about was this feeling between them, the way he was making her body move, as if indulging in some private dance. She clung to his shoulders as a rhythm was set up, not for one second thinking of separating her body from his.

The pleasure was growing into something that was unbidden, so strong in her body that she could barely look at one place. Her eyes moved from his to his lips, then down to his exposed chest between the opening of his waistcoat and shirt. When he moved his lips back to hers again, kissing her, she reached for him, pushing off his waistcoat and pulling at his shirt and cravat, desperate to touch more of him.

He pulled back from the kiss to help her, shedding the clothes to the side of the rococo settee, before he returned that arm around her waist and used it to turn the two of them together. With his fingers no longer pleasuring her, Violet whimpered, wanting more of the Duke's touch.

To her surprise, she did not have to wait long. With her back to the settee, he braced himself above her, kissing her on the lips one last time before he made his way down her body.

First, he planted a kiss on her chest above the neckline of her gown, then the kisses traveled. Across her bosom, and down her clothed stomach, then beneath the risen gown to her bare hips and the top of her thighs. This time, when her legs were parted, Violet lifted herself up on the settee, wanting to watch what the Duke would do next.

He moved back toward her center, but not with his fingers this time, with his lips. The kiss to her core made that pleasure shoot so far through Violet that she tilted her head back, trying to hold in her breathy moan as much as possible. She could scarcely believe what he was doing to her. She'd heard of such things before, whispered by Mary and the other maids in the corridors of the house when they didn't think she was around, yet she had never expected it to feel as it did.

It was as if her entire body responded to such a simple touch. The more he kissed her center, pleasuring her with his tongue alone, the more she couldn't control what she felt for him. She wanted to cling to him, and even reached down at one point, winding her fingers in his hair as she had so often fantasized of doing.

Soon, her body took on new realms of pleasure. She imagined it was rather like being hit by an ocean, with increasingly large waves striking her body. The greatest wave struck her, and her back arched off the settee, as a final shot of pleasure sizzled through her body. The Duke's touches slowed, as her body basked in the glory of that feeling. Slowly, she came down from the pleasure, aware that the Duke stopped touching her and lifted himself up enough over her so that she could see him smiling.

"Well, that was quite something," he whispered to her. The quietness in the room made her giggle. She covered her mouth, amazed at how out of breath she was, before the Duke moved toward her again. He pulled away her hand and moved his lips to hers, treating her to another kiss. She could taste herself on him, amazed at the sensation as his body brushed over hers.

"I suppose..." she murmured after a minute, waiting until he lifted himself up enough to connect their gazes. "I should say we shouldn't have done that."

"But you're not going to." His words made her smile all the more. "Thank God. I'm glad we did that too." He moved to her and kissed her another time.

With his chest bare, her fingers wandered. She reached up and let her fingers caress the exposed muscles of his chest. It made him moan into their kiss before he pulled back again.

"You and I are going to have to return to the others soon, or they'll know we have been together."

"Yes, you are right," she whispered, though she wanted more than anything else to stay as they were, with these stolen touches between them. She began to sit up, but he didn't move quite yet.

"First, would you tell me one thing," he pleaded. She nodded, encouraging him on. "Why do you need to wed, Violet? Why are you so eager to marry that you have set your sights on my brother?"

"I do not know how to explain it." More than anything was she tempted to tell him the truth in that moment, but she couldn't. It would be betraying Penelope's confidence. "I must marry, that is all. It is imperative, not out of choice, but necessity. Your brother intends to marry, does he not?" Her question made the Duke close his eyes, as if he could sense what was coming next. "You have declared you will never marry too."

"That I have." He moved off her then, standing to his feet and reaching for his shirt, pulling it back over his body.

The words made an ache develop inside of Violet. This one was of pure sadness. There was something gutting to her that even after what she and the Duke had just shared, he still would not consider the idea of marriage.

Was it all just excitement to him? Nothing more?

"I should go back first." Violet stood to her feet and lowered her skirt, before turning to a mirror and fussing with her hair, trying to make it look half decent.

"Before you go." The Duke appeared in front of her once again with something in his hands. "This is for you."

Violet fell still, staring down at what he was proffering toward her. It was a sketchbook, beautifully bound in dark red leather, with crisp white pages between the leaves.

"You bought this for me?" Violet asked in surprise.

"Well, you needed a new one, did you not?" He pushed it quickly into her grasp and stepped away, apparently nervous. Violet couldn't stop smiling as she took the book. It was truly beautiful.

"Thank you. I love it."

"Good, that is all I wanted."

What does this mean?

Violet lifted her eyes and looked away from the book, watching the Duke across the room as he continued to dress.

"Go now, Violet, back to your family. I will follow later. Trust me, your reputation is safe. No one will hear about this."

She knew he was trying to be kind, but there was something in those words that hurt her all the more. She nodded and held tightly to the sketchbook as she left the room, feeling as if her thoughts had stayed behind with the Duke in that room.

Why would he give me such a gift, something that a lover would give to another? Yet vow in the breath before that he could never marry any woman?

Chapter Fifteen

"Seb? Are you quite well? You seem distracted tonight."

"I am well, Benedict, thank you." Sebastian was growing tired of lying to his brother as they traipsed through the assembly rooms. Ordinarily, Sebastian would have been happy to give such an assembly a miss, but he found he couldn't resist tonight. The moment Benedict had mentioned it, and the fact Miss Hathaway was to be there, Sebastian had agreed to go too.

"You look positively wild," Benedict said in laughter as they reached a drinks table where he poured out claret for the two of them. "Must have been all that riding you did today. I know you like to ride, Seb, but you have barely been in the house these last two days. What has made you ride so much?"

"Call it longing to be back on the continent and riding across those wild landscapes. I miss it." It was a longing, but not the reason Sebastian had ridden so much in the last two days. He had ridden with the intention of distracting himself from thoughts of Violet, but it had done little good.

Each time he closed his eyes, he pictured he was with her again. He thought of the way her body had moved above him as he had pleasured her with his fingers, then he thought of how she had moaned, digging her hands into the rococo settee when he had kissed her very center, driving her to an oblivion of pleasure.

"Seb? Are you with me?"

"What was that?" Sebastian took the glass of claret proffered to him, shaken out of his thoughts by his brother who was laughing at him again.

"Everything I say is simply drowned out by you this evening. Something must be on your mind."

"I am sorry." Sebastian took a big swallow from the claret, hoping it would help enough to calm the whirring of his mind. "I'm not meaning to be rude; I am just distracted."

"Care to tell me what is on your mind?" Benedict asked, smiling at him. Sebastian came close to telling Benedict in that moment. After all, what would be so awful in telling Benedict that Sebastian was charmed by Miss Hathaway? Benedict had hardly declared a wish to court the lady.

I would be betraying my promise to Violet, would I not? The vow I made would be left in the dust!

Sebastian knew he couldn't do that. He downed the rest of the wine glass in one, watching as Benedict's eyes widened.

"Whatever is on your mind, it's clearly upsetting you." Benedict proffered forward the claret carafe and Sebastian happily took it from him, topping up his glass once again.

"It will pass in a few days, I'm sure. I am simply..." Sebastian struggled for the right word.

Enamored? Entranced? Or am I just a fool!

"Relax, brother. All you need is a little bit of distraction." Benedict clapped Sebastian warmly on the shoulder. "I am sure there are plenty of ladies here tonight that can distract you."

"You are the one who searches for comfort in a lady's smile, Benedict, not I." Sebastian spoke the words teasingly with mischief, prompting his brother to laugh warmly.

"Perhaps so." Benedict nodded. "Yet I am sure we can find someone to distract you tonight." He turned Sebastian to face the crowds in the assembly rooms.

Sebastian looked at it all with cool detachment. He saw the myriad of eager mothers and fathers that often looked in their direction, clearly sizing them up as eligible gentlemen for their daughters. Young ladies that were also glancing their way had elaborate headdresses or feathers in their hair, and some wore so much jewelry that they glittered, as if they had been dipped in silver. The gentlemen laughed raucously, drinking claret and brandy, with some of their laughs matching the violin music in volume.

"Any lady turn your eye, Sebastian?"

The question made Sebastian burn with guilt as he looked back at his brother. All he could think of was the heat that had been between him and Violet. It burned within him, a reminder of the pleasure, before the guilt returned. If his brother had developed an affection for Violet, then Sebastian was very much in the wrong.

"No," Sebastian replied quickly. He had barely finished the word when a new group of people walked through the door on the other side of the room. Flanked by two standing candelabras, their faces were lit by the warm light.

Sebastian's eyes flitted past Mr. and Mrs. Notley, and their daughter. His gaze went straight to Violet, on the arm of her sister.

Violet...

It had become so natural to him two nights before to address her by her Christian name. Now, he found he could think of her in no other way.

His eyes danced over her gown, taking in her full appearance. Tonight, she had returned to a Pomona green dress. It was beautifully bold, striking in the way it matched the greenness of her eyes. Her golden hair was swept up into a simple chignon, with a few curls teasing her cheeks. The look was elegant indeed.

"Miss Hathaway and her family have arrived." The words escaped Sebastian with a heavy breath. He knew what was about to happen, even before it occurred. Benedict smiled and walked off in their direction, leaving Sebastian to trail behind him.

As soon as Benedict reached the group, he greeted them all warmly. Violet was not quite as effusive in her greeting though as she had been before, something Sebastian watched with interest. When he arrived and bowed to her, he watched her the whole time. Her gaze held his as she curtsied.

Everything has changed now.

It was as if the air had shifted between them. He knew her better, and despite his good sense, he did not wish to go back to the way they were before.

"I hope you have come tonight eager to dance, my lord?" Mrs. Notley said. She already had a hand on Violet's back and was pushing her forward, clearly desirous to see her dance with Benedict.

Sebastian cursed under his breath, but there was nothing he could do to stop it.

"I have indeed. I would be blessed if both the Miss Hathaways would grant a dance to me tonight," Benedict answered quickly with much politeness.

"We would be delighted, my lord," Violet said, though her smile wasn't quite a full one.

As Benedict offered her his hand and she took it, the two of them walking off to dance together, Sebastian watched. He found he couldn't take his eyes away, even when Violet looked back at him. Their eyes connected for a few seconds, before she looked away again, as if his look had burned her.

"What a delightful sight this is, your Grace, do you not think?" Mr. Notley said, moving to Sebastian's side. "Your brother and our niece. They make a handsome pairing, do they not?"

Sebastian's hand tightened so much around the claret glass, he feared he was in danger of breaking it.

"Yes, so they do." Sebastian kept his true thoughts to himself. "If you would excuse me, there are friends I must greet." He bowed and extricated himself from the situation as quickly as he could, before walking around the room.

Rather than greeting any friends or acquaintances, Sebastian chose a dark corner where he poured himself another glass of claret and watched as Violet and Benedict danced together. They smiled at one another sweetly, but Sebastian knew Violet well enough by now to see that her smiles were not completely genuine. She kept looking away from the dancefloor too, as if she were looking for someone.

Is she looking for me?

As Benedict took her hand to perform certain steps of the routine, the envy burned within Sebastian. He could have happily torn Benedict's hand off Violet in that moment.

I am losing my mind!

He swallowed more claret, aware that he was drinking a little too quickly, though he didn't stop himself. If it helped him to deal with the jealousy he felt and how much he watched Violet, then fair enough. When the dance ended and Benedict escorted Violet from the floor, he laid a gentle hand on her back. That soft touch made something snap in Sebastian.

With a heavy thud, he placed his wine glass down on a table beside him and crossed the room, his body tense, and his face adopting an impassive look. When he reached Benedict and Violet together, the two looked startled at his sudden appearance.

"Seb, how are you feeling now? Any better?"

"Better?" Violet asked, stepping forward. "Your Grace, are you unwell?" She looked truly concerned at the idea. It didn't help, but what bothered Sebastian more was that she was still addressing him as 'your Grace'.

Should she not be calling me something much more intimate after what we shared?

"I am well enough, thank you," Sebastian said quickly, his eyes only on Violet. "Miss Hathaway, I know I am not the great dancer my brother is, but would you dance the next with me, please?" He held his hand out toward her.

"What a good idea! A dance! That will cheer your spirits, Seb." Benedict clapped him on the shoulder before walking off, clearly assured of the outcome. Sebastian waited in limbo for a second, staring at Violet, not so certain of what her answer would be.

She glanced from side to side, clearly aware that people were watching the two of them, before she nodded and placed her hand in his. The moment her hand touched his, Sebastian felt a calmness take over him. He lowered their hands down at his side and walked her back toward the dancefloor. The touch of her hand made him cling to her, and he was aware of how tightly her fingers curled around his hand in response.

When they reached the dance floor, the opening notes began for a waltz. He smiled a little as he bowed and she curtsied, thrilled that he could have the chance to be so close to her again.

As he took her in his arms, he was extremely aware of every place that they touched. He thought of the gentleness of her fingers on his shoulder, so unlike the way she had clung to him with vigor on his settee. He thought, too, of their hands and their fingers pressed together. Moving forward and leading her into the dance, he brushed his thumb against the side of her hand, an intimate touch, one that made her breath hitch.

"What are you doing, your Grace?" Violet murmured after a few seconds of silence, her eyes intently on Sebastian's.

"Dancing a waltz," he whispered. "No more 'your Grace,' Violet. I do not think I can stand to hear you calling me that."

"What do you mean?"

When they nearly collided with another couple, she looked afeared of being overheard. With his hand upon her waist, he pulled her away from the other couple, avoiding the collision. She gasped at that touch and tilted her head up higher, so close that had they been alone, he could have kissed her.

If only...

"Call me by my name, Violet, please. My name is Sebastian." As he led her around the floor, her lips parted, as if he'd asked her for something shocking.

"I cannot do that!"

"Why not?"

"Because you are a Duke!" she pointed out, her eyes wide. "To address you as such would be an intimate thing." He raised his eyebrows, reminding her of what they had already shared. "Do not speak of that night."

"Why not? You seemed very happy at the time."

"Your Grace!" She clung tighter to his hand with the word. He adjusted the way they were holding hands, entwining their fingers together. In the middle of the floor and hidden by the other dancers, it would have been a difficult thing for any observer to see. Her eyes shot to the way they were holding hands and she chewed her lip, apparently nervous. "Do not do this to me, please."

"Do what?" he asked. All he had wanted was to be close to her in this moment, and he had that at last.

"You are toying with me," she said accusingly, turning a glare upon him.

"Toying with you? No. That is not what this is." He spun her away from another couple, their movements abrupt in his surprise at the words.

"Then what are you doing?" She turned her head up toward him. "You have declared you will never marry a woman, and you know I must marry. Yet you are now encouraging me to care for you."

"Is it so wrong to acknowledge that there is something here?" he asked. With the words, he rocked her gently from side to side, their movements so close, that for a second, their bodies brushed together, before she stepped back a few inches, creating space between them again. "You and I both feel it."

She didn't answer for a second, though her breath appeared to hitch higher.

"A bond," she murmured eventually. The word made his smile grow.

"A bond." He rather liked the way she put it. "It's sensual too, exciting." He shifted their fingers together another time, aware of the way her touch made a tingle pass through his body.

"Yet it can lead to nothing, can it?" she whispered. "Not when I have to..." She broke off and looked away from him. He couldn't see where she looked, and he was sure he didn't want to know out of fear she may have looked for Benedict.

"Dance with me for a minute, Violet. Think of nothing else, other than this dance, please." He was certain now the claret was making him listen to what his body wanted rather than his mind. After all, if his logic was with him, he would have put distance between them, yet the mere thought of her leaving his side at this moment gutted him.

Violet did as he asked. She danced with him only and said nothing more. Every so often there was a stolen touch. The way he held her waist would be slightly more intimate, and she would curl her gloved fingers over his a little more.

When the dance ended and they bowed and curtsied to one another, Sebastian didn't know what to say. He searched for anything to utter, but Violet beat him to it.

"I cannot do this." She curtsied to him another time and hastened off, slipping between other dancers so fast that she made others around them glance his way, wondering what he had done or said to make a lady run from him so quickly.

Sebastian cursed under his breath as he looked around the room. Soon enough, he found Benedict looking at him with anger in his face.

I know, brother, I know. I have caused this mess.

Sebastian didn't hesitate in his next decision. He left the dancefloor, ensuring those gossiping had just enough time to look away and think of other things. Once they had looked in another direction, he took his chance and followed Violet out of the room.

Chapter Sixteen

Violet was pacing in some distant room to the Almack's Assembly Rooms. She hadn't really looked at what path she had taken. All she had wanted to do was escape the ballroom, to escape the way the Duke was looking at her.

Sebastian.

Now he had asked her to call him that, she couldn't get the name out of her head. Each time she thought of it, the very name conjured thoughts of him. She turned back around again and paced the other way, thinking of how he had held her as they had danced together. That single dance had brought something sharply into focus.

If I did charm Lord Westmond enough for a marriage, could I ever be happy with him?

She knew the answer. The very thought made her stop pacing and blink, trying to stop the sting of tears that had crept into her eyes.

No. I could not be happy. Not after knowing his brother as I do now.

Violet returned to her pacing, but it didn't last long, for the door crept open. She spun around, looking toward it out of fear. As a face appeared there, visible in the moonlight that filtered in through the tall arched window behind her, her heart thudded harder.

"What are you doing here, your Grace?" she whispered as Sebastian appeared. He closed the door behind him, but not before glancing up and down the corridor, clearly checking he had not been followed.

"No. No more 'your Grace.' I have just asked you that." He crossed toward her in the room.

Something in the back of Violet's head told her she should run and escape him now. Every time she was near him, he seemed to have this power over her. So much so, that the last time she had been intimate with him. Could she really risk doing such a thing again?

"Sebastian." Her whisper of his name made a smile appear on his face. For a second, she returned that smile, before she realized what she was doing, and the smile faltered. "Why did you ask me to dance?"

"There is nothing wrong with asking you to dance, Violet." He inched closer toward her and reached for her hand. The moment he touched her, she felt her resistance wither away. She let him take her hand, watching, entranced, as he lifted that hand to his lips. Even though it was gloved, he kissed the back, and held that kiss for a few seconds, never once looking away from her eyes as he did so.

"We shouldn't be here," Violet murmured.

"Yet again, you are not running away from me." His words made her angry at herself. Why was it that every time he was near, her good sense abandoned her? "Stay a little longer yet, Violet."

She had no wish to go anywhere. Instead, she took another step toward him, moving so close that he smiled as he bent down toward her. Violet raised herself on her toes and closed her lips to his. This kiss was a slow one. It may have started as something chaste, a press of lips together, but soon, a hunger developed to it.

The sensuality of it made Violet move her hands to Sebastian, clinging onto the lapels of his tailcoat. His own hands came up to gently rest on the curves of her waist. It was such a soft touch that she couldn't help but compare it to the passion he had shown her in his library a few days before.

When they did part from their kiss, they didn't go far. They stayed in each other's arms.

"We shouldn't be doing this," Violet whispered after a minute. "I know that, yet I can't seem to stop myself anyway."

"Too powerful, isn't it?" Sebastian murmured and moved his lips to her again. This time, he trailed a path up her neck, where he found a sweet spot beneath her ear. As he playfully nipped her there, Violet gasped and curled her fingers around his lapels even more, just needing to hold onto him. "Tell me something, Violet."

"What?"

"What do you want from life?"

"Life?" Violet blanched, startled by the question. "How do you mean?"

"What do you want for your future?" Sebastian trailed more kisses down her neck, now giving attention to her collarbone in such a way that she arched against him.

"To be happy." The words fell from her lips. "I don't want to be with my uncle and aunt anymore. I wish to be far away from here, somewhere distant, somewhere that Penelope could be cared for." She swallowed, keeping her next thought to herself.

And her child too.

"Is that why you want to marry? To escape the life that you're living?" Sebastian asked, his voice gentle as he lifted his lips from her and connected their gazes.

"Not exactly. That is out of necessity. If I could marry as I chose to, then I would choose someone that I..." She faltered, unable to say the words. Sebastian just waited for her to resume; his hands still soft on her waist. He drew one of them up and down, making a tingle of pleasure shoot through her and reminding her of what he had done to her on that rococo settee. "I would marry someone I care about. Someone that excites me." Sebastian smiled a little at her words. "Yet that life is impossible."

"Tell me your secret," Sebastian pleaded with her. "Why do you have to marry now? Why, Violet?"

"It is not my secret to share." She shook her head, showing she could not speak of it.

"Then... whose is it?"

Violet couldn't let him think anymore. If he did so, then he might just guess the secret concerned Penelope. She raised herself on her toes and kissed Sebastian another time, desperate for that touch.

He kissed her back with full vigor, but then she parted from him, settling back down on her heels again.

"I must go. Before someone realizes we are both here." She slipped away from him, aware that he lowered his hands from her as reluctantly as she stepped back from him. She hovered in the doorway for a few seconds, looking back to him in the moonlight, before she disappeared.

As she walked away, the guilt grew worse within her. It wasn't just that she had been trying to charm his brother that made her feel so guilty, it was now that she also felt as if she was betraying Sebastian.

Oh, what do I do now?

Chapter Seventeen

"Seb? You and I need to talk." Benedict practically collared Sebastian as he walked out of the assembly rooms.

"At home, Benedict. I just need to leave this place at this moment." Sebastian shrugged on his frock coat and placed his top hat on his head, before hurrying down the steps toward his coach that had been brought around. Benedict hurried to collect his coat and hat too, but he didn't waste time putting them on as he hastened after Sebastian.

The two of them moving quickly made splashes in the puddles across the darkened street. In the last few minutes, the heavens had opened, and heavy rain was pouring down, bouncing off Sebastian's hat and dampening the shoulders of his coat.

As Sebastian stepped up into the coach, Benedict followed him. The two fell into the coach, sitting opposite one another. The light in the coach may have been poor, but Sebastian could see enough through the shadows to be able to tell his brother was glowering at him.

"You have not stopped glaring at me since I danced with Miss Hathaway." As he spoke, Sebastian had to remind himself to call her Miss Hathaway, not Violet.

Does he wish to court Violet after all?

Sebastian felt the mere thought made him sick. He had always vowed not to marry. He had made that decision long ago, yet now he was tempted. The thought of Benedict standing at an altar beside Violet was urging Sebastian to bump Benedict out of the way and take his place.

Could I marry? Should I tell Benedict I am considering the thought?

"She ran off, Sebastian." Benedict's words were immediately harsh. "Do I need to remind you that you have already embarrassed this woman once at a ball? Now, you have embarrassed her again."

"I didn't embarrass her!"

"Then tell me why she ran away from you." Benedict sat forward, practically balancing on the edge of the coach bench as he tossed his top hat on the seat beside him. "She is a good lady, a fine woman, yes?"

"Yes," Sebastian answered eagerly.

"Kind, respectable, interesting."

These are not enough words.

Sebastian had more words he wanted to use to describe Violet. Passionate, outspoken, bold, intelligent, and creative, were just a few of the words that popped into his mind. He stopped himself from saying them, waiting for his brother to complete the speech he had clearly worked himself up to say.

"She does not deserve to be treated badly, Sebastian."

"I didn't treat her badly." Even as Sebastian said the words, he thought of the moment he had shared with Violet on the settee. He had compromised her, but not out of a wish to hurt her. It had happened because he couldn't resist her, just as she appeared unable to resist him.

"Then why did she run away from you?"

"We had a little argument. That was all. Calm yourself, Benedict. I caught up with her and apologized to her. All is well again." Sebastian tried to persuade his brother, but he was not convinced Benedict believed him. Benedict's eyebrows were raised, and he shook his head after a few seconds.

"I am missing something here."

"What do you mean?" Sebastian asked, trying to sound innocent. A fear was growing in him now. It was just possible that Benedict truly did care for Violet, and if that was the case, then Sebastian was an awful brother for what he had done.

Please, do not tell me that is the case!

"What do you think of Miss Hathaway, Seb?" Benedict asked. He sat abruptly back on the coach bench, with his arms folded across his chest. "Tell me the truth, what you really think of her."

"You know what I think." Sebastian shifted where he sat. He tried to fidget with his frock coat in an effort to give himself something to do. When it was not enough to distract his mind from the conversation at hand, he reached for a tinder box that was kept under the bench, and lit the lantern between him and Benedict, that swung from the ceiling of the coach.

"You think she is only showing attentions my way because she is after a marriage for advantage?" Benedict asked slowly.

Sebastian accidentally burned himself on the iron wool. He blew out the flame and shook his hand, trying to calm the singe before he attempted to light the lantern a second time.

"I think there is a reason she is doing it, but what that reason is, I do not know."

"Then it's not possible she could just be a good-hearted lady?"

"I didn't say she wasn't." Sebastian froze as the lantern took light. The glow that emitted from that single flame cast an orange hue around the carriage, and on Benedict's face. "I think her..."

"What? You think her what?"

Captivating!

"I think she is very interesting," Sebastian murmured. "Yet if you are asking me if you should consider courtship with her, Benedict —"

"We are jumping ahead a bit here."

"Are we?" Sebastian sat forward, his head nearly tapping the lantern in his sudden eagerness to speak. "If you are asking me that, then my honest answer is that I do not know. I want you to marry for love, and to be truly happy. If Vi — I mean, if Miss Hathaway is anything short of that, then do not consider it. I beg of you."

A silence descended on the carriage. It was only disturbed by the rocking of the carriage to and fro, and the sounds of one of the horses whinnying beyond the window.

"Benedict?" Sebastian said after a minute of suffering in this silence. "Will you not say anything?"

Benedict tilted his head to the side slightly, his eyes narrowed, and the corner of his lip tilted up in a lilting smile.

"What!?" Sebastian said, finding his patience was wearing thin thanks to the liquor he had consumed that night.

"You called her Violet."

"No, I did not." Sebastian shook his head quickly.

"Fine, you did not, yet you nearly did."

"It was simply a slip of the tongue."

"A slip of the tongue?" Benedict sat forward again. "You nearly call a young lady by her Christian name, and that means nothing, does it?"

"I was simply thinking earlier this evening what a nice name it is. I meant nothing by it." Sebastian shrugged, praying his brother believed him.

Here was his opportunity to come clean. He could tell his brother the truth, that he was completely entranced by Violet Hathaway, and despite his vow to never marry, he was finding himself imagining what it could be like to marry Violet. Yet there was something that stopped him from doing so.

I made a vow. One for Benedict's future happiness. It is the right thing to do, and no good can come from changing my mind or even voicing my true thoughts on Violet.

Sebastian made a quick decision. He would merely be tormenting himself with a possibility that could never be, even if he mentioned the mere idea to Benedict.

"Tell me this, Benedict, I beg of you." Sebastian needed to understand his own thoughts. He and Violet could not be together, but he needed to know if he would be tortured by the sight of her constantly throughout his life, teased by the possibility of what could have been. "What do you think of Miss Hathaway? You have said you are looking for a wife. Are you considering Miss Hathaway could be that woman?"

For a second, Benedict said nothing. He scratched his jaw and shifted in his seat, then he looked up again, finding Sebastian's gaze with his own.

"She is a fine woman, but no more than that have I thought."

"Does that mean you have ruled her out as a possible wife, or you are still considering it?"

"Seb? Why would my answer matter to you that much?" Benedict's question left Sebastian sitting back on the coach bench again. He shrugged it off, pretending to be nonchalant.

"It doesn't matter. I am invading your privacy and I apologize for it," Sebastian spoke quickly. "I will not ask again."

Yet Sebastian felt the words were uncomfortable on his tongue. All he wanted to do the entire journey home was ask if Benedict intended to court Violet or not.

Chapter Eighteen

"Pen, let me feel your head again." Violet reached for Penelope's temple. She had no fever, but she was clammy from the hours of having been sick. Beside them, Mary took the chamber pot away that had been used for Penelope's illness.

"It is not getting any better, is it?" Penelope said, her tone rather weak. She tilted her head back on the pillow, making her dampened hair fall loosely across the linen covers.

"I wish it was," Violet murmured, worried for her sister. She sat forward and pulled the covers around Penelope another time, trying to make her more comfortable.

All night, Violet had been awake. Each time she attempted to sleep she would dream that she was back in Sebastian's arms, which would force her to wake again. Now morning had come, and she had discovered Penelope was back to being ill, and it gave her something else to worry about.

"How are you feeling now, Pen?" she asked, her tone gentle. Penelope rolled over on the bed and practically hugged Violet's legs from where she was sitting beside her.

"I have heard women say before that all the difficulties of pregnancy are worth it when the child arrives. Oh, I hope so! Because this feels…" She trailed off and held a hand to her mouth.

"Mary! Mary! Quick, another chamber pot." Violet stood off the bed, releasing herself from Penelope. As Mary reappeared from a door, carrying another chamber pot, Violet took it from her and thrust it onto the bed, barely getting there in time. As softly as she could, Violet held back her sister's hair, making soothing sounds and patting her back.

Once the sickness had passed, Penelope fell back limp on the bed again, and Violet sat with her, holding onto her.

"Thank you, Mary."

Once more, Mary hurried off with the chamber pot, wrinkling her nose at the smell.

"Something must be done," Violet whispered softly. She laid Penelope down on the pillows and brushed back her hair from her face. "Pen, it is time you saw a midwife, or a physician of some kind. Someone, at least."

"You know I cannot," Penelope murmured, her voice frail and her cheeks white as milk. "If anyone came here, then our Aunt Deborah would realize something was amiss."

"I know, but what if we were to go to them?" Violet's words made Penelope lift her head off the pillow. "I have heard before that some physicians can give a tonic or something to help soothe bouts of sickness. Is it not worth going to see if someone could help?"

Penelope looked excited by the idea and raised herself on the bed, pushing back her dampened hair from her forehead.

"I would like that, but how could we make it work?"

Mary appeared once more beside them, with a fresh chamber pot that she placed beside the bed, in case it was needed.

"We couldn't go to any well-known physicians," Violet whispered. "Perhaps not even anyone used by the ton, for if you were seen there, gossip could spread."

"I have an idea," Mary said softly. "I have a cousin who works near Hyde Park, on the cheaper side of town, Miss Hathaway. She is a healer, and many go to her for advice, but certainly no lady or gentleman from the ton. If you went to her, no one would recognize you there."

Violet slowly fell to her feet, still holding onto Penelope's hand.

"That could work, could it not? Pen, what do you think?"

Penelope seemed to chew over the thought for a minute. She tilted her head from side to side before turning to face Violet.

"When could we go?"

"Give me a few minutes. I will arrange the carriage at once."

Chapter Nineteen

"No carriage available?" Violet scoffed as she steered the horse forward down the street, pulling her pelisse high up around her face to avoid being seen by those passing. One glance back at Penelope showed she was equally unhappy, looking rather nauseous atop her horse, with Mary trailing on behind them on her pony. "No carriage? Yet a carriage can be used to take Louise to her dress fitting."

"Perhaps you should have told our aunt you wanted the carriage for a dress fitting yourself so that you could impress Lord Westmond. That would have certainly prompted her to produce a carriage," Penelope said with a sigh.

"I could hardly tell her that. She would have then insisted on coming with us." Violet shook her head in dismay and urged Mary on again through the roads, to come to the front and lead the way.

They had long since left the main streets of London and were in the back alleys behind Hyde Park and the forest that backed onto it. More than one passing trader and worker looked their way, clearly startled to see women of the ton in these parts. When they, at last, reached the house, Mary was the first to jump down from her horse and knock on the door of a tiny building.

The door was opened in a hurry by a young smiling woman on the other side, so large that her apron strained against her waist.

"Mary, this the woman you tell me about?" she asked, turning her gaze on Violet.

"No. This is Miss Penelope." Mary gestured to Penelope behind her.

Violet jumped down from her horse and helped Penelope down from her own.

"Still feeling sick?" Violet whispered to her.

"You hardly need me to answer that question," Penelope murmured, her face so pale that she was the color of the clouds above.

"Best come in, Miss Penelope. I'll see you alone." The rather buxom woman beckoned Penelope forward.

"It's all right," Violet assured Penelope, squeezing her hand. "You go. We'll wait here with the horses."

Penelope nodded and went inside. The young, rounded woman offered them a restrained smile before she closed the door. The rather loud sound made Violet flinch and turn to look at Mary with a questioning gaze.

"That is your cousin?"

"Yes," Mary said, shifting between her feet as she held the reins of her horse and Penelope's. "She is rather known for her sharp manner."

"Yes, I can see why." Violet looked back and forth across the street, searching for something to do whilst she waited. She was met with curious glares that stared her way.

"I'm beginning to think this was a mistake, Miss Hathaway," Mary whispered, moving to her side.

"A mistake? Why?" Violet asked.

"Because these parts can be dangerous for a lady like you. See the way they look at you?"

Violet could see what Mary meant. She didn't have much desire to stay where she was and at the end of the street, she could see a patch of trees, their autumnal leaves dancing in the wind.

"Is that the back of Hyde Park?" Violet asked, glancing toward it.

"Yes, Miss Hathaway. There is a patch of woodland behind it."

"Then I shall take a turn there for a while with the horse. I will be back soon."

"Are you sure?" Mary looked nervous at the idea of letting her go alone.

"Quite sure. As you say," Violet paused and gestured to the people around them. "I am being watched here." Violet did not like the idea of giving any thief a chance to steal her purse. She climbed quickly into the saddle and rode toward the park at the end of the road.

The horse grew excited beneath her, galloping as they reached the tree line. Violet only glanced back once, ensuring that Mary was well and safe with the horses before she rode into the trees.

The sound of the people and the busy street disappeared behind her, and the cacophony of workers and horses moving back and forth faded too. Violet grew lost between the trees, riding with wild abandon, so madly that the horse's hooves striking the earth beneath her were the only sounds she could hear.

More than once did she have to bend down beneath a passing branch, but she didn't care. For a few brief minutes, out here and alone with the trees, she was able to forget the woes of the world. She didn't have to worry for Penelope and the child, and neither did she have to fear what she felt for Sebastian. She could think only of the trees as they danced from side to side, as if their wind was their music.

Violet was uncertain how long she had ridden for, but she was coming down to a slow canter when a figure appeared up ahead. Through the tree trunks and the branches that danced like waving arms, a man had stopped atop his gray horse. The animal was snorting, as if annoyed at something, and the man riding him was laughing.

"Calm yourself, Gray, have we not done enough riding these last few days to even satisfy your hunger for the wilderness?"

That voice!

The horse snorted another time.

Violet urged her mare forward a step, where she at last had a good look of the man ahead of her. It was Sebastian atop the horse, though he had currently stopped and was checking the time on his pocket watch. When Violet's mare snorted too, as if in agreement with the other horse, Sebastian sharply looked up.

The moment their gazes connected, Violet felt the wind had been taken from her body.

"Violet," he spoke, pocketing the watch quickly. "Are you following me around now?" he asked with that usual mischievous smile.

"No, I just..." She glanced behind her, realizing she could not talk of why she had come here. "Excuse me." She turned the horse quickly and tried to ride away again.

"Wait, Violet!" Sebastian called after her, but Violet didn't listen. She just had to keep on going and ride away from him. The horse moved with vigor beneath her, as fast as she could with Violet pulling on the reins so. "Violet!" The closeness of Sebastian's voice showed Violet did not need to turn around to see she had not lost him. He stayed with her, never once backing up.

When Violet tried to turn down a path, to head between a clump of trees and head back to the street, she found her path was blocked. Sebastian had ridden along a different path to her own, and jumped a fallen log, ending up in her path instead.

"Woah!" Violet pulled on the reins of her horse, stopping the mare from going any further and colliding with him. The animal squealed in surprise and backed up a little, as Violet turned an accusing glare on Sebastian. "You spooked her!"

"You rode away, I was merely trying to catch up with you."

"When someone rides away from you, it means go away, Sebastian. It does not mean chase me down." She flicked the reins, about to urge the mare to walk past him, but Sebastian reached out and took hold of her reins, pulling her to a stop beside him. His hand was so close to Violet's on the reins that she thought of the small distance between them, thinking how easy it would be to reach out and touch him.

"Something is wrong." Sebastian's eyes were on her face. That intense look made her wriggle in the saddle, but she couldn't escape. "Violet, something has happened. What is wrong?"

"It is nothing."

"Then if it is nothing, surely you can tell me of it, yes?" His questioning gaze made her wither under that look.

How easy would it be to tell him everything?

"It is nothing. It is just Penelope. She... I'm worried for her. That is all." Violet couldn't say anymore, how could she? When she looked away from Sebastian, trying to keep her emotions in check, she lost the battle. Tears sprung to her eyes and her breath hitched. She kept her gaze through the trees as her vision blurred, somehow hoping that if she didn't look at Sebastian, he wouldn't notice her crying.

"Violet? Oh no, you are not doing this right now."

"Doing what?"

"Crying and pretending you are not!" Sebastian released the reins of his own horse and jumped down, standing between the animals, before he slid his hand along Violet's own reins, placing his hand over hers. "Come down, Violet, please."

She didn't have the heart to refuse him. She looked about, through her blurry vision, she didn't think anyone else was around, so she slipped down off the saddle, her hand still in Sebastian's.

"What has happened?" Sebastian was gentle as he turned Violet in his arms. She sniffed another time, but she couldn't stop the first tear as it leaked out of her eyes and down her cheek. Sebastian lifted his hand

and rested it against her cheek softly, as he used his thumb to dry the tear away. "You said you are worried about Penelope. Has something happened to her? Is she well?"

Violet wanted to lie and say all was well, but there was something about being in this moment with Sebastian that stopped her from uttering such a lie. When her breath hitched and the tears came harder, Sebastian embraced her.

"I've got you, Violet," he whispered, pulling her toward him. "Nothing is wrong here, nothing we can't mend, I promise you that."

Despite the fact he did not know what he was comforting her for, somehow, his words helped. She rested against his chest, clinging to him as much as she could, with one of her hands in his and her other curling around the edge of his frock coat.

When he moved his lips to her forehead and kissed her there, the effect made Violet's body freeze within his grasp.

What she and Sebastian shared, she knew, wasn't just about excitement. It was about so much more than that. All this time she had been falling in love with Sebastian, but only now here in this moment had she realized that was what it was.

I'm falling in love with him.

She lifted her head from his chest, watching as he looked at her. Another tear escaped and once again did he lift that hand, drying that tear away.

"I didn't expect to find you out here of all places," he whispered. "I've been escaping here most days at the moment."

"Why is that?" she murmured quietly.

"I'm struggling to arrange my thoughts. I find I can't take them off a particular lady at this time." He offered her a sad sort of smile with the words, showing who he meant. It made her heart ache for him.

I wonder if there is a chance that he could look at me as I do him? If I am so much on his mind, is it so mad to think so?

"Violet, I hate to see you crying." He dried another tear. "Will you not tell me what is wrong?"

"It's Penelope." Violet found the words falling from her lips. She was taking this chance. It was a leap of trust, praying that she could trust Sebastian with this secret, but she knew him well enough by now that he did not gossip, nor was he one that talked of scandals. "Please, you mustn't tell anyone."

"Very well, but what is it that I must not tell people?"

"Penelope. She... she is with child."

Chapter Twenty

"She's with child?" Sebastian found himself repeating the words, almost woodenly. Something numb had passed through his body as he tried desperately to understand. "Miss Penelope is with child? Who? Who would leave her so?" He was immediately angry.

Sebastian did not know Miss Penelope very well, but he had seen her enough to know she was sweet, reserved, and quiet. Any man who would do this to her was cruel to leave her in such a situation.

"Violet? Who left her to fend alone?" Sebastian asked, doing his best to keep his voice quiet.

"What does it matter now?" Violet said tearfully, sniffing and trying her best to stop herself from crying anymore. "He courted her, then he left her. He as good as discarded her as if she was rubbish to him. Now, everything is so..." She held up a hand between them, letting her fingers fall slack to show how everything was falling apart.

"God's wounds." Sebastian was thinking quickly. He closed his eyes and tipped his head back, his mind working fast as the realizations slotted into place. "*This* is why you told me it was a necessity that you married. You were doing it all for your sister, weren't you?" He opened his eyes again and looked down at Violet. She nodded wordlessly. It prompted Sebastian to curse under his breath, feeling he understood Violet even more than he did before.

She was putting her sister first, constantly. When she talked of marrying for love, it was what her heart wanted, but she also said it was an impossibility.

"Often it is the women in these situations that marry quickly," he said slowly, watching as Violet shook her head. Around them, the birds tittered and the wind whistled, masking some of Violet's voice as she continued on.

"Penelope made it clear to me she could not imagine marrying at this time. She couldn't do it. What was I supposed to do, Sebastian? Leave her as she is without help? I have no money, no connections, no home to call my own in which to house her and the child. I had to do something. I have to now!" She was insistent, her tears coming fast even as she tried to stop them.

Sebastian held onto her, unable to let go of Violet just yet. He had one hand in hers, and the other wrapped softly around her waist.

Here, she is safe, in my arms.

"So, you set your cap at Benedict, because it is known he intends to marry and has the money you need."

"I'm sorry," Violet murmured.

"Sorry? What are you apologizing for?"

"For doing this! All of it. For trying to catch your brother's eye when in truth, I do not want to. I do not want any of it, but I did not know what else to do." The despair on her face was real, that was plain to see.

"I know. I can see that, Violet." He pulled softly around her waist, drawing her toward him. He was very glad the horses were on either side of them, so that if any passing walker in the distance of the forest looked their way, they would not be able to see the position Sebastian and Violet were in now. Once Violet was nestled against him, he lowered his forehead to hers. It was an intimate action, one he hoped reassured her. "Violet, I can see why you did it. You were protecting your sister."

I probably would have done the same to protect Benedict if our roles were reversed.

"I was. In my effort to help, I have only failed, haven't I?" Violet said miserably. Sebastian felt a small kernel of relief begin inside of him.

"You have no wish to marry Benedict, do you?" he asked, needing to hear the words.

"No." She shook her head. He sighed, glad to hear the words. "Yet I must do something, for Penelope's sake."

"Yes, something must be done." Sebastian lifted his head off Violet's again. "If only I could find a way to help you. Surely, there is something that could be done."

Violet sniffed, evidently trying to halt her tears. He held her hand tightly in his own, not wanting to let go of her yet, not until he was certain she was comforted.

"Violet, I will help you if I can, I promise you that."

"Do you truly mean it?" she asked quietly. When her lips tilted up into a small innocent smile, he began to think his words had worked, that was until he heard what she had to say next. "Does that mean that you would abandon your promise not to marry?"

Sebastian blinked; certain he had heard her wrong for a second.

"Wait... what did you say?"

"You said you wanted to help," Violet spoke quickly, "and I need to marry."

Sebastian dropped her hand. His other arm was still around her, for he was finding it difficult to walk away from her, but her words had shocked him to his core.

Yes, he might have fantasized about what it could be like to wed Violet, but that was all it was.

A fantasy.

"I am not offering to marry you, Violet," he whispered. "What I said before is true. I made a vow not to marry. For the sake of another, I must keep to that vow." Violet shifted in his arms. She closed her eyes and more tears leaked out. "Violet, wait –"

"No. No." She backed up completely, so that his arm fell away from being around her. "You really intend never to marry? Never?"

"Never. I told you as much."

"Yet you..." She gestured between them. In that moment, Sebastian felt raging guilt. It made him feel small, as if he was a withered boy standing before Violet, no longer a man.

"I know what I did."

"You were charming, you kissed me so many times, and you and I... in your library... we..." She was barely making sense now, almost frantic and shaking her head back and forth between her tears. "Oh god, what have I done."

"Violet, all of that was natural." He stepped toward her, but she backed up from him. "What passed between us was a thrill –"

"Yet that was all it was, wasn't it? Just a thrill? A passing excitement?" The passion and boldness of her words made him fall still, feeling that guilt so strongly through his body that he could have sworn his hands shook at his sides. "What have I done?" Violet whispered, more to herself than to him at all.

"Violet, I still want to help," he called to her as she reached for her horse, clearly so eager to escape him that she didn't wait. She didn't even glance back at him.

"You can help. You can help by vowing never to speak a word of this to anyone."

"Violet?"

"Swear it." She pulled herself up into the saddle, turning her gaze upon him. "You clearly keep your vows well, so I beg of you, vow it to me now, and I will ask no more of you, Sebastian."

Her words cut him deeply. He stood still and nodded at her, feeling as if a wall was being rebuilt between them.

"I give you my vow, Violet. I will not speak a word of what you have told me today of Penelope."

"Good. Then that is that. When we see each other again at balls, you will not ask me to dance, nor will you kiss me in darkened corners where no one can see us."

Her instruction made him reach out for the horse behind him. Gray snorted, pushing his nose forward, clearly wanting to ride again. At this moment, it only angered Sebastian further. His eyes found Violet's where he saw those green orbs were full of fresh tears that were on the precipice of falling.

"Goodbye, your Grace." The word and her use of his title had a finality to it. It ended things, as if they had never been close at all.

"Violet, I'm sor −" He didn't manage to finish the word. She flicked the reins of her mare and galloped away, leaving him with fresh soil kicking up from under the horse's hooves, dirtying his breeches.

He watched as she disappeared between the trees, uncertain what feeling swayed greater within him. Was it guilt? Fear? Or maybe, it was just pure melancholy.

I'm so sorry, Violet.

Chapter Twenty-One

When Violet reached the edge of the trees, she worked hard to stop her tears. She had not stopped crying since she had left Sebastian's side, knowing what she had done.

By sharing Penelope's secret, she had increased the chance of discovery. What was more, she had burned any possible bridge between herself and Lord Westmond now. There was not a chance Sebastian would let his brother give her attention after this. Especially not after she had as good as suggested a marriage between her and Sebastian, and he had rejected her so.

It was all fleeting excitement to him, was it not? He doesn't look at me as I do him. He has not been falling in love with me, as I have him.

Violet sniffed another time and pulled the horse out of the tree line, heading down the busy street toward the house where Mary was standing outside.

"Miss Hathaway, you are back." Mary's smile faltered as she took a good look at Violet. "Is all well? Have you been cry–"

"All is well. The wind has been strong today." Violet tried to laugh it off and waved a hand at her face. "My eyes are quite sore. I think I got some soil in them from all that riding." Mary nodded, but Violet was not convinced she had managed to persuade her of that lie.

Before anymore could be said between them, the door to the healer's house opened, and Penelope stepped outside.

"Penelope!" Violet hurried down from the horse and moved to her sister's side. She pushed away all thoughts of Sebastian or his brother and focused on Penelope.

She is the most important person. I must think of her and nothing else.

"How are you?" she asked, relieved to see Penelope smile.

"All is well with her," the healer called from the doorway. "Sounds like the two of them are doing very well." She gestured down to Penelope's stomach as she spoke. "Quite natural to be so sick, though I have given her a tonic which should help quell some of the worst of it."

"Thank you. A thousand times, thank you," Penelope said gushingly to the healer.

"You're most welcome." The healer offered another smile and then closed the door again.

"See?" Mary said with a laugh. "She has a rather brusque manner, but she knows her business very well."

"Thank you for this, Mary," Violet said. After she had helped Penelope back onto the horse, she went to the maid's side and squeezed her hand, a silent sign of friendship. "What would we do without you?"

"My pleasure. I am just glad Miss Penelope looks so happy now."

"I am. Very happy indeed." Penelope looked down to her stomach as she spoke.

That simple smile filled Violet with relief. It seemed most of what had plagued Penelope these last few days was fear. That fear there could be something wrong with the child.

All will be well. I have to believe that.

As Violet climbed into the saddle and turned to lead the way, her own smile dropped, but she hid her face. She kept replaying what had happened with Sebastian in her mind. The pain of the rejection stung, as if her heart had met with a wasp's sting, but there was more that worried her now.

It seems I must find another man to persuade to marry me now, even though my heart isn't in it.

Chapter Twenty-Two

"I do not think you have said two words together this morning. For God's sake, Seb, say something."

Sebastian looked up from his breakfast plate, uninterested in the food that was there. The scent of the cooked meat hung in the air, along with the bread. Despite the scents, he was not concerned with eating. He was content to sit back in his seat, his mind elsewhere, as the chair creaked beneath him.

I am back at Hyde Park, with Violet beside me.

All night, he had not stopped thinking of what had passed between Violet and himself. He thought of the pain she was in, and the need to do something for her sister, then he thought of the guilt he suffered from too.

I want to help her, but as much as the idea of marrying Violet fascinates me, I cannot do it.

"Seb?" Benedict as good as barked the word.

"What was that?" Sebastian turned his focus beside him, to see Benedict was sitting forward from his chair, as good as waving his fork in front of Sebastian's face in the effort to capture his attention.

"Good lord, you are miles away this morning. What has you so worked up?"

"I am not worked up."

"Fine. Will you explain the heavy shadows under your eyes? How about your inability to talk? Or your rather slumped posture this morning? You have been an altered man since you came back from your ride yesterday," Benedict pointed out, seemingly in a hurry as he ate his breakfast. He ate with speed, mopping one piece of cooked ham against another on his plate, before pressing it between his lips.

I cannot tell him.

It would betray his promise to Violet, and it would be unkind to her sister, Miss Penelope.

"It doesn't matter. I am in my own world, as you say." Sebastian sighed and picked up his coffee cup, deciding that would do for breakfast this morning. "Is there a reason you are so eagerly eating that you are in danger of choking?"

"I will not choke," Benedict said with a smile. "I am in a hurry, that is all."

"Whatever for?" Sebastian sat forward, aware of the butler's entry and how he moved straight to Benedict's side.

"The carriage is ready for you, my lord."

"Good, thank you." Benedict nodded in appreciation at the butler. As the butler hurried off again, Sebastian couldn't hold back his curiosity.

"Benedict, where are you going this morning?"

"To see the Miss Hathaways." As Benedict moved to his feet, so did Sebastian. His movement was so abrupt that the chair scraped beneath him along the floorboards. He placed his hands on the table too, the movement harried and jerking. "That seemed to put the fright of death into you." Benedict laughed at his own words, yet his eyes didn't leave Sebastian's face. "What is wrong?"

"You cannot go there. Not anymore, Benedict."

"Ha! Don't be ridiculous." Benedict stepped around the chair. "Your objection to Miss Violet Hathaway is really going very far now if you intend to stop me from seeing her family altogether."

"No, you do not understand." Sebastian crossed the room. He reached for the door and blocked his brother's exit, so he could not leave just yet. Placing a hand firmly on the door frame, he blocked the door completely.

I cannot let him see Violet now. She needs to be visited by a man who can marry her, and she has agreed, she cannot marry Benedict.

"Benedict, please, I beg of you." Sebastian implored his brother, aware that his tone was rather desperate. So much so that Benedict's eyebrows lifted sharply across his temple. "Do not go see the family today."

"Why not?" Benedict folded his arms across his body and jerked his chin higher, clearly having no wish to follow orders without an explanation.

"It is not good for Miss Hathaway."

"Ha! Since when are you concerned with what is good for her?" Benedict laughed and tried to reach for the door handle, but Sebastian stepped in the way before his brother could reach it.

"I have always been." Sebastian uttered the words with more feeling than he had intended. He took hold of the lapel of his brother's jacket and shook it to get his attention. "Pray, listen to me, brother."

"You have my attention." Benedict stood rather still, his eyes unblinking, evidently startled by the sudden change in Sebastian.

"Miss Hathaway... she... she is in need of something."

"In need of what?"

"I cannot speak of it, or it would be betraying a confidence." Sebastian's words came fast, jumbled together, prompting Benedict to shift on his feet and angle his head to the side, to better watch his brother. "Your kindness to her must end there. As kindness only."

"How do you mean?"

"I mean that the lady needs to marry," Sebastian spoke quickly and quietly, praying his brother would listen to him and abandon his endeavor to see Violet at all. "I do not believe you wish to marry her. You have not intimated that you wish to."

I hope you do not. I cannot bear the thought of you marrying her, Benedict! My heart will not stand it.

Sebastian's heart seemed to thump harder in his chest at the mere thought.

"Therefore, I beg you. Do not give the lady any hope of something that can never be. She deserves more than that, and she cannot afford for her time to be wasted." When Sebastian finished his spiel, he stood still, breathing heavily, aware that Benedict had not once looked away from him.

There was a minute of silence. The only thing that disturbed that peace was Sebastian's heavy breathing.

"It seems there is something of a bond between you and Miss Hathaway, brother," Benedict said slowly.

"A bond? No. No, that is not what it is. I merely feel..." Sebastian struggled for the right word, running a hand through his hair.

"Protective? Of me or her?" Benedict asked with a smile on his lips. "It used to be me, now I think you are protective of her."

Sebastian released the door and stepped away, frustrated. Benedict seemed eager to cause mischief, and that was hardly helping.

"Please, Benedict, I ask you this. Do not go, and do not give Miss

Hathaway hope of something that cannot be." Sebastian held his brother's gaze one last time.

Benedict shifted his weight between his feet and scratched his chin, deep in thought.

"You have somewhat perplexed me with this conversation, brother," he said with a sigh. "Yet I have said I will go, and I shall. I will not break my word on that. I shall see you later." With these final words, Benedict left, and the door closed softly behind him.

As soon as he was gone, Sebastian capitulated into the nearest chair, hanging his head in his hands. He wasn't sure what thought he feared more. Was it the prospect of Violet remaining unmarried and the chaos that could ensue for her and her sister? Or was it the idea that Benedict could marry Violet which upset him more?

৩৯৯

"Oh! This could be it. Come, Louise, let us invent a reason to be gone this morning. We shall visit Bond Street, to see the modiste." Deborah grabbed Louise's hand and jerked her to her feet so quickly from the piano that an unnatural chord rang out from the piano keys.

"Surely that is not necessary," Violet pleaded from her place by the window. They had all seen at the same time who their caller was.

The Marquess of Westmond.

Violet felt uncomfortable and clammy at his approach, with her palms turning sticky and the hair on the back of her neck rising.

Why is he here? Has his brother broken his word to me and told the Marquess the truth of my situation?

The mere idea made her swallow around a painful lump in her throat.

"I believe it is," Deborah said firmly. "It is high time his visits became something more. A courtship, perhaps?" Deborah was flustered, hurrying around the room and waving her hands in the air as if they were fans. "For that, you must have time alone with him."

"But Mama?" Louise was most put out, clearly trying to get her mother's attention, but little good it did.

Within seconds, Deborah took Louise out of the sitting room, and they hurried to the front door, collecting their pelisses, and readying to leave. Violet was left alone in the sitting room, with a maid tucked in the corner, breathing heavily. She longed for Penelope to be here too, but her sister was taking a nap. Something that was much needed at the moment.

It left Violet quite alone as the Marquess of Westmond approached the house and was let in by the butler.

"I cannot do this," Violet murmured audibly. Knowing all that had passed between her and Sebastian, she knew she couldn't be charming and flirt with the Marquess anymore.

This must come to an end.

Breathing deeply, she stood away from the window and waited for the Marquess to be shown into the room.

"The Marquess of Westmond, Miss Hathaway." The butler announced her guest.

"Thank you." She smiled and nodded, waiting for the butler to retreat as she curtsied to Lord Westmond, and he bowed to her. "How good to see you again, my lord."

"And you." He looked around, clearly aware that she was not usually here alone. "Have I come at a strange time? Your sister, your aunt, and cousin, of course, are they joining us?"

"My sister may join us in a short while," Violet spoke hurriedly.

"I see." Lord Westmond must have sensed the awkwardness in her tone, for he stood perfectly still and looked around the empty seats.

This is not the way it was supposed to go.

"Forgive me, Lord Westmond, but may I speak plainly to you?" she asked, hurrying forward to his side. He looked startled by her approach, with his eyes wide. "I wish to speak to you as a friend. Openly and honestly."

"Yes, of course you may." He nodded, then gestured to one of the chairs behind her. "You seem to have made yourself quite panicked, Miss Hathaway. Shall we take a seat?"

"Yes, perhaps so." She hurried to sit and urged him to do so too, then she glanced toward the maid. She knew well enough Deborah would have asked the maid to report back to her later everything that passed, so Violet chose to whisper to make it as difficult as possible. "Forgive my plainness, but I believe you will have noticed as well as I, my aunt's rather... fervent expectations that have been placed upon you."

"Ah, I see. Very plain indeed," Lord Westmond said with an amused smile. "Yes, I am not immune to the way she has pushed me toward your side, Miss Hathaway."

"I apologize for her forthrightness and any discomfort it has caused. I want you to know..." Violet thought only of Sebastian in that moment. She thought of the thrill he had shown her and the happiness, then it gutted her, reminding her she could never have a marriage with such happiness now. "I wish the best for you, as a friend, but I..."

"Allow me to guess." Lord Westmond smiled and rested his elbows on his knees. "You have no attachment to me beyond that of a friend?"

"I confess, I do not." She was rather relieved to see the gentleman still smiling softly.

"Do not apologize for it," he said gently. "It is natural. Judging from what I have seen, and heard, your affections lay elsewhere, do they not?" Violet held her breath, so startled by Lord Westmond's words she could have fallen off her chair. "I can see your surprise," Lord Westmond declared with humor. "I may be something of a fool in some ways, but I am not wholly blind. You and my brother... though I am not sure what is there, I believe there may be something. Am I correct?"

"Well…" Violet looked down into her lap and fidgeted with her hands, unsure how to put the feeling into words. "Any bond there may have been, my lord, I fear was imagined on my part. That is all it ever was."

"Imagined? That was not quite my judgment on the matter." Lord Westmond shrugged as if the idea perplexed him. "I may not always understand my brother myself, but I did honestly judge there to be an attachment on his part. If that is not the case, I am sorry it has caused you pain. Please, allow me to say this, Miss Hathaway, for I am grateful for your honesty. I wish you the best too, as a friend."

"Thank you." Violet smiled. A weight had been lifted from her mind with this conversation, yet now another greater weight sank within her stomach. It was emphasized the moment the door opened and Penelope hurried in.

I am so sorry, Penelope. I have failed you.

"Ah, Penelope, there you are." Violet adopted an upbeat tone and stood to her feet to welcome her sister into the room.

"Here I am," Penelope said with a smile, then she turned her focus on Lord Westmond, and that smile grew greater. "Lord Westmond. How lovely it is to see you again."

"And you, Miss Penelope." He bowed to her.

"I am glad you are here. I was hoping to talk to someone about this latest music piece I have heard, and I knew you would be interested." As Penelope hurried off to collect the sheet music, Lord Westmond followed her, apparently with eagerness.

It was then Violet traced the extent of Penelope's smile. It was vast, reaching up to her eyes, and was clearly heartfelt.

Oh lord, have I been so blind?

Violet began to see a hint of something that Penelope was keeping from her.

Is it possible that Penelope cares for Lord Westmond?

Chapter Twenty-Three

"Have you read this!?" Deborah's irate voice ricocheted around the dining table before the scandal sheet was thrust in front of Violet's eyes. The paper crinkled, and the sound crunched near Violet's ears.

"I cannot read it when you are shaking, Aunt." Violet tried to calmly take the scandal sheet away from Deborah but ended up having it thrust toward her so abruptly that the paper curled in the air and then fell into her dinner plate.

"I cannot believe it. How cruel it all is!" Deborah boomed as she marched around the table.

"What is happening, dear?" Walter said from his place at the head of the table.

"Ask her. Ask our niece, go on." Deborah gestured madly at Violet. "She clearly already knows all about it. I confess, I suspected as much myself at the ball, but I did not want to believe it."

Violet shook a little before turning her eyes down to the scandal sheet, then sighing with a little relief. The article spoke of the Marquess of Westmond.

'Indeed, Lord Westmond's quest for a wife goes on. What is plain to see is that any interest he may have had in Miss Violet Hathaway has long passed. At the Rumptons' ball on Sunday, they did not dance together once, and spent very little time in each other's company altogether.'

The ball had passed just two days ago, and it was true Violet had barely spoken to Lord Westmond throughout the event. The true damage that was done by the article was only revealed further down though, as the writer had speculated on what flaws Violet had that must have driven Lord Westmond away. The writer had laid all her flaws bare for every reader in London to see.

"How could you do this, Violet? To us?" Deborah asked wildly. Beside Violet, she felt Louise take the scandal sheet out of her hands. On Violet's other side, Penelope reached for her hand under the table.

"I was not aware any connection I had to Lord Westmond concerned you, Aunt," Violet kept her voice calm, though it only seemed to make the matter worse. Deborah planted her hands on the back of a chair as she abruptly stopped pacing.

"Do not be so insolent! Your marriage to a marquess would have elevated this family. You know as much."

"There was never any question of marriage, Aunt." Violet still attempted to keep her voice level, though the lump in her throat was growing now. It was the guilt that put it there, with the temptation to cry, the guilt that by falling for Sebastian, she had ruined everything for Penelope. "Lord Westmond and I are friends. That is all."

"How can you speak so?" Deborah demanded, with her voice still wild. "You have failed. Quite miserably."

I am aware.

Louise's snigger beside Violet made her tense, but not as much as Penelope, who Violet caught sight of glaring in their cousin's direction.

"It seems dear Violet was not enough to hold his interest, Aunt. Hardly much of a surprise there." Louise sniggered again.

"Louise, do not speak so. You only make yourself look cruel." Penelope's words were so bold compared to her usual self that Violet cricked her neck by turning to look at her sister so sharply.

"Oh, we had such hopes." Deborah wailed and paced again. This time, Walter moved to his feet and hurried to her, trying to calm her.

"It will all be fine, dearest," he murmured.

"How can it be? That scandal sheet has painted Violet as unworthy of affection. You think any gentleman will marry her after she has been spoken of so? No! Of course not." Deborah gripped her husband's arms, as if they were the last thing keeping her standing. "What did you do wrong, Violet? Were you uncouth? Unladylike?"

An image shot into Violet's mind. It was of the moment she had shared with Sebastian in his library. The freedom, and the excitement.

"No." She felt as if she was lying in that moment.

I bent the rules of decorum when it came to being a lady, yes.

"You have ruined this family, Violet. I hope you realize that!" Deborah boomed. When Louise sniggered another time, Violet felt as if someone had plunged a knife into her chest.

To be lambasted, ridiculed, and then laughed at, made her feel very small indeed.

Penelope's hand tightened in Violet's, but at this moment, it was not enough to calm her.

"If you would excuse me." Violet released her sister's hand and stood to her feet.

"Where are you going?" Deborah followed Violet as she moved toward the door. "I am not done with you yet!"

Violet felt her patience snap. Whether it was down to her aunt's insistence on meddling in her life, the sudden shift between being overly kind and overly distraught, or the comments that were made about her mother, Violet knew she couldn't stand any more of her aunt.

"Well, *I* am done." Violet turned sharply in the doorway, facing her aunt so fast that Deborah wobbled on her feet, nearly colliding with her. "You can berate and scold me all you like, but I do not have to listen to it, merely because I am not marrying a man you hoped for me to marry."

"Insolent child. If I wish to censure you, then you will stay in this very spot to hear it." Deborah pointed a finger at the ground, showing she wished Violet to stay exactly where she was.

"No." Violet tilted her chin higher. "I will not." With these final words, she turned on her heel and hurried out of the room. She was aware of more commotion behind her, of Deborah wailing, of Walter trying to comfort her, and a pair of hurried feet too, but Violet didn't stop to hear more.

She hastened from the room and moved to the stairs, taking two at a time in her eagerness to be in her room. When she reached her chamber, before she could turn around to close the door, she found the door opened wider, and Penelope stepped in.

"Pen," Violet said softly, beckoning her inside. Penelope went straight to her and the two of them embraced. Violet clung to Penelope. With her fingers curled in the folds of her sister's dress, she begged that touch could tell of the pain in her heart. "I am so sorry."

"Do not apologize, Violet."

"How can I not? I have not done as I promised I would do. I have not protected you." Violet felt the tears, but she held them back. She closed her eyes and pushed away that stinging feeling. Only when she was certain those tears would not fall did she stand back and release her sister.

"Is this all that troubles you, Violet?" Penelope's words made her stand rigid.

No. I miss him.

The thought of Sebastian came back to her. She thought of the way they could talk easily together, comparing notes on paintings and challenging one another, with such flirtatious smiles that she was soon weak.

I cannot speak of it. I must put my sister first.

"Yes. That is all," Violet lied and took Penelope's hand, drawing her down to a chaise longue nearby. "Now, tell me of how you are feeling. You seemed sick again this morning. Is your new tonic not working?"

"No, it is," Penelope assured her with a nod and laid a hand over hers, playing with her fingers.

Violet remembered what she had seen a few days before, how eager Penelope had been to talk to Lord Westmond.

I wonder if my suspicions are founded.

"Is there anything you wish to tell me, Pen?" Violet asked, urging her on. Penelope looked up, her breathing suddenly stuttered. "If you were not sick this morning, then I must conclude that you were avoiding seeing me for another reason altogether. Please, tell me what it is."

Penelope seemed to shake a little. She fidgeted, looking around the room, back at their clasped hands, then to Violet's eyes again. "Would it have anything to do with Lord Westmond?" Violet kept her voice as gentle as possible.

The effect was instant.

"Oh my god. You know?" Penelope said in a gasp. "Oh, am I truly so plain to read?"

"No. Indeed, you are not." Violet shook her head. "My suspicions that you felt something for Lord Westmond were only raised the other day when I saw your smile in his presence. Never do I think I have seen you smile in such a way."

"Violet! I longed to say something."

"Then why didn't you?" Violet asked, leaning toward her sister with a kind of desperation. "If you mean to tell me that I have been setting my cap at the very gentleman you have developed an affection for, then how in the wrong have I been. There are not enough words to describe the wrong I have done!"

"No, no." Penelope was insistent, shaking her hand. She shuffled closer toward Violet on the seat and took both of her hands, interlocking their fingers together. "You did nothing wrong. You were trying to help me. I hardly expected to feel for Lord Westmond what I feel."

"What a mess we are making of things, are we not?" Violet cracked and a small laugh escaped through her sadness. "You with child, me trying to marry to help you, then trying to ensnare the very man you care for. Oh! It is as good as a Shakespeare play, is it not?"

"Ha! Yes, I suppose you are right." Penelope laughed too, giving way to mirth, though there were tears in her eyes. Violet wondered if they both needed the laugh at that moment, to contend with the pain of it all. "What is that play called? The one with the fairy rushing all over the place making people fall in love with their wrong counterparts?"

"*Midsummer Night's Dream.* The fairy, Puck, is it?"

"That's the one!"

"He has been quite mischievous here, it must be said." Violet shook her head in a kind of despair. "Oh, Pen, I am so sorry. I wish you had told me sooner."

"I am sorry too." Penelope opened her arms and pulled Violet in for a second embrace.

This time, Violet showed no inclination of pulling back from her sister very quickly at all. She clung to her sister, resting her head on her shoulder as the tears sprung to her eyes.

What a mess I have made of everything!

"Do you have any idea if Lord Westmond cares for you too?" Violet asked eventually, her voice just a whisper.

"No. I do not believe he does. He is a kind man, caring, friendly, but beyond that? No, nothing." Penelope lifted her head a little, urging Violet to do the same. "Even if he did... if by some wild hope he could care for me, I could never court him, Violet, and keep this secret from him." She slowly lowered her hand down to her stomach and rested her fingers there, as they trembled.

Violet placed her hand over Penelope's, resting it on her stomach and the child within.

"I would have to tell him," Penelope whispered, as another tear escaped down her cheek. "I am not so great a fool as to think a man could accept raising another man's child as his own very easily. The kindness, the benevolence, not to mention the acceptance... it would have to be immense for him to accept such a thing."

Violet wanted to believe it was possible, but like Penelope, there was no reason to think it was. Lord Westmond had been kind to Penelope, and had certainly danced with her, but Violet had never seen him take her hand in a certain way. She had never seen him whisper in her ear, as Sebastian had done with her. She had never even seen Lord Westmond smile at Penelope, as Sebastian had smiled at her.

Enough! I must stop thinking of him.

"What a mess we have made," Violet said another time. "Come here, sister. I am so sorry for your pain." She hugged Penelope.

She couldn't tell her sister of her own heartbreak, for Penelope was suffering enough. She did not need more pain to contend with. It was a pain she would have to deal with herself.

After some minutes of silence in their embrace, Penelope eventually broke that peace, with a question Violet was unsure how to answer.

"Violet, what are we going to do now?"

Chapter Twenty-Four

T he painting that stood at the end of the hall seemed to tower over Sebastian. He was not pleased by its sight. He would have happily gotten rid of the painting some time ago, had Benedict not pointed out to him that it would have been odd to the staff for them to do so.

The gentleman in the painting was older than he was, much older, though the features were remarkably similar. The dark hair was there, along with the tall frame and that rather strong glower. It was that glower and those thin lips that were pressed together that haunted Sebastian so, for at some point, those lips had started taking in life, and those hurtful things were always pointed in one person's direction.

"Do I dare ask how long you have been standing there?" a voice called to Sebastian. He glanced away from the painting long enough to see Benedict approaching him. He was hurrying down the stairs before he stopped at Sebastian's side and turned his focus on the painting too, "Staring at it doesn't make any of it better, you know."

"Perhaps not. At least it is somewhere to direct my hate," Sebastian murmured, aware that his words made Benedict lift a hand and pinch the brow of his nose.

"Our father is long gone, Seb. Little good comes from hating him now."

Sebastian supposed Benedict was right, but still, the hate lingered.

Maybe you can forgive, Benedict, but I cannot. If you had heard what our father had said, you would be the same.

"Are you going to tell me what is wrong today? Or shall I stand here and guess?" Benedict asked and turned to look at Sebastian. "You and I both know it cannot merely be the memory of our father. He has been gone long enough."

Sebastian sighed and reached into his tailcoat pocket, pulling out the scrap of paper that he had been re-reading all morning. It didn't seem to matter how many times his eyes lingered on those words, for their meaning was still just as painful. He passed the scandal sheet into his brother's hands, aware he had crumpled the paper.

"Turn to the article about you," Sebastian whispered. Benedict did so. Sebastian watched as his brother's eyes danced back and forth across the article, then his brows quirked together.

"Good lord, they do not hold their punches when it comes to Miss Hathaway, do they?" he murmured, seeing the very same thing that Sebastian had seen in the article.

"It goes on." Sebastian thrust a finger at the sheet. "Look here. Whoever wrote the article is seditious, for they took great delight in comparing all your dance partners from the ball to Vi – I mean, to Miss Hathaway, and pointing out how their virtues were better than hers. God's wounds, what kind of person would do such a thing? They must get pleasure out of causing misery."

"Am I supposed to ignore the fact you nearly called her Violet again?" Benedict asked.

"Yes." Sebastian was sharp as he snatched the article back, letting his eyes tarry on the words another time.

How is she supposed to marry now?

The thought disgusted Sebastian. In one fell swoop, the writer of the article was stirring a dislike toward Violet.

"Rumors and words like this soon pass, Seb," Benedict assured him with a clap to his shoulder, just as Sebastian returned his focus to their father's painting. "Give it a few months, and no one will remember an article like this."

"Brother, you do not understand." Sebastian waved the scandal sheet in the air, crumpling it so much that it practically cut into the pads of his fingers. "This will impair any chance she has of marrying soon. She does not have months."

"What does that mean?"

"It doesn't matter." Sebastian held his tongue, realizing how close he had come to betraying the secret. Scratching his face and pushing that hand up into his hair, he felt the stress and panic overtaking him.

I would help her. If I could.

He could not stop thinking of their moment together in the library. Yes, there had been passion, certainly, and a life with passion was something that sounded very alluring, but there was more to it too. Now he had not seen her for a few days, he found he missed Violet.

As he had ordered a new painting the day before, he had wanted her opinion of it. He had arranged a visit to Somerset Gallery too and found that he longed to invite her to go with him. She was there in his mind, constantly as a presence, yet he wanted that presence by his side.

"Seb, tell me something," Benedict spoke slowly.

"What?" Sebastian set his glower on their father.

"Why does it bother you if Miss Hathaway doesn't marry?" Benedict's words made Sebastian look sharply at his brother, feeling a twinge in the muscles in his neck at the suddenness of the movement. He was met by a somewhat playful smile on his brother's lips. "Surely it does not matter to you, does it?"

"No." The word came surprisingly quietly from Sebastian to which Benedict's smirk turned into a full smile.

"That was a bad lie."

"No, it wasn't."

"So, you accept it was a lie?"

"Oh, be quiet." Sebastian looked away from his brother and walked off, yet he did not have the escape he wanted, for Benedict followed him.

"Care to tell me why you are lying?" Benedict called, with his pace persistent.

"I didn't say I was!" Sebastian called back, yet Benedict laughed as he followed.

"If I didn't know any better, brother. I'd say Miss Violet Hathaway has gotten rather under your skin."

◈

"You have a plan?"

"I do." Violet moved to her sister's side. Penelope laid down the embroidery as Violet closed up her sketchbook. She had been working on a sketch of Sebastian when the idea had occurred to her. It seemed no matter how many times she told herself she had to forget Sebastian, her heart would not listen.

One sketch of him had turned into many, and there were few times she could be seen without the sketchbook in her hands at present.

"What is the plan?" Penelope asked with eagerness.

Violet sat beside Penelope on the settee as they both glanced toward the door. It was firmly closed, blocking out any chance of their aunt, uncle, or cousin passing the door, and seeing them talking together conspiratorially.

"You and I know we need money," Violet whispered quietly, "yes?"

"Yes."

"With money, we could get a house and provide for the child." Violet gestured toward Penelope's stomach. The slight movement made Penelope lift a hand and rest it across her belly. "If we cannot get that money by marrying, then we must get it another way."

She could see Penelope's confusion, for her hand lowered from her stomach and her eyes focused on Violet, making the skin across her eyelids wrinkle a little.

"What if I was to become a governess, Pen?" Violet offered. At first, Penelope said nothing, but she cocked her head to the side as if she were a blackbird, eyeing her carefully in the garden. "Think of it. I could write off for a position at some country estate. I am well taught, our mother always made sure we were educated. It is something that could work."

"And us?" Penelope glanced down at her stomach.

"With the money I earn, I could rent a small house for you and the child to live in. Far away from here."

"We'd leave London?" Penelope was amazed at the idea, with her eyes going wide. "That could be a difficult thing to accomplish."

"No, indeed. Very easy. Perhaps even better for us." Violet spoke with eagerness, realizing what a good plan it was. "Away from London, there are fewer people to see you with the child, and if we chose somewhere remote enough, people would not know you either. We could lie and say you had been widowed."

"Oh..." Penelope sat straight, her eyes lighting up a little. "You think it could work?"

"I think it is worth a try." Violet nodded eagerly. Secretly, there was another reason she wished to leave London, but she saw no point in telling Penelope of it.

I need to be away from him.

When she had caught sight of Sebastian the other night at a ball, it had pained her more than she had thought possible. He seemed to be drinking a little too much and spent most of the evening in a corner. He didn't dance all night and he didn't talk to any ladies either, showing something was wrong with him.

Does he miss me as I miss him?

"Perhaps it could work." Penelope sat forward, showing sudden eagerness. "The question is, do you know of such a governess position?"

"I could write off and begin inquiries, could I not?" Violet said with excitement and stood to her feet. She left the sketchbook behind her on the chair, not thinking of it. She took hold of the idea with enthusiasm. "We have friends that own country estates. I could write to our friends this afternoon and see if they know of any such positions. What do you think?" She began to wander the room, her excitement making her pace back and forth.

"Yes, yes, it could just work." Penelope inched forward on the seat again, then she accidentally placed her hand on the sketchbook and looked down at it.

Violet thought no more of it and turned away, walking on.

"If we went somewhere remote enough, the rent for a house could be cheap too. We might even be able to afford a member of staff to help you with the child." She smiled; knowing the promise of another life was in reach made her heart thump hard in her chest. "What do you think?"

"Is there another reason you wish to leave London, Violet?"

"What do you mean?" Violet turned around and stopped dead. She felt hollow as she saw what Penelope was doing, as if her heart had left her chest and thudded outside of her body. Penelope was sitting quite calmly, turning the pages of Violet's sketchbook, her eyes wide on the drawings. "Oh, Pen," Violet gasped. "Do not look at that." She lifted her hands to cover her mouth, knowing the moment was too late, regardless.

"These drawings..." Penelope murmured. "They are exquisite." Then she turned the book around and showed Violet one of the drawings of Sebastian. "Yet they are all of the Duke of Ashbury."

Violet felt her hands begin to shake as she held them over her mouth, watching as Penelope drew her own conclusions.

"You are in love with the Duke?" Penelope asked, standing to her feet abruptly.

I am. I do love him!

"Shh!" Violet begged, aware that she could hear footsteps outside of the door.

"But... Violet, look at these!" Penelope was gesturing to the sketch-book another time.

"Pen, please." Violet crossed the room, very aware those footsteps beyond the door were getting closer and closer. They sounded firm and heavy to her ears too, as if someone had a purpose in striding this way.

As the door opened, Violet snatched the notebook off her sister and closed it firmly.

"Penelope!" Deborah's voice boomed. The door opened wide, swinging so much that it clattered against the wall. Deborah stepped in, with her hands on her hips, as behind her, Louise walked in, pushing forward a rather panicked-looking Mary, who was holding onto some bed sheets. "Your maid has been hiding your bedsheets, I hear."

Oh no...

Violet could feel the impending moment, even without the words having to be said.

"It seems she has been hiding the fact you have not bled. For months."

Chapter Twenty-Five

Violet felt Penelope's hand was suddenly in hers. The pressure of her fingers was weak, limp, as if she could barely hold herself up at all. Violet subtly moved in front of her sister, as if to protect her, even as Deborah marched into the room.

Poor Mary hurried on behind her, clutching at the bedsheets. Violet shot a quick look Mary's way. She knew how hard the maid had worked to hide those bedsheets. It was hardly her fault if the ruse had eventually been noticed.

"Aunt, please —" Violet began, but Deborah did not let her finish before she was shouting again.

"Do you have any idea what position you have placed us in, Penelope?" Deborah's voice was so loud, Violet could have sworn the chandelier above them rang out. "This family... it is ruined. All of us! We are ruined."

"All of us?" Louise squeaked from behind her mother, placing her hands on her cheeks. "But... this cannot affect me, surely?"

"You think not? Wake up, Louise! This is the way the world works." Deborah marched toward her daughter with her hands on her hips, then swung around and faced Violet and Penelope again. Behind her, Violet could feel her sister flinching at that look. "Once this is out, we will all be tarred by the same brush. Think of it. My niece, harlotted herself away, and now pregnant. What will the world think of us?"

"Harlot," Penelope whispered behind Violet, the word barely audible at all. Violet could feel her sister was about to cry in the gasping of her chest that rose and fell again.

"To think I let my sister's daughters into this house." Deborah threw her hands to the ceiling, as if talking to God himself, and not to them. "If I had only known this would happen. Oh! How could you do this to us Penelope?"

Violet felt a fury begin to burn within her stomach. Any truly caring aunt would have uttered other words by now.

Did she not want to ask after the health of the baby? Penelope's health too? No, none of that mattered. All that Deborah was concerned with was censuring Penelope for the mistake she had made and her reputation.

I see the man involved bears no responsibility in her eyes, does he? She hasn't even asked who he is.

"She can be made to marry, can she not?" Louise asked quickly, stepping forward. "Mama, if Penelope marries, then all would be well."

"Let me guess." Deborah turned sharp eyes in Penelope's direction. "The father has long since fled, has he not?" Penelope didn't need to nod for Deborah to read the truth. "I thought as much. A foolish woman you are, Penelope. You have given yourself away and risked us all. Well, I hope that one night was worth it."

"That is enough." Violet felt the words sharply escape her lips, so swiftly that she almost spat with the words.

"I will deal with you later, Violet," Deborah warned with a lifted hand. "Your lack of surprise shows me that you knew. This will not be stood for. You should have told us."

I never would have done that.

Violet took a firmer hold of her sister's hand, relieved to find that now Penelope clung to her a little tighter.

"As for you." Deborah rounded on the maid who was still carrying the sheets. "Pack your bags. You are to leave this house."

"What? No!" Violet stepped forward with the words. "Mary did nothing wrong."

"Nothing wrong? Do not give me that, Violet." Deborah shook her head madly, so fast that the curls which had been excessively curled to frame her cheeks bounced with the movement, back and forth. "I cannot have a maid under my roof that would conspire in such a manner." She marched toward Mary and snatched the sheets from her arms. "Go. Now!"

"Mary?" Violet called to the maid. "I am so sorry."

Mary hastened from the room. She nodded, showing she knew of how truly sorry Violet was, but it was not enough.

Poor Mary has lost her job! It cannot be!

"Was that really necessary?" Violet asked her aunt once Mary had gone.

"Oh, it was." Deborah was firm. "Now, we must think of something."

"Something?" Louise stepped forward. "Mama, they must be sent away."

Violet did not object to this idea. It could at least facilitate her plan to become a governess and send money to her sister for the child.

This could work.

Penelope must have sensed the same thing too, as her hand wound together through Violet's.

"No. If we send them away, the ton will know of it." Deborah began to pace around the room, dropping the bedsheets in the nearest chair and brushing them away from her, as if they were tainted. "There will be whispers and suppositions in the scandal sheet about their sudden departure. No, it is not something we can do. We must look for an alternative path."

"My life is being planned for me," Penelope murmured, so quietly that only Violet could hear her.

"You are right, Louise, Penelope must marry," Deborah spoke with sudden finality.

Violet felt her jaw begin to drop. Her aunt spoke as if marriage was an easy thing to accomplish.

"I cannot marry," Penelope said suddenly, her voice at last loud enough for her aunt to hear her.

"Did you dare speak to me?" Deborah snapped, turning to face Penelope with such venom in her tone that Violet felt her sister step further behind her.

I will keep her safe. Always.

"She can speak to who she likes," Violet said, but her aunt didn't appear to hear her. "You and I know, Aunt, if Penelope marries, the husband will realize soon enough when the baby comes early that it is not his. What do you think he will do to Penelope then? Cast her far into some country house, never to be seen again?"

"At least the ton would not know of it." Deborah walked toward her daughter. "The news would not affect us then." She preened one of the curls that fell out of Louise's updo.

That is all she cares about.

"I'm tempted to be sick with disgust," Violet whispered. Penelope heard her for she pulled tighter on Violet's hand.

"What was that?" Deborah flicked her head in Violet's direction.

"Nothing," she lied.

I will have to get Penelope out of this house, long before any such marriage can be arranged.

"Who would marry her so quickly, Mama?" Louise said, her tone fervent.

"Well, that needs some thought." Deborah walked away. She moved toward a chair and tried to sit, but she barely sat still for long. She was soon on the very edge of the chair, with her eyes wide. "Oh... now, *he* is a possibility."

"Who is a possibility?" Violet said, no longer attempting to keep her tone plain.

Deborah didn't answer, but she got to her feet. Pushing past Louise, she hurried from the room.

"Come on." Violet pulled on Penelope's hand, dragging her away. The two of them followed, along with Louise, trailing after Deborah as she hastened through the house.

A series of doors were opened, slammed shut, and opened again by Violet as she hurried on behind her aunt. A path was created through the house, one with a clear destination.

Our uncle's study.

When they arrived there, Deborah swung open the door without knocking. Violet walked in behind her, still clinging to Penelope's hand, as Louise followed too. Violet saw that Walter had already been told.

He was sat by his fireplace, staring into the low embers that burnt there, with such a heavy crease to his brow that it seemed as if a permanent mark would be left on his skin. At their entrance, his gaze turned on Penelope.

Violet could see the hatred there. It made his eyes narrow, rather like a cat's.

"I have got it," Deborah declared to her husband.

"Got what?" Walter said. "A way out of this predicament? Such a thing seems impossible." He shook his head and leaned back in his chair, making it creak beneath him. "Our family will be ruined by this, Deborah."

"Not if she was to marry. If she were to marry by special license within a few days, then all would be hushed up, before anyone could know."

"By special license?" Violet released Penelope's hand and strode forward, realizing the horror that was afoot.

It would not give me time to find a governess' position and get us out of this house!

"You cannot do that," she pleaded. Deborah waved a hand in front of Violet, silencing her.

"Enough." Deborah cast a glance Violet's way before turning to face Walter another time. "Walter, what of Viscount Haywood?"

Haywood? I know that name.

Violet took a step back, racking her brain for where she had heard it before. Slowly, Walter looked up from the fireplace where he had been staring, and that crease in his brow began to soften.

"Think of it," Deborah pleaded, moving to the chair beside her husband. "Has he not told you he wishes to marry?"

"He has. Again and again." Walter began to nod slowly.

It was then Violet remembered where she had heard the name. She had read it in scandal sheets, many times. Stepping back, she held a hand to her mouth, thinking of what an awful man could end up marrying her sister.

"Viscount H-haywood?" Penelope stammered. "But he..."

"He is an adulterer, and a lecher," Violet said, snapping with the words. She stepped in front of her aunt and uncle, determined to be heard. "He is known for his cruelty to women. He was taken to court for hurting a woman last year. The scandal sheet said as much!"

"He was not convicted." Walter shook his head, clearly disbelieving the claim. "Lord Haywood is a friend, a good friend. He needs to marry and he needs an heir." He pointedly glanced Penelope's way and down at her stomach. "Something tells me he wouldn't mind how that heir was obtained, as long as it happened."

"Is this not promising?" Deborah said, moving to the edge of her seat. There was a sort of excited energy to her now. One that made her eyes dart back and forth. "You could see him. Today, Walter. Tell him of the situation, be plain, and see what he says."

"You would give Penelope to an odious man like that?" Violet felt the anger made her words shake. She nearly hiccoughed in the middle of her question, so frightened of the idea of Penelope being at the mercy of such a man that it made her tremble.

"He is not so odious as people think." Walter shook his head. "He merely believes in tradition. He will have his say in his own house, that is all."

"What of all his affairs?" Violet asked, her tone wild.

"They have perhaps made it a little hard for him to marry," he acknowledged slowly and glanced back at Penelope again. "I think that is why he would be amenable to such an offer."

Violet turned her eyes on her sister, watching as poor Penelope staggered backward. She reached for the wall behind her and clung to it, clearly keeping herself standing.

Louise appeared to be sighing with relief on her other side.

"So, this could work?" Louise asked her parents excitedly. "If Penelope is married to this man, no one would need to know of the scandal, would they?"

"Just so, Louise. Just so." Deborah nodded, then flicked her eyes to her husband. "Well?"

"I'll write to him now, and send an urgent message. With a little luck, I will be able to see him later today. He is in town at present." Walter moved abruptly to his feet and crossed the room. Reaching for his desk, he pulled out paper and an inkwell. His movements were so harried that he nearly tipped the inkwell over more than once.

This cannot be happening.

Violet felt as if her sister's life was disappearing before her. As if she were trying to grab onto sand, but it just kept slipping between her fingers.

Penelope leaned on the wall, seconds from tears, as Deborah and Louise talked together, making plans for a hurried ceremony, and how to obtain a special license. Meanwhile, Walter wrote his note so hurriedly, the paper was scrawled with tiny black lines.

I must stop this.

Then an idea occurred to Violet. It was horrific, awful even. She would be binding herself to a life that she would hate, but for Penelope? Oh, she would do anything! She could not bear to see Penelope suffer this sadness, nor be forced into a life with this man.

"Wait!" Violet called loudly above the hubbub in the room. Deborah and Louise looked to Violet, and Walter barely glanced up from his letter.

"Not now, Violet," Deborah warned.

"No, I have to say something. If you are going to wed Penelope to this Lord Haywood, then you are under a misapprehension of what has happened here, and I cannot let the truth go unknown for any longer." Violet could see her sister stepping off the wall, turning to look at her with wide eyes.

"Explain yourself, Violet," Walter said from the desk. "What misapprehension are we suffering from?"

"Penelope's bedsheets were not the ones being hidden by Mary." Violet could see her sister across the room with her jaw falling low. Penelope began to shake her head back and forth. Violet widened her eyes on Penelope momentarily, urging her to be silent and not say a word.

If this is to work, if I am to save Penelope from this fate, my aunt and uncle must believe it.

"You mean to say that you…?" Deborah gestured a hand at Violet.

By now, Violet had seen Penelope's actions often enough to know how to act. She raised her hands and placed her palms flat to her stomach, glancing down, as if there was something there she was trying to protect.

Someone.

"I do not understand." Deborah looked between Penelope and Violet, clearly uncertain what to think. Fearful her aunt would not be swayed, Violet stepped forward, ready to convince her. "Why would you let us go on, saying Penelope is the one with child, if it is you –"

"Penelope was trying to protect me, but I cannot let her do that anymore." Violet swallowed past a lump in her throat, feeling the tears begin to prick the corners of her eyes. "If you want convincing, then I suggest you visit my chamber. In the cupboard beside my bed, you will find a tonic for morning sickness."

Violet could see Penelope swaying another time, amazed at her words. Violet sighed with relief, knowing that she had some spare tonic for Penelope in that cupboard, and it would likely be enough to convince her aunt.

Deborah said nothing, but she walked to the door, opened it wide, and called a maid to her. It was a matter of minutes for the tonic to be collected and returned to the chamber. Once the glass vial was in Deborah's hands, she hurried to place it down on Walter's desk, as if she feared merely touching it would infect her with the same scandal.

"Then it is true," Deborah murmured, with her hands shaking.

"Oh my lord. Is it the Marquess of Westmond's child?" Louise said, stepping forward.

"No!" Violet snapped, so loudly that even Deborah flinched. "The father wants nothing to do with the situation."

"Goodness. Violet is the one with child." Deborah backed up, colliding with a chair. "Violet, how could you do this to us?"

Violet looked away from her aunt and turned her focus to her uncle. Walter picked up his quill once again and dipped it in the ink pot, clearly returning to his letter.

"Very well. If Violet is the one with child, then she is the one who must marry." He began to put the quill to the paper. "Get out of my sight, Violet. I cannot stand to look at you any longer."

She was glad for it. Violet crossed the room and took hold of Penelope's hand, dragging her out of the room so quickly that Penelope nearly tripped on the door jamb. When they reached the staircase, Penelope pulled sharply on her arm.

"Violet, what have you done?"

Chapter Twenty-Six

"He is here." Walter's words made Violet swallow and close the cover of her sketchbook. From beside her, Penelope took the sketchbook and hid it behind her back.

"Are you sure of this?" Penelope whispered in Violet's ear.

"You asked me that all evening and all night." Violet glanced at her sister. "You do not need to hear my answer again." She reached for Penelope's hand and squeezed it softly once.

It had been a long night. Violet had made it plain to Penelope that she did not regret what she had done. She would do anything to protect Penelope and her child from a man like Lord Haywood. Penelope had cried and pleaded with Violet not to condemn herself, but it had done little good.

My mind is made up.

As the door opened, Violet slowly stood to her feet and released Penelope's hand, looking around the sitting room.

It was an awkward affair. Louise had been practicing at the piano again, though somewhat distractedly, and Deborah was anxious. She kept clasping and unclasping her hands together, curling her fingers like a cat's claws. Walter moved away from the window at their guest's entrance, keen to greet him.

"Lord Haywood, so good of you to come." He eagerly bowed and shook his friend's hand. Only when he stepped back was Violet allowed a proper look at the man she was to marry in a mere few days' time.

Lord Haywood was a striking figure, and an unpleasant one. His features were sharp, with a rather crooked nose, and his fair hair curled inwardly toward his neck, slicked with so much wax that his hair appeared quite drenched by it. Rather small and blackened eyes turned in Violet's and Penelope's direction.

He looked between them like a hunter, selecting which pheasant to choose first, clearly wondering which woman was to be his bride.

"I was glad to come," he said with a sudden smile.

That smile turned Violet's stomach. She couldn't help comparing him to Sebastian.

Lord Haywood is nothing like him.

She longed for Sebastian's charming smile, and how those eyes could make her heart flutter.

Stop thinking of him!

"I must admit, I was not just intrigued, but eager." Lord Haywood turned his eyes back to Walter.

Violet exchanged a panicked look with Penelope. They didn't need to speak for that look to be understood. They were both fearful of the man's eagerness to marry.

"Well, I know for how long you have wanted a wife of your own, Lord Haywood. Allow me to introduce my niece to you, so you may judge her for yourself." Walter gestured toward Violet. She was careful to keep her lips closed, or she would have happily snapped at him that she didn't care for being judged. "Here she is."

Walter reached forward and took Violet's elbow, steering her into the middle of the room. Violet attempted a smile, but it didn't go very far and it didn't last long. It quickly faded away.

That scent...

It was awful. Viscount Haywood wore a ridiculously strong cologne, one so full of musk that it tickled the back of her nose.

"Miss Hathaway?" Lord Haywood stepped toward her and took her hand, lifting it quickly to his lips and kissing the back.

A memory shot across her mind. She remembered when Sebastian had given her such a touch and the thrill that had passed through her then. The mere memory of it made a lump form in her throat.

No more tears. I have shed enough of them.

"Lord Haywood." She curtsied to him and tried to retract her hand, but he didn't let her. He kept a firm hold of her hand, his fingers curling around her own in a pincer-like fashion.

"She is a beauty, indeed, you were not lying, my friend," Lord Haywood said, turning to acknowledge Walter beside him. "Yes, I can see the arrangement working."

Violet glanced across the room. She could see Deborah trying to subtly wave a hand at her, urging her to speak.

"You do me a great kindness, my lord," Violet said falsely, trying to play her part.

"A pleasant voice too," Lord Haywood approved with a nod, though he still did not speak directly to Violet. "How far along is she?"

"Well, I..." Walter did not answer straight away.

"No use being shy." Lord Haywood shook his head and returned his focus to Violet. "I know the wedding must happen quickly because of your situation, Miss Hathaway. I must know, how far along are you?"

"A few months." Violet was careful not to glance back at Penelope, fearful of giving any hint of the truth.

"Very well."

"Does that mean you accept the offer, my lord?" Walter said far too eagerly for Violet's liking. Once again, she tried to retract her hand from Lord Haywood's, but he did not let it happen.

"I am considering it." He kept his eyes on Violet for a moment. She felt examined as his eyes darted down her body and up again.

Her heart longed to be somewhere else. She wished to be back in that library with Sebastian, kissing him, exploring him with the passion that they had shared. She did not want to be here!

"May I have a moment to speak with Miss Hathaway in private?" Lord Haywood asked, turning his focus on Walter. "Her sister can stay to chaperone, if you like."

"Yes, of course. Come along, dear." Walter was full of enthusiasm as he collected Deborah from the other side of the room and then Louise, ushering them to the door.

Violet's eyes tarried on Louise. She did not miss the way that even Louise had paled, and her eyes darted back and forth. She hovered in the doorway for a minute, looking uncertain, before her father snatched her away and closed the door.

Even Louise is no fan of this gentleman.

The moment the door was closed, Violet managed to retract her hand. Unsure what to say, she stood perfectly still, staring at Lord Haywood and waiting for him to begin. She grew aware that beside her, Penelope took a seat, watching over them.

"I will endeavor to speak freely to you, Miss Hathaway," Lord

Haywood said, his tone deep. "You have read the scandal sheets that utter my name, no doubt."

"I have."

"Then you know I am no saint, and I do not pretend to be." He didn't blink, not once. The effect made her heart rate slow, to something that was barely recognizable in her chest. "I wish to marry, so that I may have an heir. In fact, I am determined to make that happen. If you are to have a son..." He paused and glanced down at her stomach. "Then that child will be my heir."

"Is that something you can accept?" Violet half-hoped he wouldn't. At least then, whilst her uncle and aunt flapped around trying to find another man for her to marry, she could have more time to escape this predicament.

"It is." His words made her shoulders slump. "I am under no illusions. I would be doing you a service to marry you, saving you from disgrace."

Violet's eyes flicked momentarily to Penelope, seeing how she shuddered in the chair.

"In return for the favor I extend to you, I will ask for something in return."

"What is that?" Violet asked, returning her focus to Lord Haywood. He was still examining her with those dark eyes, unblinking.

"I am the master of my own house." He spoke firmly. "I have my rules, and they will be followed."

Violet clamped her hands together, knowing exactly what Lord Haywood was trying to tell her.

He intends to run my life.

"Where will I live?" she asked, trying to keep the nervousness out of her voice.

"At my country estate." Lord Haywood spoke quickly. "The rules will be followed, Miss Hathaway. I wanted you to know that now."

Violet hoped her trembling did not show through as she clamped her hands together. In the end, she nodded, unsure of what else to do.

"Excellent, then I will speak to your uncle, and we will arrange the special license." With these words, he was gone. He hurried from the room and let it close softly behind him. The moment he vanished, Penelope was on her feet reaching for Violet.

They clasped hands, but neither of them said anything. For the moment, there was nothing more to say.

❦

VIOLET KEPT LOOKING OVER THE SKETCHES IN HER BOOK. THERE was one, in particular, she was fond of. Sebastian was in the library as she remembered him from that night, sitting back with a book in his hand, and his waistcoat unbuttoned with his shirt sleeves rolled up.

It was a fine drawing, so real that she could remember being back there with him.

"What would you think of me now, I wonder?" she murmured into the air as she laid a finger over the sketch of his face.

It still hurt, the memory of how he had rejected her, but she could not blame him for it.

Who would marry me when they knew the reason I had to marry? He is a duke... he has no reason to marry someone so in need.

The clock struck midnight over her mantelpiece. Turning her eyes on it, Violet waited, listening to the light-toned tinkle as it echoed around the room. Penelope was due to come to her room any second. Violet had requested Penelope to do so earlier in the evening.

As if on cue, there was a light tap at the door.

Violet hastened to her feet and hurried to the door, letting Penelope in. Just like her, Penelope was dressed for bed, with her hair loose around her shoulders.

"Violet, what is the reason for all of this?" Penelope said, crossing the room.

"It is necessary." Violet hurried away. She reached for the mantelpiece where, beside the clock, she had laid a string purse tied tightly. She began to untie those laces as Penelope gasped behind her. "What is it?" Violet looked around.

Penelope was standing over the sketchbook, tracing the drawing with her fingers. She smiled sadly, as if the picture gave her both pain and happiness, then she lifted her eyes to Violet.

"Would you tell me what this means now? What it was that you would not tell me the other day?" Penelope whispered into the air.

"If you wish," Violet capitulated. She walked forward, carrying the purse in her hands. "You were right, Penelope." She cast a glance down at the purse. "I do love him."

"Oh, Violet." Penelope moved toward her.

"No, please, do not say anything," Violet begged of her sister. "I lost my heart to the Duke when I should not have done, and that was an error on my part."

"An error? It was hardly something you intended to happen, was it?"

"I know, I know." Violet walked toward the sketchbook, looking down at that drawing again. Sebastian was smiling up at her, that same mischievous look he always wore. "It happened without me really knowing it. One thing led to another, and then..." She lifted the cover and closed the sketchbook, hiding the sketch from view.

"We have both been holding onto secret hearts, have we not?" Penelope whispered. Those words urged Violet to look up from the closed sketchbook. "We fell in love with two brothers." She smiled a little. "What a thing to happen."

"Yes, I suppose so." Violet smiled too, though it didn't last. "Let it be the last we talk of the Duke." She slid the sketchbook away. "I was wrong to ever place hope on him."

Penelope looked as if she desired to say something, moving forward with her lips parting, but Violet knew it was time. It was time to reveal to Penelope the extent of her whole plan.

"Penelope, listen to me." Violet opened the purse and showed it to Penelope. "This is for you."

"What is it?" Penelope's eyes widened when she saw the money inside. "Good lord! Where did you get all this?"

"It is everything I own. I sold a few things too, to raise some money. I want you to take it." She pressed the purse into Penelope's hands.

"Why?" Penelope asked, her eyes darting between the soft purse and Violet's eyes.

"Because I do not need it where I am going, do I?" Violet shrugged. "At least this way, you have something to take to get away from here. You can go somewhere, far away, find a cheap house to rent with what you have here, and find a home for you and your child. That is what I want."

"Violet, please."

"I will find a way to get money out of the Viscount too. I will send it to you, every month. I know he has his *rules,* as he was so keen to point out to me, but there must be a way to get some money from him. Even if I tell him it is for a fine dress or other such nonsense, that will do. I will send the money to you and you can live free, with your child."

Penelope pulled Violet sharply into an embrace. It was so sudden that Violet fell into her sister, nearly toppling the two of them over.

"Can't breathe, Pen!" Violet cried out, struggling with the tightness.

"I cannot believe all that you are prepared to do for me." There was a gasp to Penelope's breathing, showing she was holding back tears. As she released Violet from the tight hold, they shared a sad sort of smile. "You are kindness itself."

"No, I am not." Violet felt an image come back to her. It was of the moment she had stood with Sebastian by their horses, mistakenly believing he would be willing to marry her.

I asked him to marry me... I should not have done that.

It didn't matter that her heart had wanted it as much as her head, she had asked it for Penelope's sake.

"I will write to you. Every week," Penelope said as she looked inside the purse again.

"I am counting on it," Violet said with vigor. "I wish to hear about everything, and I want to know too how my niece or nephew are faring. I will send gifts, you can count on that. All will be well again, I promise."

"Oh, Violet." Penelope sighed, as if the conversation was the hardest they had ever shared. "When should I go?"

"That is the next thing that is hard to say." Violet breathed deeply, building the courage to do so. "It will not be long before you start to show. Even before that, one of the other maids could wash my sheets and discover I am not pregnant." She wrinkled her nose at the thought. "Pen, I think you must go tomorrow."

Chapter Twenty-Seven

"Not enough pheasants today," Sebastian muttered as he lifted the gun and fired into the sky another time. The beaters were far ahead in the trees, rustling up the pheasants and urging them into the air. The gun dogs ran after them, collecting the shot pheasants and bringing them back to Sebastian's and Benedict's feet.

"Little wonder. You seem to have shot them all these last few days," Benedict murmured, shifting his weight between his feet.

"I needed the distraction," Sebastian explained as he took another shot at the sky. He caught the tip of a pheasant's wing and it came down, falling fast.

Violet.

Nothing seemed to work to distract himself from thoughts of her. All he had decided in the last few days was that he couldn't bear the thought of her not being in his life. Come what may, they couldn't carry on like this.

I need to see her again.

"I have noticed." Benedict sighed and adjusted his stance, looking at the gun in his hands.

As Sebastian lowered his weapon and waited for the beaters to do their job, he glanced Benedict's way, noticing something odd.

"Is there a reason you are not shooting, brother?" Sebastian's question was met with an odd shrug. Benedict fidgeted, nearly dropping the gun at one point. "This is usually one of your favorite sports."

"I have little appetite for it today, that is all." Benedict cocked the gun regardless and aimed at the sky. When the next pheasant appeared, he took a shot, but he missed by a mile.

"You are as distracted as I am," Sebastian mused as he reloaded his own gun. "Yet you wish me to tell you what is wrong."

"You refused to do so," Benedict added wryly.

That is because you have guessed.

"You did not need me to say it," Sebastian murmured and raised his own weapon. When two pheasants appeared above the trees, he fired two shots, catching them both and bringing them down.

"Good shot." Benedict's tone lacked enthusiasm.

"There was a time such a shot would have got a roaring applause from you." Sebastian lowered his weapon with the barrel still smoking and turned to face his brother. "For God's sake, Benedict. One of us moping is bad enough, but two of us? No. That is too much even for me to bear. Tell me what is wrong."

"I..." Benedict did not go on. He fidgeted where he stood before passing his weapon to a groundsman that stood with them, clearly having had enough of the shoot. "My mind is elsewhere."

"Well, as you will not tell me any more, perhaps I should take a leaf out of your book, and play a little guessing game. Are you thinking of a woman?" Sebastian asked. To his dismay, Benedict nodded slowly.

Oh god. Do not say it.

The weapon fell limp in Sebastian's hands. He thought of the number of times Benedict had bugged him about Violet, and if she was the woman on his mind. It irked, to the bone, but now it offered up a new possibility.

I cannot bear it if he is going to tell me that Violet is the one who plagues his mind too!

Sebastian hurried to reload his weapon. He took a step away from his brother, closer to the trees, and raised it once again. Lots of pheasants shot into the air this time, so many that he couldn't catch them all. Two fell to the ground through the branches before he grew aware of footsteps behind him.

"Will you not ask me what lady bothers me, brother?" Benedict asked. Sebastian glanced at his brother, seeing the pain in his features.

"Perhaps I fear the answer." Sebastian walked forward again, yet this time, Benedict was close behind him. Around their feet, the gun dogs hurried, offering up more pheasants that were collected by the groundsmen.

"You never did like their family, did you?" Benedict asked. Sebastian froze. He felt the accusation clear in the air, even with his back turned to his brother. "I swear, Seb, I do not understand you at times. You outrightly said again and again why seeing the Miss Hathaways was a poor idea, yet you clearly have a fascination for Miss Violet Hathaway, do you not?"

"Benedict!" Sebastian spun around to face his brother. "We should not speak of it."

"Why not?" Benedict asked wildly, walking forward with his arms outstretched. "What is so wrong to speak of it? You think I have not seen the way you look at her?"

Sebastian looked away. He kept his eyes on the trees, trying to think only of the pheasants, though it was pointless. Violet kept coming back to him, as did his brother's words.

"I made you a promise, Benedict. Long ago."

"Wait... is that what this is about?" Benedict took Sebastian's shoulder and shook it for good measure. Sebastian turned around to face him, aware of the sudden redness to his brother's cheeks and the wildness of his hair, as if he had tugged on the tendrils. "That is why you will not speak of this?"

"If you are so eager for us to talk, then you talk first." Sebastian had had enough. He waved a hand at Benedict, half afraid to hear the words, but also burning with curiosity.

I have to know. I need to know if Benedict is in love with Violet too.

The moment he had the thought, he stumbled back, realizing what it meant.

When did I realize I was in love with her?

"You wish me to talk? Fine! I will talk." Benedict gestured toward Sebastian. "What do you wish to know?"

"Tell me why you have been miserable ever since we came back from that ball," Sebastian said, hurrying to reload his weapon. "Tell me why you will not stop bugging me about Violet – I mean, Miss Hathaway."

"You did it again."

"I know I did!" Sebastian lifted the weapon, ready to fire at the birds. "Part of me does not want to know it, but we must talk of it, mustn't we? Very well, tell me, Benedict. Tell me why you are so miserable at the moment."

"Because I am afraid to hear what you will say to what I have to tell you," Benedict said slowly.

"Then speak of it!" Sebastian kept the gun trained over the tops of the trees, ready for the birds to emerge.

"Fine. I will. I'm in love."

It is what I feared.

Sebastian began to lower the gun.

"With Miss Penelope Hathaway."

"Penelope!?" Sebastian swung around.

"Watch that gun!" Benedict barked, backing away with his arms lifted.

"Relax, my hand is nowhere near the trigger." Still, Sebastian unlocked the weapon and tossed it to the side. Scarcely able to believe what he had heard, he hurried toward his brother, grabbing his shoulders and shaking him for good measure. "Did you say Penelope? Miss *Penelope* Hathaway?"

"Do you need your ears checking?" Benedict asked with a smile. "That is what I said."

"But…" Sebastian released his brother. "Your attentions, they were to Violet."

"That was just to show I was ashamed of how you treated her at the ball, Seb. I was kind to her, nothing more. She is a fine woman, I do not deny that." He shook his head emphatically. "Yet Penelope? Well, she is someone quite special."

Sebastian watched, wide-eyed and slack-jawed, as Benedict's smile grew.

"We were much thrown together at times. She's nervous with people, but with me? She opens up more. Especially these days. I think I only really knew it at the last ball, when I danced with her." Benedict sighed, with a kind of contentment. "I am in love with her."

Sebastian was breathing deeply, uncertain what to say or feel.

He doesn't love Violet? Thank God!

"Why didn't you tell me?" Sebastian snapped, taking another step forward.

"Oh, are we completely open with each other?" Benedict asked with a laugh, though he took a step back, clearly a little nervous. "You do not tell me what is in your heart, do you, brother?"

He gestured to Sebastian so strongly, it made Sebastian flinch. "You refuse to tell me what you think of Miss Hathaway, though you have called her Violet so much that it is very noticeable what you really think. I know what you think of the family, Seb. When I started seeing the sisters, you said again and again how I should not associate with them. How could I tell you I was thinking of marrying the younger sister?"

Sebastian lifted his hands and covered his face for a minute, realizing with all this new information what had really happened around him.

"I am such a fool." He shook his head, then turned back to look at Benedict.

I know something he must know.

"Benedict, listen to me." Sebastian reached forward, taking one of his brother's shoulders, and looked him in the eye. "If you wish to give your heart to Miss Penelope, then I give you my blessing, with all my heart."

"You do?" Benedict asked excitedly, his smile so full, the creases in his cheeks reached his eyes.

"Yet... there is something you must know before you do this." Sebastian breathed deeply. It was not his secret to share, and he had promised Violet to keep it quiet, but things had changed now.

Benedict could be the man to help Penelope out of her situation. Yet if that is going to happen, he needs to know all the facts.

"Do you remember I told you before that Miss Violet must marry?"

"Yes. I remember."

"It is for her sister's sake. She is..." Sebastian breathed deeply.

Please forgive me for revealing this secret! It is for the best.

"She is what?" Benedict urged him on.

"Miss Penelope is with child, Benedict." Sebastian let the words hang in the air, watching as Benedict's face changed. Rather than shock, it was more realization.

"Oh..." He began to nod slowly. "That explains so much."

"What do you mean?"

"I knew she was hiding something. Each time I asked her to dance, she would question if she truly was the person I wished to dance with. I thought that was her nerves." He shook his head in bemusement. "Who is the father?"

"A charmer and a rake," Sebastian declared with a sigh. "He seduced her and left her, Benedict."

"Penelope." Benedict breathed out her name. "She deserves so much more kindness."

"That she does." Sebastian released his brother's shoulder. "I have told you I give you my blessing, and that still stands, but if this goes any further, Benedict, you need to know what you are taking on. You would be accepting to save Miss Penelope from her situation. Not to mention, you would be raising another man's child."

To Sebastian's amazement, Benedict smiled once again.

"Of all people, Seb, do you think *I* would look down on an illegitimate child?" He practically laughed at the idea, shaking his head.

Sebastian sighed. The matter of Benedict's parentage wasn't something they discussed aloud very often.

"No, I suppose not," Sebastian said with a smile of his own. "You would do this then? You are considering asking Miss Penelope to marry you?"

"Very much so." Benedict seemed incredibly happy.

Not knowing what more to say, Sebastian took hold of his brother and pulled him into an embrace. It was a quick thing, yet much needed. Sebastian felt such relief course through him, he didn't know how to put it into words.

It was the relief that his brother had found happiness, and the relief that Violet's situation was about to be made so much better.

"Your Grace! Lord Westmond! There is a young lady running this way."

Sebastian stepped back from his brother, looking in the direction of the house to see his manservant was right.

"Is that...?" he began, watching as the woman was running quite wildly, her gown flapping around her legs and her hair falling down from her updo.

"It's Penelope!" Benedict cried out.

Chapter Twenty-Eight

"Miss Penelope? What is it? What is wrong?" Benedict was hurrying forward to meet her.

Sebastian hurried on behind his brother. He gave quick instructions to his manservants to end the shoot, then he followed. One glance at the house in the distance showed that Miss Penelope had arrived by carriage.

It is early for visitors.

Turning his gaze upon her, he watched as Miss Penelope reached his brother. Now Sebastian knew what to look for, he saw the blush in her cheeks as she looked at Benedict.

It seems my brother has reason to hope, after all!

"Lord Westmond. Forgive me for coming in this state." She stopped in front of him, holding a hand to her chest as she tried to catch her breath. "I know this is hardly proper."

"Think nothing of that." Benedict took her arm, holding her up as she continued to pant. A small smile crept through the panicked look before it vanished once again. "You are in shock. Come, we should get you to the house."

"First, I must speak to your brother." Miss Penelope kept her hand in Benedict's.

Sebastian's eyes flicked down to those hands, watching at how fervently those fingers were clasped together.

Theirs will be a true love.

Sebastian smiled a little more. It was everything he had ever wanted for his brother, to marry for love.

"Your Grace, I must speak to you," Miss Penelope begged. "I know I am calling unannounced, but I cannot afford to wait, for the very event I fear is about to take place may be determined by a license today."

Sebastian's smile vanished and he stepped forward, his boots moving through the long grass.

"What event, Miss Penelope? What has frightened you so?" he asked, moving to her side.

"It is Violet."

"Violet? What of her?" Sebastian didn't even try to use her formal title now. When Benedict looked at him with a humored smirk, Sebastian narrowed his eyes. "Not the time, Benedict."

"Agreed," Benedict said quickly. "Go on, Miss Penelope."

"She is to marry!" Miss Penelope's words made Sebastian's stomach drop. For a second, he couldn't hear anything, not Miss Penelope's heavy breathing, nor the barks of the gun dogs as they were rounded up. All he was aware of was his own heartbeat, thudding in his chest.

"Marry? No. She can't." Sebastian had an awful imagining. He pictured Violet walking to the altar in an ivory gown, of the kind that would hug her curves, yet he was not the one to greet her at the altar. Another man was.

She cannot marry anyone else.

The sudden thought crushed him.

How has it taken this to make me realize that?

"Who? Why is it this soon?" Sebastian asked wildly, his tone so panicked he feared he was not making sense.

"She is doing it for me." Miss Penelope glanced at Benedict, looking nervous before she turned her gaze on Sebastian again.

"We know of your situation, Miss Penelope." Sebastian sought to reassure her. Rather than looking comforted at all, she looked horrified. Her lips parted and she backed up, but Benedict was there, holding her gently.

"There is no need to fear," Benedict said softly to her. "We will not tell a soul, you have our word."

"Thank you," she murmured, smiling at Benedict, before looking back to Sebastian again, her expression abruptly serious. "My aunt discovered my... situation. Yet Violet claimed I was not the one in trouble. She said that *she* was. She could not bear the thought of them marrying me to Viscount Haywood, so she has volunteered herself to save me from such a fate."

"Haywood?" Benedict repeated, his nose curling instantly.

"That scoundrel!?" Sebastian spluttered, hardly believing his ears. "The man is odious, reprehensible..."

"Monstrous?" Benedict offered.

"Any ill word you care to think of!" Sebastian had never known such anger or panic. He backed up from the two of them, turning in a mad circle through the long grass as he plunged his hands into his hair. "She cannot marry such a man."

"She did it for me," Miss Penelope's voice was so soft, it was a stark contrast to Sebastian's own. He turned to see her, with tears in her eyes. "Violet may be my sister, but she is also my greatest friend, your

Grace. She would do anything to protect me, and it pains me that I cannot do the same for her. So, I must do the only thing I can." She took a step toward him, releasing the hold she had on his brother, before reaching into a bag that was threaded over her arm.

Sebastian held his breath, recognizing exactly what she had taken out.

The sketchbook I gave Violet!

She passed it into Sebastian's hands, urging him to take a look with a nod of her head. Sebastian flicked through the pages. The moment he saw his face staring back up at him, he felt a smile tug at his lips.

"She loves you, your Grace," Miss Penelope whispered, her voice nearly lost in the wind that buffeted him.

Sebastian continued with the sketches. The words had filled him with a kind of hope he had not known before. It reminded him of the pleasure and pure unadulterated happiness he had felt in the library when he was with Violet.

"Seb!" Benedict's voice made Sebastian snatch his gaze up from the sketchbook. "Do you intend to just stand there?"

"No." Sebastian stepped forward, appealing straight to his brother. "The vow I made you. I promised you I would never marry."

"Let me guess, you wish to be released from it?" Benedict asked, a smile appearing on his lips. "Believe me, brother, I happily release you. I never wanted you to make such a vow in the first place."

"What vow?" Miss Penelope asked at their side.

"I will tell you soon." Benedict looked to her. "I think there is much I need to say to you."

Sebastian reached for his brother's hand. Benedict took it and shook it heartily.

"I hope you know I never asked for that promise, Seb," Benedict said with a smile. "I was never bothered with the idea of being duke someday."

"If I never marry, you would be."

"Who cares! I'd rather see you happy." Benedict clapped Sebastian on the shoulder and released his hand. "Go, now! Before she marries another man."

Sebastian took off. He tucked the sketchbook into his pocket before he ran with such vigor across the field that his boots tore a path through the long grass, and his footman ran on beside him.

"Your Grace! Your Grace? What is the rush for?"

"Fetch my horse. At once, if you please," Sebastian called back. "I must get to Miss Hathaway's house. Now!"

The moment he reached the driveway, Sebastian issued more orders. His horse was brought around within seconds, saddled and ready with the reins. The dark horse neighed, clearly happy to know he was about to be ridden wildly again.

"Just like our rides on the continent, old friend," Sebastian said as he pulled himself into the saddle. "Fast and without restraint. That is what we need today."

Sebastian only paused long enough to look across his lawn out toward the tree line. At this distance, Miss Penelope and Benedict were very small, but he could see them clearly enough to be able to trace the way they were standing together.

Benedict was speaking intently to Miss Penelope, and he had her hand in his, holding it toward his chest.

He is speaking of his heart. He is a good man. In fact, Benedict is the best of men!

Sebastian felt a swell of love for his brother in that moment, before he tugged on the reins of his horse. The steed snorted and took off, racing down the drive so fast that the gates appeared within seconds. The groundskeeper had barely pulled back the gate in time for Sebastian to shoot through on his horse.

"Fast now," Sebastian muttered to the horse. "If she is to marry soon, then there is no time to waste."

"Violet, where is Penelope?"

Violet had not answered. No matter how many times her aunt plagued her with this question, she stayed silent. Sat at the breakfast table, beside Louise and the empty chair that usually belonged to Penelope, she kept her eyes down on her plate, where she kept poking at morsels with her fork that she felt unable to eat.

"Violet?" Deborah snapped her name this time. Violet slowly looked up and met her aunt's gaze with a slow smile.

"She has chosen not to join us for breakfast this morning."

"That doesn't explain why she has gone from her room," Walter spoke up, walking into the room so swiftly that the heels of his hessian boots struck the floor noisily. He stopped by Violet's side and leaned down toward her, his eyes so narrowed that barely any of the irises were visible at all. "This is the time you explain yourself, Violet."

"Perhaps Penelope just wanted a new life." Violet shrugged. "I can hardly blame her for making such a decision and wanting to be away from this house."

"Ungrateful whelp!" Deborah wailed. As Walter walked around to comfort his wife, Violet lifted her teacup and hid her smile behind the china rim.

She is gone. At least now, Penelope is safe from them and their interference. She can carve a life for herself and her child.

"I hope you do not behave like this when you are wed." Deborah waved a dismissive hand in Violet's direction. "To think you will talk to Lord Haywood in this manner, after all he is doing for you to save your reputation. To save this family. I hope you treat him with respect, Violet."

"Respect," Louise murmured, rather uncertainly. The oddity of the tone made Violet turn her head in her cousin's direction. "I do not imagine Lord Haywood has much respect for anyone, Mama. He hardly seemed the... kindest of men." Louise clearly chose her words carefully.

"Since when are you so outspoken!?" Deborah cricked her neck in her daughter's direction. Louise shrugged but offered no words. Her quick glance in Violet's direction though said much.

In a way, it was a comfort to Violet, to see her cousin was not happy about the situation. She evidently disliked Lord Haywood as much as Violet did.

A firm knock at the door silenced Deborah's wails. Violet slowly looked up to see her uncle straightening his waistcoat and adjusting the cravat around his neck, clearly trying to appear a perfectly respectable gentleman.

"That will be Lord Haywood," he said, turning his gaze on Violet. "Come to discuss the special license. Up." He flicked his fingers at Violet, ordering her to her feet.

Violet chose not to move. She sat rigid in the chair and stared back at her uncle.

"I am not a dog to call to your heel by clicking your fingers." Violet's words were unwelcome. She could see it in her uncle's complexion which turned a funny shade of purple.

"Violet, I do not have the time to stand here and lecture you on the error of your thinking." He rounded the table and took her wrist, jerking her up to her feet. "You will see your betrothed and you will behave as a lady should. Though judging by your recent behavior..." he shot a glance down at her stomach, showing exactly what he was referring to, "Behaving as a lady should, is something of a difficulty for you."

Violet chewed the inside of her mouth, refusing to say anymore. She quickly understood that little good could come from arguing with her uncle at this moment.

I have agreed to this wedding, have I not? I must accept it, for Penelope's sake. By the time any of them realize that I am not the one who is with child, she will be far away, and somewhere safe.

Stepping into the entrance hall and wincing at the tight grip her uncle had on her wrist, footsteps followed behind her. Deborah had grabbed Louise and was dragging her forward too, despite her protestations.

"I do not have to see this man again, Mama!"

"Quiet child."

On cue, the door was opened by the butler and Lord Haywood stepped inside. There was a spring to his step, so light of foot that it betrayed to Violet just how excited he was by the upcoming event.

He truly is in need of a bride and an heir!

"Mr. Notley, how good to see you again. I have news." Lord Haywood addressed Walter directly, barely looking at Violet at all. The two gentlemen bowed to each other as Violet released her wrist from her uncle's grasp and rubbed the sore spot he had created on her skin. It had turned pink and a peculiar hue of red in the time that he'd had hold of it.

"News? What is it?" Walter asked with eagerness.

"The special license. It has been obtained." Lord Haywood smiled with these words and turned his focus on Violet.

She found herself gulping at the strength in that stare.

I cannot escape this fate now.

The thought cut deeply through her mind as she became aware of the butler trying to close the door, only for it to be blocked by another person. Violet felt her hand taken by Lord Haywood.

"How does a wedding in two days' time sound?" Lord Haywood asked, his smile so great the skin around his eyes crinkled.

"What wedding? There will be no wedding!" a voice boomed from across the room.

Violet snapped her gaze away from Lord Haywood and looked to the door to see the very person who had swung open the door. He was stumbling inside, visibly sweating from riding, with his hair wild and his tailcoat disarrayed.

Sebastian!

"Lord Haywood?" His eyes flicked to the Viscount. "Take your hands off my betrothed."

What did he say?

Chapter Twenty-Nine

S ebastian could see the shock on Violet's face. With her jaw agape, and those large eyes wide, she stood perfectly still, with her hand limp in Lord Haywood's grasp.

"What the devil?" Lord Haywood's spine stiffened, and he jerked his head back and forth, looking between Mr. Notley and Sebastian, clearly seeking an explanation.

"You heard me. Release my betrothed." Sebastian strode into the room, walking quickly toward Violet. When he offered his hand to Violet, it was the moment of truth.

Will she accept?

He was giving her the escape she so needed, he now just had to pray she would forgive him for stalling.

I should never have turned her down! The moment she spoke of marriage there in Hyde Park, I should have leaped at the opportunity.

Her gaze was clearly uncertain, questioning him, so Sebastian held his hand firmly outward, begging her to believe he was being genuine. At last, she moved. She placed her hand in Sebastian's and took her other hand out of Lord Haywood's grasp.

Her fingers were warm beneath Sebastian's own. He took her hand and used it as an opportunity to separate her from Lord Haywood's side, pulling her forward a little bit and putting himself between the two of them.

"What is going on?" Lord Haywood asked wildly, looking around the room and seeking an answer.

Sebastian was well aware of the shock on Mr. and Mrs. Notley's faces. The two were staring as if they were at a theater, watching a scene unfold with no explanation.

"Violet, what is happening?" Sebastian feigned innocence at the situation. "Have your aunt and uncle tried to force you into a marriage?" Turning to face her so only she could see his expression, he winked, urging her to play along.

"Well... yes," she murmured eventually. "Lord Haywood has acquired a special license."

"Then such a special license can be torn up," Sebastian spoke with finality and turned back to Lord Haywood. "I do not know under what pretense you have been brought here, Lord Haywood, nor how you have been persuaded to marry Miss Hathaway here, but any illusion of marrying her you may have, ends now. Miss Hathaway and I are to marry."

"Oh my goodness," Mrs. Notley gushed and wafted a hand in front of her face. "A duchess for a niece."

Sebastian felt a hatred curdle in his stomach as he glanced her way. To think such a woman could manipulate her niece so, and now delight in the prospect of a more advantageous match sickened him. He could feel it upset Violet too, for her fingers curled through his, clinging onto him tighter.

"I have had enough of this." Lord Haywood marched forward with the words. "I have an agreement with Mr. Notley here. A gentleman's agreement. Out of my way." He tried to push past Sebastian, and grab hold of Violet again. Sebastian felt the thrust against his arm and saw the way the Viscount's fingers stretched out flat toward her. The thought of Lord Haywood touching her disgusted Sebastian, especially when he could see where Haywood was reaching.

He was not trying to take her hand, or her arm, he was trying to grab her waist, to fling her out of Sebastian's hold as if she were a *thing* that could be moved around at his will.

Sebastian didn't hesitate. He lashed out and grabbed Lord Haywood's outstretched hand, then thrust it behind the Viscount's back and used it to shove the man away. Lord Haywood stumbled on his feet, grunting in shock before he managed to find his balance again. In that time, Sebastian put himself firmly back in front of Violet and took her hand once more.

"Did you just...?" Violet whispered in his ear, clearly so shocked she couldn't quite finish the sentence.

"Any man that would try to touch you so deserves what he gets, Violet." Sebastian held her gaze for a beat, before he turned his focus back on the Viscount.

"Mr. Notley?" Lord Haywood turned his eyes on Mr. Notley. He adjusted his tailcoat, as if he could shake off the incident that had just occurred. "You told me she was unattached, unwed, and in need of a husband. How could you deceive me so? I will not be treated in this manner!"

"I did not know," Mr. Notley shook his head back and forth with vigor. "I do not understand, Violet never said anything of the sort." He turned an accusing glare in Violet's direction, clearly needing an answer.

"That was my doing," Sebastian said, thinking on his feet. "I did not wish to make the betrothal public just yet as I had affairs to get in order."

"What affairs?" Lord Haywood asked.

"They hardly matter." Sebastian knew the lie was falling thin, but nothing could change the endpoint now. He had to get Lord Haywood far away from Violet, and that was all that mattered. "What concerns me is your wish to marry my betrothed. Any ideas you had upon her end now, Lord Haywood. Have I made myself clear?" He felt his voice shake a little with anger.

Lord Haywood's eyes turned down toward Violet. That single look made Sebastian stand taller, feeling that hatred growing into pure venom.

Such a man does not deserve her.

Sebastian had not only heard enough vile things about Lord Haywood to convince him of his character, but Sebastian had witnessed often enough his awful actions too. More than once had Sebastian been in a gentlemen's club when courtesans were called in. The way Lord Haywood treated the courtesans had disgusted Sebastian.

Such a man should never be allowed near a woman at all.

"Abundantly clear." Lord Haywood kept his voice level as he looked back at Mr. Notley. "It seems our arrangement is at an end, Notley. I will remember the betrayal." With these words, he turned on his heel and headed for the door.

"There was no betrayal, my lord. No intention of deception, I assure you!" Mr. Notley had to run to keep up with the fleeing figure of Lord Haywood. "Please, do not let our friendship be at an end because of this misunderstanding."

"Misunderstanding?" Lord Haywood turned back around with an accusing glare. "This is a humiliation! To discover my betrothed is already betrothed to another. Do not write to me again." He turned another time and reached for the door, hurrying out so fast that the tails of his coat whipped behind him.

Violet visibly breathed a sigh of relief. That sound made Sebastian step closer toward her.

"All is well now," he murmured.

"I do not understand," she whispered, for only his ears to hear.

"A duchess? Oh my goodness! Violet will be a duchess!" Mrs. Notley was so elated, she could not stand still. The mere sound of her voice irritated Sebastian so much that he cringed, looking away from Violet's aunt.

"Not another word, Aunt, I beg of you," Violet said hurriedly, then pulled on Sebastian's hand another time, clearly wanting an explanation.

"I will be an aunt to a duchess."

"Aunt!" Violet snapped again. Mrs. Notley turned around as if startled to hear Violet had spoken at all. Seeing the surprise there, Sebastian knew he could not stand for it anymore.

He had no intention of letting Mr. and Mrs. Notley take advantage of the match, especially after the way they had treated both Violet and Penelope.

"Allow me to make myself clear and speak plainly." He addressed the words to Mr. and Mrs. Notley, looking between the two of them with firm vigor. "This marriage is between Violet and I. Whether you are even invited to the wedding at this point is debatable after the way you have treated Violet and her sister."

Mr. Notley said nothing as he stood by the front door, turning away from the retreating figure of Lord Haywood. Mrs. Notley fell quiet and placed her hands to her chest, as if trying to quell her quickening heartbeat beneath her ribcage.

"We were only doing what we thought best," Mrs. Notley said eventually.

"Did you ever ask after the health of the child? Or of your niece?" His words showed he knew of their secret. At once, Mr. Notley hung his head, but Mrs. Notley did not. She stared back at him, as if baffled by his questions. "No. You thought of your own position only. If you would excuse me, I wish to speak with my betrothed in private."

Taking a firmer hold of Violet's hand, he pulled her free from the room.

"But I —" Mrs. Notley clearly intended to stop them, but Miss Notley stepped in her mother's way. She said nothing, but the obstacle was enough to make her mother fall still.

Sebastian took the opportunity to tow Violet far away. They moved through a door to a sitting room, but he didn't want to give the family a chance to listen in, so he reached for a door that led out onto the garden, and carved a path between the trees. Within a few seconds, they were at the far end of the garden, swathed in greenery, with only glimpses of the house visible beneath the warped bark of the trees.

"What is going on?" Violet cried the moment they could both be certain they were alone.

"Penelope came to see me." Sebastian kept his voice level, watching as Violet's shoulders crumpled. "She told me of what had happened. Of how you volunteered yourself to marry such a man in order to protect your sister. What a selfless act indeed, to give up your life so."

"I would never hesitate." Violet shook her head. "I would do anything to protect her."

"It made me realize what a fool I was." Sebastian took Violet's hand another time and lifted it to his lips, kissing the back of it. That same thrill shot through his body, the one he had always known whenever he was near Violet. He had felt it that first night at his house in the picture gallery when he had stolen a kiss, and in his library.

This burning passion   it cannot fade

"Why are you a fool?" Violet asked, her eyes on where he was kissing her showing she was equally affected.

"Because I clung to a resolution I had made long ago, purely out of spite. I was prepared to allow that to ruin both of our lives. Violet, I do not want to live without you. The thought of seeing you marry any man, let alone a man as vile as Lord Haywood, disgusts me," Sebastian spoke with emphasis, shaking his head.

"What resolution? Sebastian, you are not making much sense."

"I know. There is so much I want to say, I am uncertain what order to say it in." He stepped closer to her and kissed her hand again. Her other hand lifted from her side and found the lapel of his jacket, clinging to him. That touch gave him the confidence to go on.

She must learn of everything now.

"Violet, my father on his deathbed, impressed on me the need for me to marry and produce an heir, for *his* sake. All he was concerned about as he laid dying was that Benedict would never become duke." Sebastian watched as Violet's eyes widened. "Benedict is illegitimate. He is my father's son, but not my mother's. He is my brother in every way though, nothing will change that."

"I do not understand," Violet said in a small voice. "What father would dismiss his son so after raising him."

"He was never kind to Benedict." Sebastian closed his eyes, feeling the memories come back to him. There were hours of torment and things said to Benedict that could never be undone. "He was cruel and unloving. He raised him out of necessity, not love. I couldn't bear it. So I vowed to my father to defy him. I promised not to marry, so that Benedict would be a duke someday."

"Oh." Violet gasped before revealing a sad smile. "I understand. You put your brother first, as I put my sister first."

"It seems we are very alike." Sebastian moved his head toward Violet's. "Yet I am done clinging to that resolution now, Violet. Benedict told me this morning he has no wish to be duke, and I cannot bear the thought of you marrying another man."

"So, wait, you are truly asking me to marry you? This isn't part of a ruse just to help me escape?"

"A ruse? Of course not!" Sebastian said with a laugh, tilting his head closer to Violet's. "I love you, Violet, and if you can forgive a fool, would you marry me?"

He kissed her then, unable to resist, pressing his lips eagerly to hers, impatient for her answer. When she kissed him back, that familiar thrill shot through him. Her hand slipped beneath his tailcoat and clung to his waistcoat, as his other hand found her waist and held her to him.

When they parted, both breathless with their chests rising and falling, Sebastian didn't step far back. He kept his eyes on Violet, waiting for her answer.

"I do not think I have ever known this sort of happiness before. Yes, Sebastian, I will marry you," her whispered words urged him to kiss her again.

Epilogue

Violet felt a hand to her back as she said goodbye to her guests. That simple touch made a thrill pass up her spine, reminding her of what could be about to happen. Angling her head, she shot a smile Sebastian's way.

"You cannot keep touching me like that," she whispered.

"It is hard to stop," he confessed, moving his lips so near to her ear that the hairs on the side of her neck stood on end with anticipation.

"How can I keep a calm countenance to say goodbye to our guests if you continue like this?"

"I rather like this game." He was mischievous, passing a hand around to her waist with such slow promise and burning fingers that Violet giggled.

When people passed in front of her, she had to step out of Sebastian's hold, so that her guests would not see what was afoot.

"What a charming wedding breakfast that was!" Deborah gushed, hurrying forward and leading her husband and Louise behind her. She curtsied to Violet, in a fashion she had never done before. Violet had to work hard to maintain her smirk, and make sure she didn't laugh too loudly. "Congratulations, my dear. I am delighted for you, more than I can say." She kissed Violet on the cheek, showing a warmth of affection that Violet had not felt much of before.

Violet glanced Sebastian's way, seeing he was uncomfortable with the action. Since the wedding date had been set, Violet had been open and honest with her family, encouraged on by Sebastian. She had told them of the cruelty they had shown her in forcing her into a marriage, and the embarrassment of their longing for advancement.

You showed no love.

It was these words that had affected her aunt and uncle most. Deborah had apologized, most assiduously, and promised to be kinder. Walter had apologized too, and stepped far back. He seemed to understand that a degree of separation was only natural now. Deborah had adopted a more humble and modest stance. Violet couldn't help wondering if Deborah hoped in time that she would be more involved in Violet's life again, still wanting advantage.

Time will tell, I suppose, if this is a genuine change or one with an agenda in mind.

Walter wished them well too, then took his wife's arm and tried to lead her away, leaving Louise behind. Louise shifted a little on her feet, then she took Violet's hand, taking it as a truly loving cousin might.

"I am very happy for you, Violet," she said with genuine warmth. There was something in that tone that made Violet break. She knew Louise was not to blame for what her parents had done. Pulling on her cousin's arm, she drew her in for an embrace.

"Thank you, Louise. Perhaps we could write to each other?" she offered, as they stepped back again.

"I would like that." Louise's smile grew wider, then she shot a glance at her parents' retreating figures as they stepped out of the door and toward the carriage that awaited them on the driveway. "I might not tell my mother for the time being."

"If you think it's best. I will see you soon." Violet squeezed her cousin's hand in parting one last time, then Louise left.

Violet felt movement at her side as Sebastian stepped closer. She turned her gaze on him, admiring him in the handsome tailcoat and dark black trousers he had worn for their wedding. His waistcoat was midnight blue, embroidered with pockets of stars that had a habit of drawing her eyes downward.

"Eyes up, love," Sebastian whispered mischievously in her ear. "Our last guests are about to depart."

"You sound very excited about that."

"Oh, I am." He whispered the words to her with a seductive smile.

Violet turned her eyes forward as the last pairing left the dining room where the wedding breakfast had been set up and walked toward the two of them. Penelope was on Benedict's arm, the two holding tightly onto each other, laughing about something that had clearly tickled them greatly. Benedict seemed a little in his cups, happily having indulged to celebrate his brother's wedding.

"I hope you can make it into the carriage at this rate, Benedict," Sebastian said with a laugh and stepped forward, taking his brother's shoulder to steer him toward the door. "You have people to take care of now, need I remind you."

"I am perfectly in control of my faculties," Benedict said with a happy smile as he moved his hand to take hold of his wife's.

Violet couldn't stop her smile as she looked between her sister and her new brother-in-law.

The day Sebastian had proposed, he had brought her back to his house, where Violet had discovered that Penelope and Benedict had confessed their feelings for each other. Benedict, as the good-hearted man he was, had stressed repeatedly how he intended not just to take care of Penelope, but her child too.

'I will love the child as my own.'

The kindness of the words he had uttered still brought tears to Violet's eyes, making her blink them away to stop them from falling.

"I intend to keep them safe, don't you worry. And have no fear, sister," he called back to Violet as he stood in the doorway with Penelope. "I will take care of my wife."

"I am glad to hear it. Now that you are off on your honeymoon, I hope you will write lots of letters?" Violet called to Penelope as she hurried down the steps.

"There will hardly be a day I do not write!" Penelope called back as they moved toward the carriage.

Violet stood in the doorway to the house with Sebastian beside her, as he wrapped an arm around her waist, and teased her with his hand upon the curve of her hip another time.

"It will not be every day, I grant you," he whispered for only Violet to hear him. "Married couples tend to have other things on their mind." Violet held in her giggle as they waved to Benedict and Penelope, clambering in the carriage.

Violet had already noticed the happiness of her sister. The couple had been married for just over a week now, and there had barely been a time she had seen Penelope when clothes were not being straightened or hair was being flattened, showing that she had been up to mischief with Benedict mere moments before.

The door began to close.

"Speaking of married couples…" Sebastian whispered in her ear.

"Yes?" Violet said, tilting her head up toward Sebastian, in anticipation.

"Would you like to see your new chamber?"

Violet couldn't resist. She said nothing, but placed her hand in Sebastian's and let him lead her away.

As they passed the staff moving to the dining room to clean up, they nodded and smiled in parting, then hastened up the stairs. Toward the top of the staircase, they moved so quickly, both impatient, that they tripped on the steps. They only stopped themselves from falling by reaching out to take each other's arms, laughing away.

When they reached the chamber, Violet could not admire its beauty. It was stunning, to be sure, with cream curtains and bold mahogany furniture, but her mind was elsewhere.

Sebastian.

"Do you have any idea how much I have thought of our night together in the library?" he whispered to her as he shed his tailcoat and moved toward her.

"As much as I have, I hope," she murmured, and reached for his clothes. She was not slow, but urgent. Her fingers pulled at his waistcoat and cravat, urging them off. He began to chuckle softly at her speed, then he matched it, reaching for her gown and undoing the laces at her back.

Violet gasped every time he touched her. His hands elicited a new sort of pleasure as his lips found hers in a kiss. Her gown was slipped down her body, so that the silk tickled her arms with the promise of what more touches could happen. Sebastian only parted from the kiss when he urged her to turn around so he could access the laces of her corset.

She laughed as he hurried her, indulging in the moment.

This is one of the reasons I love him.

It wasn't just about the passion, it was about the happiness. The freedom to be with him and laugh even when the desire burned so strongly was enough to make her feel intoxicated.

The corset was dropped to the floor and the chemise was lifted over her head. The moment her body was exposed, goosebumps raised across her skin.

"God, you are beautiful," Sebastian whispered in her ear, moving his lips to her neck as he stood behind her. She gasped at that touch and tipped her head back, wanting more of those kisses. When he reached for his trousers, she reached back, urging them off too.

When they were both bare, he turned her around and moved her toward the bed. Violet tried to look down to see their bodies together, but she was distracted by his kisses. Each one was a thrill to her, sending tingles through her body that culminated in a wetness developing between her legs.

As they reached the bed, he lowered her down slowly to the mattress, then parted her legs. Lifting from the kiss momentarily, he held her gaze.

"The first time... it will –"

"I know." She nodded, having heard of such things before. She didn't care in this moment if it would hurt, she simply wanted to be with Sebastian, completely.

"Trust me?" he murmured.

"Can't you tell that by now?" she added mischievously. He smiled and moved toward her, kissing her again. When his fingers wrapped gently around her thighs, spreading her legs, she held herself tightly, preparing herself for the feeling.

The thrill grew stronger as his length slid toward her center. The moment he entered her, she felt that pain. She made a sound into their kiss, unable to stop herself, yet what startled her was how quickly the pain passed. By the time Sebastian began to rock their bodies together, finding a rhythm, the pain was gone, and it had been replaced by a pleasure that was even greater than that they had shared in the library.

Each movement their bodies made together elicited tingles through Violet. She clung to Sebastian, finding she constantly needed to touch him. Sometimes she braced herself against his biceps, other times she wrapped her arms up across his back and held onto his shoulders, anchoring herself to him.

He never stopped pleasuring her. He constantly kissed her as he made love to her, dotting kisses to her neck, her breasts, and then back to her lips again. His hands moved from the bed beneath her to touching her, caressing her hips and her thighs.

Violet could feel the pleasure building. It was a slow burn, yet seemingly not fast enough for Sebastian. His face was red and the moans he was emitting grew faster, showing he was near his edge. He reached down to their connection and brushed a bundle of nerves on Violet, just above their connection.

That touch sent her over the edge. She felt her body clamp down on him as she bucked toward him with the last throes of pleasure. Sebastian peaked too, moaning her name and lifting from her, tipping his head back to reveal the pure look of unadulterated pleasure on his face.

With them both panting, they capitulated together. Sebastian laid down over Violet as she lifted her arms around him. Tangling her fingers in his hair, she held him to her, to kiss him another time. When their lips parted, they were still both breathless, their smiles so wide, Violet thought the pair of them must have looked rather ridiculous.

"There are no words," she whispered eventually.

"I know." He sighed, with a kind of thrilling contentment. "All I can think of was how incredible that was. Oh, and one other thing."

"What?" she asked.

"How glad I am you crept off into my painting gallery the night I met you. If you hadn't done that..."

"But I did."

"Thank God!" With these words, Sebastian rolled the two of them together, and showed Violet how much more pleasure was to come.

The End?

Extended Epilogue

TWO YEARS LATER

"Again?" Violet laughed as she jerked forward in the garden chair, looking to her sister who sat opposite her, with a gentle hand resting across her stomach. "You are with child again? I thought you said the pain was like no other!"

"I did, and that still stands true, but..." Penelope trailed off and giggled, looking down to her stomach where she rested her hand. "I cannot tell you how happy this makes me."

"Then why on earth are we drinking tea? We should be drinking champagne!" Violet got to her feet and stepped away from the garden chairs.

They were at Sebastian's country estate, a house that Violet adored and considered her home much more than their townhouse. Determined to enjoy the garden as much as possible now that it was summer, the garden chairs and tables had been set up, with cakes and all sorts of treats across the surface.

In the doorway to the house, Mary was about to step outside, carrying a tea tray.

"Oh, Mary, I'm so sorry, but could we have a bottle of champagne as well?" Violet called to her.

"Champagne? Of course!" Mary eagerly hurried back inside, clearly intending to get the champagne. Violet smiled as she watched the maid hurry away.

Soon after Violet had married Sebastian, she had tracked Mary down, determined to find her again. She was not only her maid but her good friend. Mary seemed as happy in this house as Violet was, and had developed a particular interest in the carriage driver, who seemed to return her affections.

"Champagne?" Penelope said with delight as Violet moved back toward her. "We should wait for our husbands to celebrate."

"Oh, they will be back any minute." Violet flung herself toward her sister and embraced her tightly.

"Oomph! Can't breathe, Violet!" Penelope cried, making a wheezing sound for comic effect as Violet released her again.

"I am just so excited for you," Violet said as she hurried to sit down again. Leaning on the table, she looked toward her sister, seeing how great her smile was. "No wonder you arrived this morning looking so ridiculously happy. You have been holding onto this great secret."

"I have not been able to keep it in." Penelope shook her head with the words. "I wish to sing about it, with pure joy. I didn't know one child could bring as much happiness as it has done, but two? Oh, my. To think how it will change our lives."

Violet reached across the table and took her sister's hand, squeezing it softly. For a minute, there was nothing to say. They simply smiled at each other, giddy with delight.

Do not ask me what you want to ask.

Violet prayed for a minute her sister would stay quiet and not ask a question that had been so often on her lips. Since she and Sebastian had wed two years ago, Penelope had often asked if they were to have a child too.

It is a secret I shall not yet speak of.

Violet glanced down at her own stomach. At last, she had the signs of being with child, yet it was early, and she didn't want to reveal all to her sister and brother-in-law too soon. Even Sebastian didn't know yet.

"Well, if you are with child, then you have not filled your plate up enough." Violet released her sister's hand and reached for the cake stands, filling up Penelope's plate so high that it became a tower of cakes, leaning dangerously to the side.

"Violet! How am I supposed to eat all that?"

"You are eating for two now, remember? Not just one." Violet giggled and urged the plate toward her sister, rather humored when Penelope didn't object again. Instead, she delved into the cake. She grew so distracted, cutting up the honey cake and hurrying to eat it, that she didn't notice the sound of horses on the driveway, but Violet did.

Turning her head away from her sister, Violet looked to the drive where she saw Sebastian arrive first. As usual, his horse was the faster of the two, riding with wild abandon, before he drew to a quick stop by the door.

"One of these days you will beat me in a race, Benedict," Sebastian called back to his brother. Violet smiled to see Sebastian. His tailcoat was unbuttoned and his hair was ruffled thanks to his mad galloping. His appearance alone was enough to make her tingle, reminding her of all that she and Sebastian had done the night before in her bedchamber.

Behind him, another horse appeared, though this one carried two.

"You forget I am carrying precious cargo now," Benedict said and gestured down to the boy in his lap.

The baby was barely a toddler, wrapped firmly in one of Benedict's arms as he looked around the horse, his eyes wide

He looks so much like Penelope.

Violet was relieved for it. The young boy that had come into all their lives was a source of joy. A happy presence, he seemed to make their lives better.

"Penelope?" Violet said to her sister, pulling her attention away from the cake. "Your son and husband are here."

Penelope practically dropped the fork on her plate as she hurried to her feet and ran across the drive to greet her family. Violet laughed as she turned her gaze on Sebastian, only to see the way he was watching the family together.

I know what he's thinking. He is ready for a child too. Shall I tell him...?

SEBASTIAN FELT A WARMTH SPREAD THROUGH HIM AS HE LOOKED AT his nephew being lifted from the saddle and into Penelope's arms. The boy giggled and stretched out his chubby arms, before falling into Penelope's embrace. She kissed him warmly on the forehead, before turning her attention to Benedict.

"He was safe? On the ride?" she said, with clear wariness.

"Of course he was." Benedict leaned down from the saddle and kissed Penelope on the forehead. "I would never let anything happen to him."

"He wouldn't," Sebastian seconded. "That boy was very safe indeed. Benedict wouldn't even gallop whilst holding onto him." He climbed down from the saddle and watched the pair together, still feeling that warmth spread through him.

Someday, hopefully, it shall be our turn.

Sebastian was very happy for his brother. Benedict had a family he adored, and on the ride, Benedict had confessed another secret. Penelope was with child again.

As Mary appeared from the house carrying a bottle of champagne on the tea tray along with some glasses, Sebastian turned his focus on Violet, realizing it was not such a secret after all.

"I see we are to celebrate the good news." He crossed toward her quickly, then helped Mary with the tray and took the champagne bottle, opening it himself. It popped loudly and the cork shot across the garden, making everyone jump, including his nephew who wailed as Mary hurried back inside.

"Oh, Harry, have no fear, it is just champagne," Penelope assured her son and kissed him on the forehead again.

As Violet jumped up to present glasses to Sebastian to pour, he turned his gaze firmly on her, admiring her.

What a life we have.

He sighed with contentment. Never had he thought it was possible to be this happy with someone, but Violet had defied all expectations ever since he had met her. As he poured out the champagne, he thought back to the way they had spent their morning. They had spent some of the night making love, only to wake that morning and do so again. It had started off as a discussion about art, before falling into a playful bicker on who the best painter was. That argument had been settled with passion.

Seeing Benedict and Penelope were somewhat distracted by trying to pull a small jacket on Harry, Sebastian took the opportunity to kiss his wife. He moved his lips to Violet's and kissed her softly, feeling her lips mold to his own. A small breath escaped her, one of shock and thrill.

I love that sound.

When he parted from her, he could see how great her smile had become.

"What was that for?" she whispered.

"Just telling you I love you," he murmured, watching as she mouthed the words 'I love you too.'

"We are celebrating then?" Benedict said as he appeared at their side.

"Indeed we are, so drink up." Sebastian passed around the champagne glasses, humored when he saw Penelope carrying Harry in one arm, and holding a champagne glass in her other hand. "A toast, to you both, and your family." Sebastian held his glass high. "And of course, to the new addition that will soon arrive."

Benedict and Penelope exchanged a smile and then chinked their glasses together. Sebastian pressed his to Violet's as he noticed she was looking at him in an odd sort of way, with her eyes narrowed.

Is something wrong?

"Oh, dear." Penelope lowered her glass as Harry's head began to drift down and his eyes closed. "It seems slumber is quickly approaching."

"Here, shall we go put him down for a bit?" Benedict placed his glass down and then took Penelope's hand, leading her away. "We'll be back very soon."

Sebastian waved them off and turned his attention to his wife, now certain she was looking at him in an odd way indeed.

"There is clearly something going on in your mind, Violet," he said to her and topped up their glasses. "Shall I take a guess or would you like to tell me?"

"I am debating whether to tell you something or not." She chewed her lip, rather nervously.

"Well, you cannot taunt me like that and then not tell me."

"I could," she pointed out in a challenge, lifting her chin higher.

"Yes, but if you do, I will simply annoy you relentlessly by asking what secret it is that you are keeping. You may rest assured that I will not stop asking you. Even when we are attempting to sleep tonight."

"Sleep?" She repeated the word with humor.

"Well, when we are attempting to make love then," he added with a whisper, making Violet giggle warmly.

"Very well, I shall tell you my secret." Violet seemed to wait for him to place down the champagne bottle before she spoke again. Then she held the glass higher. "To us."

"Us?" He lifted his glass too.

"And to our family." With the words, she laid a hand on her stomach. The soft touch of her fingers there made Sebastian's eyes shoot down. He couldn't take a sip of his champagne, not yet, as his thoughts aligned.

We are to have a child? I am to be a father?

"You're with child?" he asked, so deliriously happy in that moment that the champagne glass nearly slipped from his hand.

"I think I am. Though it is still early, so let us keep it a secret for the time being – oh, Sebastian!"

Sebastian couldn't control himself. He placed down his glass and took Violet in his arms, nearly sandwiching her own glass between them as he kissed her.

"Something tells me you are rather happy with this news." She murmured between his kisses as he laughed. When he was done, he rested their foreheads together.

"Believe me, Violet. I am very happy indeed." He lowered a hand to her stomach and softly caressed her there with the backs of his fingers, as an image shot across his mind.

It was of a small boy, with hair as dark as his own and eyes just like Violet's, bright green.

PREVIEW: THE DUKE OF SCANDAL

Turn the page for a sweet preview of the enchanting novel by Tessa Brookman:

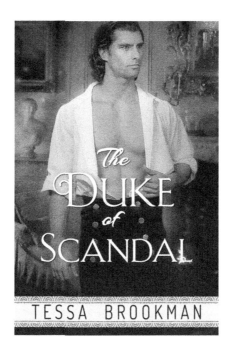

Chapter One

Erdington Estate
March 1814

"Oh, let's not walk in the south gardens today, Rose. I can't bear the view of the house at the moment," Harriet protested.

She and Rose had just stepped out of Erdington Manor house onto broad, mossy paving. Erdington was Harriet's childhood home. Rose had been her close friend since the two met at finishing school. That had been before the death of Harriet's father and the entailment of Erdington to the closest male heir. The heir being Harriet's distant cousin, Simon.

The terrace that they walked across led to wide, stone steps, flanked by carved balustrades leading down to the famous gardens. The once-famous gardens. To go with the once-famous house. But time had not been kind to either the Erdington estate or its masters.

"Nonsense, Harry. I love walking in the rose garden. The scent is incredible at this time of year," Rose enthused.

"But the house looks so woebegone with all that scaffolding around it," Harriet said.

"Then don't look at it," Rose shrugged.

She set off across the patio towards the steps. The two young women were night and day apart. Harriet was petite and fair-haired with full cheeks that flushed at a moment's notice. Rose had straight dark hair cascading down her back and dark eyes in a pale, pretty face.

"I didn't come all the way from Tedbury to sit indoors, Harry," Rose said over her shoulder as she skipped down the steps.

Harriet grumbled but caught up with the other woman, leading the way down into the gardens. They were not the works of art they had once been, a century before when the manor had been in the hands of her great-grandfather. The rose beds were still spectacular, with the plants flowering in profusion and reaching across the gravel paths which were supposed to separate different beds. Statues of famous Worthinghams were splotched with mildew and becoming gradually entwined with ivy.

"Take a deep breath. Isn't that wonderful?" Rose said.

"It is. I just don't like the sight that I know is behind me," Harriet replied.

Rose looked back over Harriet's shoulder towards the house and made a sympathetic face.

"It is rather ugly. I don't actually see any workmen though. Just the scaffolds."

Harriet swung around despite herself. The workingmen employed by Simon had been hard at work when she had woken that morning. Their incessant hammering had actually woken her earlier than she had intended. But Rose's arrival for brunch had been enough to forestall the ill mood such a rude awakening would usually bring about. Their time spent catching up after several months apart had taken her mind from the work completely.

"I had not noticed that they had stopped. Were they working during brunch?" Harriet asked, frowning.

"I didn't notice either. I was more interested in being reunited with my best friend," Rose said playfully.

Harriet smiled distractedly. "It is the middle of the day and the repairs are important. There is a veritable river flowing through the third-floor library from the leaking roof. This worries me. Rose, would it be terrible of me to want to speak to Simon to find out what is happening?"

Rose grimaced but linked her arm with Harriet's.

"A terrible imposition. But let's do it anyway. You will not be happy until the mystery is solved."

She laughed and the merry tinkle of the familiar sound brought a genuine smile to Harriet's lips. Rose had always had the knack of doing that, which was precisely why she did it. As they walked back to the house, their abortive stroll in the gardens ended, and Rose leaned close.

"Is it really bad, Harry? The...um...situation?"

She looked worried and Harriet had no desire to lie to her in order to spare her concerns.

"Simon and I do our best to keep it from Eleanor but...every day seems to bring fresh evidence of papa's cavalier attitude to money. And the pit we are sliding into gets a little deeper," Harriet said.

"Oh dear. And I thought Lord Worthingham was such an adept businessman. My own papa was immensely proud that I was attending the same finishing school as the daughter of Worthingham. He always respected the ability to make money over all things."

Rose made a face to show her opinion of such an attitude. Harriet sighed.

"Papa was a good and kind man. Too kind it seems. What he made through his estates and businesses, he lost through his charitable spirit. Simon is practically tearing his hair out."

Rose squeezed her friend's arm in an attempt to comfort her. They entered the wide drawing room through French doors that looked out onto the patio. The room beyond was mostly shrouded by dust sheets, the majority of the furniture covered as the room was part of a wing that Simon had closed, in order to allow some of the household staff to be released. Harriet had a master key and had intended to show Rose the south aspect until she remembered the sorry state of the house.

They hurried through the high-ceilinged room with its ceiling of chandeliers and elaborate plaster moldings. The wallpaper was a fine silk print of turquoise and gold, and the carpet, a royal blue. It had been Lord and Lady Worthingham's favorite room. Passing through and locking the door behind them, the two women walked along hallways with bare patches on the walls, where pictures had been sold.

Finally, crossing the still-grand entrance hall and entering the Breakfast Room, they came across the new Lord Worthingham of Erdington. Simon had fair hair and a round face with blue eyes. His face was creased in concentration. One hand held a coffee cup with the air of having forgotten it was there. The other lay across a document filled with tight-packed columns of figures. His eyes darted back and forth.

"Simon, dear. Where are the workmen?" Harriet asked.

"God's blood but I would like there to be one person in this house who does not ask me that question. They have downed tools because I cannot pay them!" Simon snarled.

Rose stopped short, a hand going to her mouth. Harriet put her hands on her hips and raised an eyebrow challengingly. Simon colored, putting down his coffee cup and then cursing as the liquid sloshed over the rim of the china.

"My apologies, cousin. And to you, Miss Mantell. I am somewhat distracted. There is a minor cash flow problem that I will resolve."

Harriet's face softened and she glanced at Rose, suddenly acutely aware that Simon would not wish to be forthcoming about money worries in front of a stranger. At least, Rose was a stranger to him, if not to Harriet.

"I'm sorry too, Simon. I should have known that you would be hard at work on the problem. You don't need us cluttering up the place."

"Actually, I was going to call you in anyway," Simon said, standing from the table at which he had been sitting and crossing the room to the mantlepiece.

A white envelope had been placed behind the clock which stood there. He took it out and offered it to Harriet.

"Your invitation," Simon told her.

Harriet frowned. "My invitation to what?"

"We all have one. The Duke of Wrexham is throwing a ball and you, I, and Eleanor are all invited."

"Oh, how lucky you are Harry. The Duke of Wrexham is one of the wealthiest men in England. And the most sought after. Why, every Lord with an eligible daughter wants to marry her off to him. I had no idea you knew the Bolton family."

Bolton was the family name of the Dukes of Wrexham. Rose crowded in eagerly to get a look at the invitation, which Harriet carefully removed from the envelope. It was written on stiff, white card with gold lettering in an exquisite hand.

"I didn't realize we did either," Harriet said, looking questionably at Simon.

He simply shrugged. "I have a passing acquaintanceship with the family. I will not look a gift horse in the mouth. We are invited and it could be the perfect opportunity to make some important connections. Everyone who is anyone will be there," Simon said.

"A passing acquaintanceship?" Harriet enquired. "I had no idea, Simon. When did you meet a member of the Boltons?"

Simon waved the question away, returning to his coffee cup and draining it. "It is of no consequence. We are invited and I shall put to Edward Bolton my business plans, and pray that he is willing to invest. It could be the making of us."

Chapter Two

"Oh, so you also received an invitation, did you?" Eleanor Worthingham said with barely concealed disappointment.

Eleanor was Harriet's cousin and Simon's sister. For reasons Harriet did not fully understand, there had always been a rivalry between them. Not on her own part, but from Eleanor towards her. She considered Eleanor to be far prettier than herself and with a more refined and fashionable wardrobe. She was also now a member of the family that owned Erdington.

The entailment that had resulted in the estate falling to Simon as the nearest male heir, instead of Harriet, also meant that Eleanor herself could not inherit. But, she was sister to the new Lord, while Harriet was merely a cousin. In Harriet's mind, that should have meant that Eleanor would be content but the younger woman never seemed to be. Harriet and Rose had left Simon to his ledgers and his worries. They had ascended to the house's second floor and the sitting room that Harriet now shared with Eleanor. The small room had once been Eleanor's alone but she had been forced to share when the room adjoining Harriet's quarters sprang a leak in the ceiling.

Simon could not afford to have it repaired, though this had been concealed from Eleanor. It meant that she was full of resentment, feeling that Harriet was receiving favorable treatment over herself. It did not make for pleasant company. Eleanor had Simon's fair hair and blue eyes. But while her older brother had a pleasant, amiable disposition, Eleanor was anything but.

"Good morning, Eleanor," Harriet said brightly, determined that she would not mirror Eleanor's hostility.

"Good morning, cousin," Eleanor replied frostily. "And to you, Miss Mantell."

Rose gave a bow of her head and then looked to Harriet for permission to sit. Harriet suppressed a smile. Such slights were beyond her to think of but Rose was an adept politician. The moment was not missed by Eleanor, who smiled fixedly as her jaw clenched in irritation.

"And in answer to your question, cousin," Harriet said, composing her skirts calmly. "Yes, I did receive an invitation of my own. So, I will be joining you and Simon on this occasion."

And I hope you choke on that fact. You thought that because I have shunned these invitations in the past, I would do so again? I do not have that luxury anymore, though god knows I would rather not be at such an affair.

She actually felt somewhat guilty at the tightly controlled look of chagrin on Eleanor's face. It simply was not in her nature to enjoy indulging in spiteful behavior. She would much prefer ignoring Eleanor and avoiding these sparring sessions. Sometimes, Eleanor made that difficult.

"I was rather under the impression that you did not care for such... what was it you called it once?" Eleanor feigned a moment of deep thought. "Ah yes, *indulgences*. I did not think you cared for such frivolous *indulgences*."

"A person can change their mind on a subject," Rose said.

And that is just what I have had to do, Rose dear. For the good of the family, though Eleanor does not know it.

"Indeed, I find that sometimes these social occasions are quite the thing. I find myself quite excited," Harriet said.

Rose looked at her briefly. Harriet knew her well enough to recognize a thoughtful look of consideration.

She knows that I'm lying but doesn't know the reason. I must keep my promise to Simon. Oh Rose, don't you realize, one cannot find a husband without mixing with society. And I cannot help Simon without a husband.

Thankfully, Rose said nothing but merely nodded as though in complete agreement. Eleanor's face had reddened and she stood abruptly. Harriet raised a cool eyebrow as Eleanor made a visible effort to control her rising anger.

"I will leave the two of you, I have business to attend to if you will excuse me."

Both Harriet and Rose gave gracious nods of acquiescence and Eleanor left the room. As the door closed behind her and Eleanor's footsteps withdrew along the bare boards of the hallway, Rose let out a long-suppressed laugh. Harriet made to shush her.

"Oh Harry, however do you put up with such a spoiled brat?" Rose protested.

"By the simple fact that I try to look for the best in everyone," Harriet replied.

She and Rose looked at each other for a moment, then Harriet laughed. "Everyone, even spoiled brats. No, no, I will not be drawn into laughing at my family behind their backs. Eleanor may be a little childish still, but that is because she is young. Do you remember being eighteen, Rose?"

"I do. Heaven forgive me if I was ever such a little...decorum prevents me from finishing that sentence. More importantly, since when did Harriet Worthingham care about a ball? I expected that you would end up married to a writer or a penniless artist. Are you seeking the approval of the county set?"

Her tone was light but her eyes were sharp. Harriet considered her response. The financial situation of her family was not her secret to tell. Simon was struggling to keep the household afloat and it was visibly aging him on an almost daily basis.

"On the subject of maturity. Perhaps I have finally grown up? One cannot spend all of one's life, say, dreaming of adventure. The world is a difficult place for women with no resources behind them...and no husband."

Forgive me, dear Rose for the lies I must tell. If Simon gives his consent I will tell you all, I swear it.

"Hmmm, a sentiment that just seems out of character but the proof is before me, I suppose. You really are going to attend?"

Harriet nodded with what she hoped was eagerness. "Yes, I really am. I intend to dance with some handsome gentlemen and perhaps, find one with whom I could be happy. Or not, as the case may be. But, I must do my duty."

Rose frowned. "Duty? I have never heard you call love a duty. And we did always swear that we would only marry for love."

So naive we were as schoolgirls, Rose. And so different. You with your family wealth behind you and all the freedom that brings.

"We did. But my circumstances demand that I look to the future and that of my family."

Rose's eyes widened. "Circumstances? By heaven, is Simon in trouble? Do you need help? You know that papa would..."

Harriet held up a hand, forcing a smile. "No, Rosie. You misunderstand. I merely speak of the duty of a daughter to her family name."

Rose did not seem convinced. "Because you know that you need only ask..."

As if I could ever bring myself to do that. It is worse knowing that you and your dear father would go out of your way to help. No, Rosie, this is for the Worthing-hams alone.

"Thank you, Rosie," Harriet said. "As usual, you are the best friend anyone could ask for. Now, Eleanor and all the talk of dances have occupied us for long enough. I don't wish to spend any more time in such talk. Not when we have so much else to talk about," Harriet said.

They passed the rest of the morning in reminiscence, about adventures and misadventures at school and since. By lunchtime, Rose went to her room to wash and Harriet took the opportunity to seek out Simon. She found him where she had left him. He looked as though he was drowning in the sea of ledgers and paper that had flooded his table in the library. As she entered the room, he looked up sharply.

"Your friend, Miss Mantell is not with you?"

"No, Simon. She is washing for lunch. We are alone." Harriet closed the library doors and turned the key in the lock. Then she crossed the room to take a seat across from Simon.

"Will you tell me what has you so worried? I know that money is short but you just seem to be more and more worried with each passing day. Is it really so bad?" she asked.

Simon looked at her for a moment as though considering lying. Then he seemed to visibly deflate. He sagged in his chair and covered his face with a hand. Harriet felt a surge of sympathy for him. Since he was a child, Simon had been a sensitive boy, most upset when he felt he was not living up to the expectations of his demanding father. His side of the family was distant from her own but Harriet had spent some childhood summers with her parents at the Norwenshire home, not far from Birmingham, in which Simon had grown up with Eleanor.

"The truth is, Harriet. We are...to use a vulgar phrase...broke," Simon said miserably. "I did not inherit as great a fortune as you may have expected from your father. It was greatly diminished by the time he died. I do not know if it was mismanagement or if someone within the estate was steal-ing. But...the truth is, we are perilously close to complete bankruptcy."

Chapter Three

Franklin House
March 1814

S oft skin and gentle, sensuous curves. Edward's first sensation upon waking was the feel of the luscious body that was pressed against him. Eyes still closed, he moved his hand from where it rested on a firm thigh, up over the glorious rounding of the hips. Fingers splayed across her stomach and rested there for a moment. The response was a murmur, delicious in its femininity and vulnerability. Then, the sinuous body squirmed against him. His hands found her round, pert bosom and gently squeezed.

"Good morning, your grace," she said in a sleepy cultured voice.

"Good morning, Alexandria. Thank you for another fascinating discussion last night. What was it we talked about?"

Alexandria chuckled, a deep, throaty laugh. "Economics, I believe."

"Ah yes. I love a good...economic discussion."

"Certainly more invigorating than anything you would get at your club."

"Do you think so? There are a few members who...went to Cambridge."

"But not you?"

"I sailed through Oxford. And I'm proud to say it barely touched me," Edward whispered.

Alexandria's hand closed around him, squeezing firmly, but Edward was already moving away. She made a disappointed noise, kicking the bedclothes away from her and lying on her back, arms spread and legs crossed coquettishly.

"It is morning, dear Alex. And there is business to be about. I cannot dally all day in bed with you."

"You've changed, darling. There was a time you wouldn't get up before dusk, and then spend all night at the club and then in my bed."

"Your bed?" Edward said with a wink.

He walked across the room to the huge, antique wardrobe, pulling open the doors and selecting a shirt and breeches.

"Most of the time," Alexandria replied, "I've missed you. My husband is an old man. All he cares about is his precious porcelain collection."

Edward scrubbed a hand through his unruly dark hair. His stomach was flat and muscled, chest and arms well defined. Like many sons of the gentry, he had taken an officer's commission in the army. Like most who did, he'd expected to spend his time at Horseguards, looking pretty in his uniform. The fine white scars that crisscrossed his abdomen stood testament along with his honed body to the fact that he had done far more than attended with the Prince Regent at court, or pushed papers for the Department of War.

After collecting an assortment of garments and casting them onto the bed, he began to dress.

"You really are an inconvenience in the mornings, Alex," he said, "if you weren't here, I would summon Rafeson to dress me. A gentleman really mustn't bother with all this nonsense."

He gestured at the cravat, tie pin, underclothes, breeches, shirt, coat, and other accouterments of the gentleman's wardrobe.

Alexandria, wife of the Duke of Richmond and, therefore, one of the elite of London society, sat up. She propped herself with her hands behind her, letting her breasts be exposed to him without shame. The sheet fell away from her stomach to reveal just a hint of her womanhood. Edward's eyes lingered there for a moment and she gave a wicked smile.

"Are you sure, Edward?"

Dark eyes locked with hers. "Yes. Quite sure. You of all people know how much work goes into arranging a ball. Especially one of this scale. Half the country is invited."

"Yes, I'm quite looking forward to it. Am I to assume that this ball to which you have attached so much significance will presage the end of our...fun?"

Edward arched an eyebrow. Then, without warning, he leaped onto the bed, kissed Alexandria, and pressed her onto her back. One hand circled her buttocks while another squeezed one of her breasts. She had time for a startled gasp before she succumbed to his passionate kisses. Presently, he lifted his head.

"Never," he whispered.

"But, rake that you are, you care too much about your name to disgrace any prospective wife by being openly adulterous," Alexandria said, winding her fingers through his shaggy dark hair.

"True. But I must see Rebecca safely married off before I can think of myself. That is the ulterior motive you're looking for behind this soiree."

He kissed her again, forgetting his own decision not to dally beneath the sheets after sunrise. Their bodies entwined and kissing became more heated, hands more insistent as touching and caressing became grabbing. When Alexandria began to undo the dressing Edward had already achieved, he pulled away. Alexandria screeched like a scalded cat and threw a pillow at him. Edward laughed.

Alexandria looked at him for a long moment, her frustrated desire putting anger in her eyes. But, Edward's easy, boyish grin was infectious. She chuckled, flinging the sheets away from her and standing, looking around the clothes Edward had ripped from her the previous night.

"My dress better be intact. You were most insistent in your disrobing of me."

Edward laughed again, putting on a silk brocade vest of black and purple, over tan breeches.

"So, do you have a prospective suitor in mind for your sister?" Alexandria asked.

"Yes, a very worthy fellow. I came across him in the army. Stout fellow, very solid. Perhaps you know him? Grantley is the name. Philip. He will be Duke of Stamford."

"Yes, I've seen him. You couldn't find someone a little less stone-faced?"

"He's not a rake like me. Almost puritan in his values, in fact. Just the kind of serious-minded man that will ensure Rebecca is taken care of. She does not need a clown for a husband."

"And you would be content with Rebecca spending the rest of her days in the distant north. Where is Stamford? Scotland?"

"Hardly. Yorkshire. Twenty miles from York. Not exactly the ends of the earth."

"It would be for me. Poor Rebecca. Have they met?"

Edward was dressed. He strode to the curtains and yanked them wide.

Pale daylight flooded the room. Beyond lay the streets of Chelsea. Franklin Place was quiet at this time of the morning. Somewhere behind the rows of townhouses, a milk delivery cart clattered, kept out of sight of the gentry to make its delivery to the servant's entrance. The houses were tall and immaculately dressed. The city beyond was misty, the highest buildings poking through in murky silhouette.

"No," he said distractedly, "they will meet at the ball."

"Then I at least hope, for Rebecca's sake, that you will have told her of your plans before she meets him."

Edward turned back from the window. London was a distraction he could do without. Once it had been his playground, but that was a long time ago. As he often did when considering his youth, he uttered a silent prayer within his head to the spirit of his father.

Forgive me papa for my callow youth. I did not know. But I will make you proud.

"Of course I will tell her. It is important that she makes a good impression. Grantley will have his pick of prospective wives. She must stand out from the lot."

"And if she rebels? Rebecca always struck me as the romantic sort. Something like you, when you were her age."

Again the boyish grin from Edward, his typical defense mechanism.

"Was I ever romantic?"

"The very soul of romance." Alexandria laughed, stepping into her dress having already put on petticoat and underskirt.

"Well, she will understand her duty as a Bolton. And she will see that duty done," Edward said with finality.

"And if she does not see it so?" Alexandria persisted.

Edward was shrugging on a coat of deep blue, studying himself in the mirror. He stopped, looking at Alexandria's reflection.

"You continue to ask. Do you think she will resist my choice for her?"

He did not believe that Rebecca would be so irresponsible. But then, once upon a time, so had he.

"She may. You are not her father."

"I am Duke and therefore father to her in all but name. She is my responsibility. And this is in her own best interest. A match with the Duke of Stamford will bring her prestige and a comfortable income for life. What more could she want?"

Alexandria's pouting lips twitched into a mocking smile.

"Love, my dear Teddy."

"Love?" Edward scoffed. "Love is for poets and fools. It is not practical. When I marry, it will be for the betterment of my family and my name. That is all."

Also by Tessa Brookman

Thank you for reading *The Rakish Duke and his Wallflower!*

Thank you for being part of this amazing journey!

Also by Tessa Brookman

Dukes of Danger Series:

Trapped with the Rakish Duke

The Duke of Scandal

Lost Dukes of London Series:

The Lost Duke and his Staggering Duchess

Seductive Wallflowers Series:

The Duke and the Spoiled Wallflower

A Virgin for the Beastly Duke

About the Author

Born in October 1995, Tessa knows a fair amount about the Regency and Victorian era. Enchanted by the Dukes and Lords, her one fascination has always been writing the stories she wanted to read.

Of course, there's more to life than writing; like taking care of a cat, two dogs, a husband and her endless cravings for adventure and travel. Having traveled to England, Scotland, India and numerous other countries, she has met friends and relatives she never thought she'd meet, with stories too wild to tell.

Her historical romances are here to bring those captivating stories to life with a touch of suspense, intrigue and happily ever afters.

Visit her on the web at www.grovechronicles.com/tessa-brookman

Printed in Great Britain
by Amazon

26923828R00148